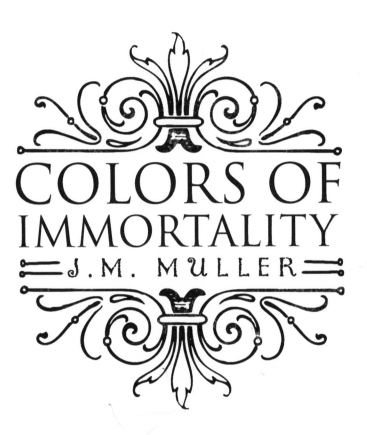

COLORS OF
IMMORTALITY
J.M. MULLER

Colors of Immortality

© 2016 J. M. Muller

Matte Print ISBN: 978-1-48356-961-1
Glossy Print ISBN: 978-1-48357-375-5
eBook ISBN: 978-1-48356-962-8

This story was derived from a mind that enjoys fantasy a little too much, and is completely fictitious. Any similarities to living people (or dead, for that matter) is entirely coincidental and should be deduced as pure happenstance. The opinions expressed by the protagonist (who isn't real) or the villains (who REALLY aren't real)—and every character in-between—belong to those characters and not the author.

This work is fiction and should be treated as such.

*For the three greatest loves of my life—Chris, Frank, and Sam—
and all the other beautiful souls walking this earth.*

CONTENTS

DAY OF POSTPONEMENT

I was screwed.

Like, big-time screwed.

That was my sole thought as I stood outside Mick's Grocery and stared across the lot. Something was wrong, although I couldn't quite determine what that *something* was.

All around me, life ambled along—carts squeaked, a bratty kid screamed, an old couple griped—everyone and everything was in fluid motion. Everyone except me. I'd morphed into a dimwitted mouth-breather, too stupid and slow to process the sight in front of me.

It was because my truck was off. With its faded paint and dented body, it was the same motorized monstrosity that it had been earlier. That much hadn't changed. Unworthy of the nobler spaces closer up, I parked it in its rightful place—far from the store. I'd always assumed it couldn't get any worse, that is, until I spotted what was wrong. It was leaning.

My eyes went straight to a single, misshapen tire.

"Son of a—" I started, stopping short when I remembered my uniform. A complaint to management about an employee swearing on company grounds was write-up worthy. Even without a name, they'd know it was me. All they'd have to say was: young, blond male, and I'd have earned my third strike. I would be unemployed in a millisecond, and it wouldn't matter that I was off the clock.

In a fit, I ripped off the idiotic bow tie I wore and shoved it into my pocket. My eyes darted from bumper to bumper in a visual sweep as I stalked across the lot.

I found no new scratches—at least no new *obvious* scratches—and my gas latch was intact. I ran my hands along the tread, searching for gashes and holes. My gut told me this wasn't bad luck, but something deliberate.

Considering the crappy start to my weekend, it wasn't a huge leap.

But the only thing out of place was a missing valve cap. That wasn't a big deal. I'd lost them before, and as long as the valve remained clear of debris, the air stayed put. Of course, someone could've purposely drained it, but the time it would take to empty the tire would require serious balls. *Unlikely.*

I let out a shaky breath, relieved that sabotage wasn't part of the equation. It's one thing to have the universe hell-bent on destroying you; it's another when an anonymous asshole takes up the job.

I used my apron to wipe the grime from my hands and unlocked the cab. I'd have to call Tony and stall him. Mr. Greenwich, my tub-of-lard boss, had made me late by fifteen *crucial* minutes.

Pulling open the glove compartment, I searched for my cell, only it wasn't there. I frantically checked my pockets, digging deep and finding only lint. Panic rolled through my limbs with each passing second. Breathing became a task, and I couldn't still my hands even if I'd tried. I looked on the floor, behind the seat, between the cushions—everywhere— and still found nothing. That's when I remembered why. It was sitting on the end table near my bed, shut off and charging. I'd completely forgotten to grab it.

Worse. Case. Scenario.

I slammed the door shut and threw my palm forward, smacking the frame with a *thwap*. I pulled back and did it again, hurling my hand into cold metal. The cycle continued until the flesh stung so sharply beneath my fingers, I was forced to stop. Defeated, I leaned against my truck and took in air. My options were bleak. Even if I went inside to use the phone, I wouldn't know what number to call. Tony was number three on speed dial, trailing only behind Gram and Sarah. That meant I'd have to ask Mr. Greenwich for Tony's number—which he had since Tony worked the produce department—but I doubted he'd give it to me. Or I could switch out the tire and haul ass to Tony's, hoping that he hadn't already ditched me which, to be honest, was a real possibility, considering his alarming level of infatuation for Candace.

I decided on the latter.

I'd just hoisted my truck on the jack when a small shadow washed over me.

"Oh, no! Did you run over a nail or something?"

That familiar voice brought an ache to my chest, and I swallowed hard before craning my neck. Behind me, Sarah stood with her arms folded across her torso, gripping her ribs in a solitary hug. Her unwashed, blonde hair was thrown into a haphazard ponytail with a few slick strands poking out. Her puffy, red eyes flickered nervously between the wheel well and my annoyed face.

"How the hell should I know?" I asked bitingly and started to loosen the first bolt.

"You haven't returned my calls."

"Yeah, I know."

"I think we need to talk."

"Talk then," I said as the bolt released its hold and began to turn. I kept my eyes trained away. It hurt too much to look at her.

Sarah crouched beside me, her shadow shrinking against the pavement to blend with my own. She rested her hand tentatively on my thigh.

Even though her palm felt much too heavy, I liked her touch and hated myself for it.

Sarah sighed deeply. That one, exhaled breath, filled with sadness, was enough to stall me. I finally met her eyes, and my anger faded at the sorrow that existed there. She gave me a grim smile before looking around. Her expression hardened while surveying the lot, transforming from grief into the distinct look of paranoia. She leaned in and said, "Something strange is going on."

Her words caught me off guard, and I pulled away. I'd expected a rehearsed apology, not … *this*. What was this exactly? A conspiracy theory? A diversion? Whatever it was, it surprised me. Sarah flinched, and having mistook my gesture for one of anger, removed her hand.

"*What*?" I asked.

Sarah repeated, "Something strange is going on." She looked from side to side and leaned in to whisper. "Something *really* strange."

"You've got to give me more than that," I said as my eyes drifted longingly to her hands. She was twisting them nervously in front of her. And part of me, despite the hurt, wished she'd return her touch. I hated myself for missing her, but I couldn't help it.

My voice must've revealed despondency—not anger—since she seemed to gather strength. Her shoulders pulled tight and her back straightened. After a moment of hesitation, she licked her lips and said, "What happened on Friday…."

That's when the world turned red. Just thinking about her actions brought heat into my cheeks. I dropped the tire iron near my feet. The impact made a clang that sent sound waves across the lot. My hands balled into fists, forcing the ragged edges of bitten fingernails to press painfully into my flesh. I sprang up, causing Sarah to sway on her heels. She splayed her palm on the pavement to stabilize her teetering body.

I crossed my arms and replied with venom, "I don't want to hear this again."

Sarah stood and took a step away, afraid of the hostility I radiated. "No," she said. "You don't understand."

"I'll tell you what I don't understand," I said as I leaned in close, making my words strong and powerful. "What I don't understand is why my girlfriend of over a year would cheat on me with the reigning douche of our high school. The past two days have been hell, and it's your fault." I nearly spat the words. "How was it, Sarah? Was Alex worth it? Are you regretting your mistake?" My tone hitched up a level.

Sarah brought her fingertips to her lips, covering her mouth and lower face. She started to shake her head as her eyes puddled with tears. "It's a lie," she said.

"Stop with the excuses. I've already heard those."

"It's the truth!"

"Bull."

That's when Sarah stiffened. "NO, DANIEL!" she said harshly. "I'm telling you that something bigger is going on." She stuck her finger against my chest. I swatted it away, but the firm look of Sarah's blue eyes made me pause.

"Sarah, we went over this yesterday, and now I'm running late. I've got places to be." I started to kneel when Sarah dodged in my way. She placed her foot firmly on top of the tire iron. "What are you doing?" I asked.

Ignoring my question, Sarah asked one of her own. "Let me guess; this place you have to be has to do with Tony's new girlfriend?"

I blinked. That was the plan, but it was beyond me how she'd figured that out. Tony and I had goals that afternoon. We were supposed to head up into the mountains where we'd meet up with Candace and her sister, Claire. My expression must have said it all because Sarah gave me a cynical smile. "That's what I thought," she said.

"I don't see how Candace has anything to do with this."

"I think she has *everything* to do with this. I did not do what everyone is saying I did." She enunciated each word carefully, "I'm certain someone slipped me something, and I think it was her." She paused as a sallow man with pockmarked skin pushed a cart filled with aluminum cans past us. She waited until he was out of earshot before continuing on in a frantic whisper. "After you left yesterday, I tried to remember what happened on Friday. It's fuzzy, but I remember Candace handing me my soda. I'd just gotten back from the bathroom. She was watching me all funny, like she was waiting for something. At the time, I thought I was overthinking it—you know, getting worked up over nothing—but now I'm not so sure." Sarah gave off an involuntary shiver and wrapped her arms around herself.

I snickered sarcastically. "You mean rum, right? Or maybe vodka? Both kinda look like soda, depending on your drink of choice."

She glared. "NO! I didn't have any alcohol."

"Suuure … that's why your voice slurred on the voicemail; too much cola. Perhaps the ice was spiked?"

Sarah rolled her eyes before her jaw squared. "DANIEL THATCHER! Dammit, are you even listening to me? That's why I think she slipped me something! Because it was only *after* I finished my drink that she tells me she has a headache and asks if I have any medicine for it. I remember going out to the car and digging around the glove box. When I found the pills, I stood up, only to hear someone come up from behind. It was dark, and I wasn't able to see who it was. But I swear *someone* was there. That's right before everything went black. Next thing I know, I'm waking up in a ditch, and everyone is saying that I made the biggest mistake of my life."

She looked around to make sure no one was listening in on our conversation.

"Look, Daniel. I know I'm asking you to take a huge leap of faith, but you gotta believe me. I really don't know why I'd do something like that. The only explanation I can come up with is that someone slipped me something."

"Sarah—"

"Take my cellphone. I couldn't find it after I woke up in the ditch. My bag was near me, but my phone was gone. After you left yesterday, I started searching again."

The harvested memories from the day before were still crisp. Sarah, confused and pale, attempted to melt into the driveway while I waved my phone in front of her face, voicemail blaring on speaker as I stage-whispered profanities in her direction. Her garbled recording boasted Alex's oral talents in comparison to my own. It's one thing to cheat, but to call up your boyfriend and brag about it was beyond comprehension—a league all of its own. The curtain in the living room billowed as her mother tried, rather unsuccessfully, to eavesdrop without us noticing. It added to the humiliation.

"Guess where I found it?" Sarah asked, yanking me back to the present.

I shook my head; I wasn't in the mood for guessing games.

"I found it in my glove box." She waited for me to react, but I didn't know what I was supposed to be reacting to. I cocked my head, confused.

Sarah, annoyed, tossed her hands in the air. "Not once, not one single time, have I ever placed my phone in the glove box," she explained. "Someone had to have put it there, like they were trying to hide it from me."

"Sarah, it was your voice on the voicemail. It wasn't like I got a text. Are you trying to say someone framed you, that you didn't leave that message? You heard it yourself. And everyone at the party saw you with Alex; explain that." I was exasperated. I hated seeing Sarah upset, but talking about Friday angered me, too. I was the victim, and her excuses just rehashed wounds that'd barely scabbed over.

It was clear that Sarah regretted her mistake, and I think in order to make peace with herself, she fabricated a new, less-painful version. I believed, *she believed*, this was all a grand conspiracy.

She started to cry. "I don't know what happened, but you gotta believe me. This is so strange. I think Candace intentionally broke us up. And...." She hesitated. Shame crept into her eyes before she looked away, embarrassed.

"And?" I prompted.

Sarah nervously shifted her weight from one foot to the other. Not looking at me, she asked haltingly, "Don't you think it's odd? Candace, I mean? She shows up out of nowhere, and now she and Tony are going out. It doesn't make sense."

"Because she's new to town or because she's with Tony?"

"You know what I mean. Tony, and, well, those two together...." Fresh tears trickled down her cheeks. When she lifted her face to gauge my reaction, I saw humiliation stamped across it. Disgust transformed her pretty features, aging it well beyond her sixteen years. Sarah may be a cheater, but she wasn't a bully. She hated when people passed judgment, and here she was, doing just that. Her hypocritical words stung.

I knew exactly what she meant. And it would be a lie to say the thought hadn't crossed my mind. Tony was awkward. Tall, thin, and prone to really bad acne—with scars to match—his cratered complexion provided a bumpy slate for features that didn't quite match up. With a nose too large and a mouth too small, he'd never pass as handsome. Candace, on the other hand, was the farthest thing from awkward. With long, honey hair, large, blue eyes, and porcelain skin, she was perfect. *Stunning.* And when paired together, it was blatantly clear they didn't fit.

Two pieces of a different puzzle: one, an image of a masterpiece; the other, a bargain-bin painting.

"Tony has charisma," I said weakly. Sarah gave me a bleak smile, as if to say, you know something's wrong, too. But I chose to ignore it and instead focused on the real issue: Sarah's cheating. "And none of that really matters. The deed is done. Everyone saw the show you and Alex put on. I wish you could take it back, but that's impossible." And in my mind, it really *didn't* matter if she was drugged. The damage was irrevocable. If I took her back, I'd be a chump—the loser who lets his girlfriend run around on him.

"But you always said we were meant for each other."

This, of all things, hit the hardest, and I had to swallow past the lump that lodged itself in the base of my throat. Sarah and I had been that odd couple that looked alike. Both of us had light hair and sky eyes. The common consensus was that we looked more like brother and sister than boyfriend and girlfriend. Sarah was miffed by this; I tried to convince her it was more of a compliment, that we looked right for each other. Now she was using my words against me.

Despite the overwhelming urge to turn and walk away, I did the opposite and pulled her into a hug. Sarah responded with enthusiasm and squeezed tightly. It was a painful embrace—physically, as well as emotionally—and I used it to hide the breaking of my face. Sadness annihilates bravado on virtually every level. I tucked my head into her hair, not caring that it was greasy and unwashed, and inhaled deeply, relishing the scent. It smelled like Sarah and reminded me how bad this really hurt.

"Please, wherever it is that you're supposed to go, don't do it. Stay." Sarah's words came out muffled against my chest. "Candace is up to something; I'm certain of it."

I bit down on my lower lip and suppressed the urge to tell her about the double-date. Sarah was already worked up, and she'd blow a gasket if she knew Tony and I were meeting Candace and Claire in the forest. She'd say it was too isolated, too odd.

"You've never been the paranoid type," I said, trying to add a bit of humor. But the heavy grit in my voice gave away my true emotions.

Sarah pulled away and looked up. "That, of all things, should concern you," she said as she wiped at her eyes.

And it did, for only a moment. A small inkling of fear crept into my heart—like a spark plug on its last fizzle of life. But that fizzle quickly died when I thought about what was to come. Monday would be the first school day since the "incident," and it was going to be brutal meeting the mocking eyes of my classmates, the gloating eyes of Alex. It was one of the drawbacks of living in a one-high-school town. Gossip was a favorite pastime. That's why I needed the date with Claire—she was to be the salve on a gaping, festering wound. It was a fast turnaround, but I owed Sarah no loyalty after what she did. I needed a rebound to prepare for the days ahead.

The date with Claire was supposed to lessen the pain, and Sarah had put me even further behind.

I walked Sarah to her car and told her that time would heal things. Her eyes sparked briefly, and I worried about giving her false hope. But I needed to get to Tony's, and I was ready to tell her just about anything to get back to fixing my flat.

After her car pulled out of the lot, it took a little under ten minutes to complete the job. Then the race was on.

When I arrived at Tony's, my eyes landed straightaway on his car, and for a moment, I thought he'd waited for me. But my optimism rapidly faded once I spotted the note tucked under his windshield wiper. Even from the distance, I could make out my name written across the front.

When I unfolded it, Tony's sloppy scrawl was nearly illegible, as though he wrote the letter in a hurry.

> Dan,
>
> Sorry man. Waited around, but you never showed. Took Eric with me. He was begging to go. Didn't want to show up without a date for Claire. Hope you understand.
>
> -Tony

And below that, in Eric's slanted print, were the words:

> Haha! Suck it, loser.

I expected Tony to go ahead without me. Eric, serving as my replacement, was something I hadn't prepared for. I crumpled the letter into a tight, angry ball and thrust it into my pocket. The day was a total wash. I drove home—sick to my stomach—knowing that I'd missed the opportunity of a lifetime.

{ 2 }

TONY'S VANISHING ACT

Eric Martin was a self-absorbed wiseass and a dick. Always had been, always will be. He was the type of kid in school who would infuriate you, only to redeem himself with some offhanded comment that was so completely inappropriate it was funny, or by taking the fall for an offense he didn't commit. A penance, I suppose.

Case in point: once Eric and I had flown a paper airplane back and forth in writing class. On it I'd written some vulgar comments about our teacher, the bifocaled Mr. Lewis. Eric caught the plane just as Mr. Lewis turned around. His bald head bobbed as he stalked over to Eric's desk, ripped the paper from his hands, and started to read. His face ripened with embarrassment, stemming from his reedy neck all the way to his cue ball scalp. He demanded to know the author, and before I could cop to the crime, Eric got cocky. He leaned back in his chair, put his hands behind his head, and in a voice that didn't falter in the least said, "I did. Just practicing my creative writing skills." He gave off his classic Martin grin before the teacher promptly issued a detention. After the lesson proceeded, Eric held up a piece of paper behind Mr. Lewis' back that said: *Detention = Nap time.* He winked, and I gave him a mock salute in lieu of thanks.

It was those moments that overshadowed his obnoxiousness.

But he was still a dick.

He was also my second cousin.

And family or not, that brawny meathead had crossed a line. Big time. Fuming over his two-faced, selfish actions, my knuckles flexed white as I gripped the steering wheel. It wasn't just the note, or Eric taking my place, that enraged me; it was that it didn't come as a surprise. Unexpected—yes; surprised—no. I figured Tony would've stopped him. Eric was a force to be reckoned with, but Tony was my best friend, and he knew what that date meant to me.

Hell, Eric knew, too, but that hadn't mattered.

And now Eric was meeting *my* girl, and all because Tony never grew a set. It was enough to tick a guy off. On the drive home, I attempted to level my anger by counting the dashed lines between solid stripes, and since I lived on the outskirts of Hicksville—aka Trestle, Oregon—I had plenty of time to practice. I'd been playing this cool-down game a lot lately. I was starting to get good at it.

At least the scenery was pleasant. Trestle, a poky, rural town wedged between two mountain ranges, was framed by farm fields and healthy rivers. To the west sat the Coastal Mountains, and to the east, the Cascades. On clear days, the scenery was incredible with breathtaking views from nearly every angle. But it's Oregon. And clear days are a rarity, especially nine months out of the year. Rain—a nasty, four-letter word for those living in warmer, friendlier climates—was simply a part of life here. Because of it, everything was green and beautiful.

I suppose it was nature's method of checks and balances. Pretty, but wet.

By the time I pulled up to the house I shared with my grandmother, I'd managed to calm down. *A little.*

Gram's place, located on a dead-end country road, was set back on a small rise. The property consisted of twentyish acres, all of which had gone to pasture, except for a small stamp of lawn and slightly-larger chunk of timber. Gram was the queen of yard flair; and like a rummage sale gone horribly wrong, every bare space was covered with offensive lawn ornaments. Little gnomes sat in flower beds, ugly flamingos leaned against trees, and tacky statues rested under noble firs—all covered in a thin layer of moss colored slime.

Her house was a charming, yellow craftsman with bright, white trim. It was large and had a great feature that, in my opinion, was priceless: a fully-equipped basement lair. Complete with a separate entrance, kitchenette, family room, bathroom, and bedroom, it was considered a daylight basement apartment. I was allowed full run of it once I came to live with her.

Sitting in the driveway, where I normally parked, was my Aunt Marie's SUV. That meant Lacey was visiting. Instantly, my mood picked up. If anyone could put me in better spirits, it was that little monster.

Sure enough, as I stepped out of my truck, her small head popped out of Gram's front door. She gave me a big smile, absent one front tooth, before running down the steps. She jumped into my arms and I picked her up, swinging her around in a hearty embrace.

"Ewww! You're all dirty," she cried.

"Really?" I asked with wide-eyed wonder.

"Yes," she answered earnestly, like I'd gone bonkers for not noticing. Then her eyes brightened. "Look, Danny," she said, pointing at her front tooth. "I lost my first tooth!"

I whistled. "Wow! Now you look like a jack-o-lantern!"

She laughed before becoming somber.

"I do not," she said seriously.

I followed her cue and agreed solemnly. "You're right, you look nothing like a pumpkin." I sat her down and chucked her under the chin. She smiled. "But now, the big question. Did you get any loot for that tooth?"

She dug into her pocket and pulled out a crumpled up bill. "Yeah, the tooth fairy came and gave me this." She displayed it proudly.

"No kidding! A whole dollar? Wow, that's a lot more than I got; must be inflation." Lacey gave me a quizzical look, unsure of that last word, but quickly moved on to more pressing matters.

"I'm gonna watch cartoons; wanna watch with me?" She tugged on my hand, skipping up the broad steps leading to Gram's front porch.

"Aw, I'm gonna have to pass, squirt," I said as I absentmindedly ran my free hand across the top of a lavender bush growing near the stairs.

Lacey's bottom lip stuck out in an exaggerated pout. She pulled harder on my hand.

"Danny! *Please!*" Her little voice was too irresistible, and I found myself relenting, despite the overwhelming desire to hibernate and stew in my own misery. This had been the worst weekend of my life. She saw me waffle and jumped up and down excitedly. Refusal was officially out of the question.

"Well … I suppose."

"YAY!" she shouted and ran into the house. "Danny's gonna watch cartoons with me," she announced happily.

Inside, I found Aunt Marie and Gram sitting at the kitchen table. Marie was patting Gram's back, as Gram shook from one of her coughing fits. Her paper skin had adapted a few more folds in the past month. Marie and I exchanged a worrisome glance as Gram collected her breath. After a few iffy moments, Gram cleared her throat and brushed Marie's hand away, sitting up with too much bravado.

She wasn't fooling anybody.

"Hi Daniel," Marie greeted warmly, as her eyes flickered between my stubborn grandmother and Lacey tugging at my hand. Gram had a doctor's appointment the following day to have her troublesome—and worsening—cough evaluated. We were careful to keep our traps shut around Lacey. Gram acted indifferent, like she was entirely well, and we were all making a big deal out of nothing.

God, I hoped that was true.

"Hey," I said with fake enthusiasm.

"So you're going to watch cartoons? Either you're the strangest sixteen-year-old boy on the planet, or you got suckered into it by a cute five-year-old." Marie winked conspiratorially at me as her voice lightened. Lacey grinned, toothless and pleased.

"Hey! I'm almost seventeen." I corrected her, not wanting to be shorted a well-earned year.

"Sorry. You're the strangest—*almost seventeen*—year-old then," she agreed, with genuine laughter.

I gave her a reproving look, feeling better. "Don't get it wrong again," I replied, before giving Lacey a big smile. She began pulling me towards the living room where the muffled sounds of cartoon music wafted in the air.

"So is it suckered or strange?" Aunt Marie pressed.

"Maybe a little bit of both," I said over my shoulder as Lacey directed me away. A thin string of laughter trailed from behind.

The rest of the afternoon was spent in front of the television in Gram's overly floral living room surrounded by the stench of lavender, watching mind-numbing cartoons and listening to Lacey ramble off on a number of topics that were absolutely unimportant to anyone except a five-year-old.

By then I'd retrieved my cell and intermittently sent messages to both Tony and Eric.

All went unanswered.

Actually, my phone remained quiet since four o'clock—which was bizarre, considering I'd been inundated with texts all weekend. After the breakup with Sarah, anonymous pricks started blowing it up with hateful texts. They called me a loser, a dumb-ass, a fool. They asked how I liked sharing my girlfriend.

I hadn't realized I had so many enemies. Skating under the radar was a talent I prided myself in. Apparently, I wasn't as neutral as I thought. All the numbers were unfamiliar, killing my chances of pinning it on anyone.

It made their taunts even more painful. What had I done to them? *Effing cowards, every last one them.*

It was one of those messages that pushed me towards Claire. Originally, I had turned down Candace's offer. After all, I'd just broken up with Sarah that morning, and my heart didn't really own a beat. Sarah was the first girl I ever cared about, and the thought of meeting up with another wasn't appetizing. But shortly after—when my phone vibrated in my pocket and I saw the text: "Can I have a turn with Sarah next? Alex said he's cool with it. Lol!"—I changed my mind.

A rebound girl never sounded better.

But even those texts had ceased. The last one I'd received came in while I was changing out my tire—and my phone sat charging at home. It simply read, "Don't trust pretty girls."

But now, silence. Which, in a bizarre way, was worse.

Even though it never went off, it didn't stop me from checking it incessantly throughout the evening. It was the unknown that made my imagination run wild. I envisioned Eric and Tony having a great time with two gorgeous girls. They would be laughing and happy—while I was stuck at home, licking my wounds.

By the time I fell asleep, my head was brimming with angry thoughts. If only one of those two A-holes would call me. I sent off a group message to both of them before turning in. The words I selected would've made a sailor blush.

And still … nothing.

I was under no ill-conceived notion that school was going to be easy the following day. I fully expected it to be bad; I just didn't know *how* bad. News traveled fast. As I made my way through the halls, stares followed my every move. Whispers and chuckles fogged the air.

I was a laughingstock.

Defiantly, I met their eyes—challenging them. I walked with as much confidence as I could muster, locking eyes with a few brazen nobodies who had the nerve to look me straight on. *Do it.* Say something and see what happens. I wanted a fight. Hell, a fight would've felt good. But no one approached me. Another tally on my long list of disappointments.

Irritated, I tossed my books inside my locker as footsteps approached from behind. I turned, expecting to see Eric or Tony, but instead met the sad and mournful gaze of Sarah.

"Not now," I said.

"I just wanted to say hi." Sarah was more put together than the day before, wearing an oversized, blue sweater with leggings and knee-high boots. She looked cute. *Icing on my crappy cake.*

"Well, I'm not in the mood to talk." I let my eyes drift around the hallway. She caught my gist and looked down guiltily at her feet. "Let's not give them another show," I said.

"Can we have lunch today?"

I gave her a preposterous look.

"No, we can't. I told you yesterday, I need some space." My voice came out in a harsh whisper, ever aware of the prying eyes and eager ears surrounding us.

"I know. I just thought maybe we could talk some more."

"There's nothing more to talk about. I'm sorry, Sarah. I know you think someone set you up, but the way I look at it, even if you were slipped something, you still made out with Alex. That's not an accident. That tells me one of two things: one, you've been harboring some sort of repressed feelings for him, or two, you and I were never that strong to begin with." I leaned against my locker and crossed my arms. "Either way, there must've been some serious issues in our relationship—issues I refused to see before—but I can't stop seeing them now. Don't make this harder than it has to be."

Sarah nodded while her eyes dampened. I fought that familiar yearning to hold her.

"I wish I'd never gone to that party," she said.

"That makes two of us."

Sarah ran her sleeve over her eyes and bit down on her bottom lip.

The sight of her was too much. I started to move away.

"I've got to go. I'll talk to you later." My words came out empty. She and I both knew I really didn't mean them.

The morning passed by much the same. Between classes, Sarah was always conveniently nearby, hovering, waiting for the moment I'd approach her with words of forgiveness.

When I walked the halls, the eyes of my fellow classmates burrowed into my back. I kept a lookout for Eric and Tony, but didn't see either of them. I also kept a lookout for Alex. I decided between morning classes—which included a nap in Economics—that I was going to take a swing. Suspension be damned.

At the start of lunch break, I sent another text to Tony. Vanishing wasn't something Tony did.

It was irritating, and the longer the silence prevailed, the more bitter I became.

Eric was a traitor; Tony, too. Tony let Eric steal Claire. Now I was isolated—ditched completely—and it looked like I'd have to spend the entire day by myself. All of a sudden I was very alone, and pairing that with the list of betrayals I'd endured—first Sarah, then Eric—I was surprised I was even at school.

A sudden notion hit me. Why not leave?

I could play hooky. No one would blame me. The thought was tempting, and as I leaned against my locker considering it, laughter rang down the hall.

My eyes focused on the group having a jolly-ass time, and in the center of the comedic cluster stood Alex. My vision hazed as my hands knotted up. When Alex pointed in my direction, my face simmered. Without thinking, I started towards the gleeful pretty boy. The look I wore must've rattled him because he blanched. That brought a bit of satisfaction. If he was scared now, just wait; I was going to make sure that perfect nose of his was forever out of alignment.

The adrenaline gave me unwavering confidence, and I hoped it would translate into a sudden burst of strength. I wanted him to hurt. I wanted my fist to crack his face. But as I approached the group, knuckles ready for the assault, his posse of followers crowded around him, one even stepping in my way. The little pansy was going to take the cowardly way out. He eagerly hid behind his friends.

"Come on, Alex," I taunted. "Hiding behind your friends?" I tried to push his pal—Steve, I think—out of the way. "That's a little wussy way to behave." If the coward wasn't going to fight, I'd at least attack his ego.

"I don't need to fight you," Alex snidely replied. "In case you haven't noticed, I've already won." His patronizing smile was all it took. I lunged at him, shoving his human shield to the side. Steve stumbled as I leapt towards Alex, barely missing him as he dodged out of my way. It took me less than a second to regain my bearings and go in for another swing. But as I pulled my hand back, one of Alex's followers grabbed me from behind and violently pushed me away. I stayed on my feet and readied myself for another go, determined to make contact with the little weasel, when an authoritative voice stalled us all.

"Cool it down, boys." It was the PE teacher, Mr. Thompson. He stepped in-between Alex and I. Built like a bull, Mr. Thompson had a broad chest like a solid sack of dry concrete. "Fighting constitutes grounds for suspension; need I remind you?" He crossed his arms over his cemented pecs and lined his feet up with his shoulders—the most no-nonsense stance in the history of mankind.

Alex acted penitent, lowering his head a fraction, while my hand flexed instinctively. Mr. Thompson's eyes narrowed in my direction.

"Now, technically, I should take you all down to the principal's office, but I think we can agree that wouldn't be beneficial to any of you. Why don't you all cool down and go your separate ways? The last thing I want to see is all of you suspended." He wasn't doing me a favor. If I got suspended, Alex would, too, and Mr. Thompson didn't want to sacrifice his golden boy right before track season.

"Sorry, Mr. Thompson," Alex said agreeably.

Mr. Thompson looked directly at me. "This is done." He said it not as a question, but as a definitive statement. He waited for my response.

"Yes, sir," I replied through gritted teeth. He narrowed his eyes further. I continued, "This is done." I repeated him, not meaning the words but saying them for necessity.

"Well, then, off to lunch." He clapped his hands and shooed us away.

I caught a satisfied smirk from Alex before he pivoted on his heel and went the opposite direction. If Mr. Thompson hadn't been staring so intently, watching my every move, I would've followed him outside. *I'd get him sooner or later.*

Instead, I retreated towards my locker, grabbed my bag, and headed out the door. I wasn't going to return after lunch. I had my fill of school for the day.

Hell, I'd had my fill of school for the year.

I almost missed it. I'd just placed my key in the ignition when I saw the note tucked under my wiper. Too lazy to get out, I rolled down the window and reached for the slip of paper. My shoulder pressed tightly against the pickup's doorframe as I grabbed the corner and tugged, pulling so abruptly that my wiper caught and lifted before snapping back into place.

Victorious, I unfolded the letter in my lap and read:

Dan-

Sorry, man. I didn't want to leave like this, but I need to get out of this stupid town and find myself. I might camp out for a bit to collect my thoughts.

No hard feelings,

-Tony

Confused, I turned the letter over, hoping to find additional information. I found some, although it wasn't what I was looking for. On the back were directions to the meeting place Candace had written down. It was beat-up and filthy looking, and in the corner there was a light red smear. It looked like blood. Or possibly ketchup. I folded the note and put it in my pocket for safekeeping.

I wasn't going to take this news lying down. I called Tony since texting didn't work. When the automated voice came through, saying the line was disconnected, my hands grew cold. I dialed Eric's number. His line went straight to voicemail.

Since when did the world flip on its axis? I turned the ignition, popped it into reverse, and pulled out of the lot. I was going to hunt down answers.

CONFUSION

This was out of character for Tony. He was one year ahead of both Eric and I, the only senior of our small group. With only a few months left before graduation, he was chomping at the bit for that diploma, determined to be the first in his family to graduate from high school. It was a big deal, so for him to skip town seemed downright unlikely.

And for him to ditch me—leaving behind a solitary farewell note and nothing more—that was messed up.

On the edge of our town in clusters are a number of trailer parks. I always thought "park" was a bit of a stretch. Really, it's just a collective group of people who seemed at peace living on the fringe of society.

As is the case with many small, rural towns, there's not a lot to do. So in order to stave off death by boredom, some people turn to drugs. Or sex. Sometimes both, and Trestle was no different. Meth was fairly rampant throughout the area, and it seemed to flow among these parks much the same as it spread through the veins of its intravenous users. Rumor had it that heroin was on the rise, too. That was according to Tony, who happened to live in one of the mangiest parks in town.

I turned into the entrance and drove past the evenly spaced sin-gle-wides lined in rows. A tweaker on his bike crossed in front of me. He clipped the speed bump I was about to cross over and contorted his body to make the bike catch air. With a cigarette dangling from his chapped lips, he flipped me the bird as a way of greeting.

I returned the gesture.

Tony's trailer was at the far end of the park. Weeds, tires, and rem-nants of a mechanical graveyard cluttered the small parcel of grass that seemed only to exist for garbage-collection. Although all the "homes" were in need of repair, I'd peg Tony's as the worst.

One of the windows had a large crack creeping up the middle and was bandaged together with the fail-safe combination of plastic wrap and silver tape. Decayed steps led to a warped front door, encased by tin siding that was in an active state of shedding its paint.

I rapped on the door with angry knuckles, and the trailer rattled as steady footsteps approached. I wasn't the least bit surprised when Tony's mom answered, wearing sweats and a holey T-shirt. She was a large, unkempt woman with bad skin and frayed hair. The material of her shirt was so thin that the outline of her bra poked through. *Nasty.* I kept my eyes averted, not needing a traumatic image burned into my brain.

Before I could say anything, she spoke up.

"Tony ain't here." She spat the words like they left a bad taste in her mouth.

"You've seen him?"

She snorted, as her reproachful gaze rested on me.

"Yeah, I saw the little ingrate. He came by a couple hours ago. Packed up all his stuff in a few trash sacks." She stopped to spit outside the door. Ugh. *Classy.*

"So he … left?" I asked numbly.

She smirked. "You dumb, boy? Isn't that what I just said?"

"Did you try and stop him?" It was the only question I could wrap my head around. Surely she would've tried to keep him home. Of all things, she needed Tony. He worked to pay her bills, although it killed him to do so. Her money went towards feeding her vices, not towards putting food on the table. But despite everything, he remained loyal, looking after her even when she was too wasted, or high, to look after herself.

"No, I didn't try an' stop him. He's eighteen, after all. And besides, after the way he treated me—"

"Do you know where he went?" I asked, cutting her off. I didn't give a rats-ass how he'd treated her. Tony was too nice to his scum-of-the-earth mom.

This time she sneered. "I don't know, and I don't care." She leaned against the doorframe and crossed her arms. "He better not show his face 'round here again. Y' know what he said to me?" She was determined to get her side across and started to pitch her voice mockingly. "He said, 'I no longer want to be a part of your life. You've failed me one too many times. I'm leaving, and I don't plan on ever seein' you again. Don't bother contacting me, ever.'"

"He said that?" I asked disbelievingly. "Tony doesn't talk like that."

"Are you callin' me a liar?" Stale tobacco clung to her breath, like musty ash from a campfire fueled by roadkill.

Yeah, actually I am, but couldn't say so aloud. If she got pissed, I'd end up with the door slammed in my face and no answers to boot, so instead I opted to lie. "No, not at all." I gave her my perfected false smile, the one I reserved for crappy customers and snooty teachers. "I've just never heard him talk like that. Was he all right?"

"He seemed fine, 'cept for the chip on his shoulder. But he's not my problem any more; 'pparently, I'm just a bad mother. Y' know what bothers me the most? I was actually plannin' on attending my first AA meetin' t'day, but I guess it don't matter now. He no longer cares 'bout me."

Pretending his words cut her deep, she started to shake her shoulders while rubbing grubby fists into dry eyes. His mom was a master manipulator, and I'd seen this type of act before. I wasn't buying it.

Behind her, to prove my point, sat a beer on the counter. Freshly opened, the cold condensation was starting to puddle at its base. I'd interrupted her daily drinking binge—an event that fueled her other addictive habits. She was putting on a show, and I was done watching.

"Well, thanks anyway."

As I turned to leave, she yelled from the door.

"If ya see him, you tell him he hurt me real bad. You tell him I don't have much time left, and he should feel awful. I could die any day, and all I'll have on my mind are them awful things he said to me. You tell him he's a terrible person, and he should be 'shamed of himself. I'll never forgive him. YOU HEAR ME! NEVER!"

Her vile words drifted heavily behind me.

"HE'S AN AWFUL PERSON! You make sure he knows that!"

I slammed my truck door, effectively blocking out the hateful air spurting from her putrid mouth. Tony didn't deserve a mother like that. No one did. People like her can't be reasoned with—personal experience taught me that. Mom with her pills and Dad with his needles, I understood firsthand what it was like to have deadbeat parents. Thinking about my painful past renewed the sense of gratitude I owed Gram. At least I had her, whereas, Tony had no one. I watched his mom turn around and go back into the personal Hell she'd created—to drink and use, to rot what was left of her pitiful existence.

Even though Tony's POS mom confirmed he'd indeed left home, I still wasn't convinced he'd skipped town altogether. Perhaps it was wishful thinking, but I held on to graduation. He wanted that diploma. He needed it. Tony wouldn't quit the race on his final lap—and senior year was just that.

I also knew his habits well. During summer months when he wasn't sleeping on my couch, he'd camp out at Emerald Grove, a local hotspot for campers at the base of the Cascades. Camping was his escape, his reprieve from the life he'd been given. It wasn't farfetched to think he was doing exactly that, hiding out in the woods as the letter indicated.

It was time to hunt down Eric; he'd know what was going on.

Eric's home life was radically different than Tony's. Eric lived in a nice, established neighborhood, filled with custom homes on large lots. As I neared Eric's drive, his truck was nowhere in sight. That pretty much guaranteed he was at Charlie's; not surprising, considering Eric stayed at his grandpa's house more than half the time.

Eric hated his stepfather, Bill, often referring to him as his home-bound nemesis. And I agreed. Bill was a total A-hole. He was egotistical, bigoted, and self-centered—a rare combination even amongst the self-serving elite of Trestle (if such a thing even existed).

So rather than deal with Bill, I bypassed Eric's house altogether and headed straight for Great-Uncle Charlie's.

Charlie was Gram's older brother and the source of my relation to Eric. Gram and Charlie were as close as two siblings could possibly be, and it was exceptionally hard on her when she lived out of state.

Ages ago, when Gram was a newlywed and pregnant with my dad, Richard, she and Grandpa Dylan moved to Maine. They traded in the Pacific Ocean for the Atlantic, a move so dramatic that Gram got weepy whenever she talked about it. But Gram wasn't comfortable living so far away. She missed the rest of her family, in particular, her brother Charlie.

So I suppose that's one of the reasons why she jumped at the opportunity to move back to Oregon. I was in kindergarten when Gram's mother passed away, leaving behind a farm that had been in the family for generations. Uncle Charlie didn't want to live there, so Gram decided to take it over.

Although Mom and Dad were clean back then, they still couldn't replace the void Gram left behind. Nothing was ever the same.

Now Great-Uncle Charlie, he'd married money. Grace came from a longstanding farming family and inherited a lot of land. Although Charlie enjoyed the outdoors, he wasn't a farmer, and neither was Grace. So they hired a manager to cultivate and work their massive land holdings. The setup was a good gig. Charlie became a forest ranger—preferring timberland to crop fields—and Grace was the traditional stay-at-home wife. They were always flush with cash, and Charlie didn't have to bring in a substantial paycheck.

Because of their ample bank account, Charlie lived in a grand country home set back amongst old oak trees. The house was a stunner. It was white and reminded me of lavish plantation homes displayed in magazines. Tall pillars supported a wide balcony, and a door made of solid cherry rested in the center. Off to the right, a large, distressed porch swing hung from the rafters.

Charlie's Border Collie, Max, barked his greeting as I parked in the circular driveway and stepped out. Max pressed for my attention by twirling in circles and yipping at my heels. I gave him a cursory greeting, patting his smooth, black fur as his tail whipped back and forth, the white tip a blur.

Eric's truck was parked near the detached garage. I breathed a sigh of relief. He was here, and I was going to get some much-needed answers. With Max at my side, I rang the bell.

Uncle Charlie answered. It took a moment to digest his appearance. The tired, disheveled man standing before me was a shell of his former self, a poor representation of Charlie's normal pristine image. His plaid flannel shirt was dirty and buttoned askew. His pants, creased, as though he'd slept in them. But it wasn't his clothes that disturbed me—it was the expression he wore on his weathered face.

Grief stricken. That's the only way I could describe it. His face, usually happy and bright, had dimmed. The lines around his eyes were deeper, his lips stretched grim and tight. Not a hint of a smile played on his face. Subtly—so slight I wasn't completely sure—I thought I saw his eyes flash with disgust.

I must've been standing there, gawking, because he spoke first.

"What is it you need, Daniel?" he asked with hostility.

Where had this come from? I took a step back, creating a distance between his negative energy and myself, worried his mood might be contagious.

"Is Eric here?" I asked, my unease so blatant that Charlie could no doubt detect it. It didn't bother him though, his jaw flexed on grated hinges while he took me in with silent revulsion. He stood inside the doorjamb, not moving, not inviting me in.

"He can't talk right now."

"Is he okay?"

Charlie narrowed his eyes into a mean glare.

"He's not feeling well," he replied.

"Can I see him for a sec? I need to talk to him about a friend of ours."

When Charlie didn't budge, I continued my futile attempt to explain, all the while trying to decipher his odd behavior.

"See, Tony … you know, the guy who hangs out with us all the time…." My words got tripped up by my tongue, which seemed to have doubled in size. I sucked in a lungful of air, composing myself. "Well, yesterday he and Eric went out, and I just found this bizarre letter saying he was skipping town. I checked with his mom, and she said he packed up all his clothes this morning. It's just very unlike him." Charlie's eyes looked blank, disinterested. I added, "And his phone's been disconnected."

I waited for Charlie to react, to open the door and step aside so I could talk to Eric, but instead, I was greeted by more disdain.

"I said he's sick, Daniel."

I flinched as he began to turn away. I reached out my hand to stop the door from shutting in my face.

"Can't I see him for a moment?" I asked desperately, my palm resting on the door with just enough pressure to keep it open.

Charlie turned back and met my imploring gaze with one full of antagonism. He wagged his finger so close to my face, I had to lean back to prevent him from making contact.

"What part of sick don't you understand?" he asked. "He's not up for visitors. Now head on out of here." He nodded towards my truck, and then pushed my hand off the slick wood before slamming it shut. The door latched, followed by the click of the deadbolt.

I'd been rejected and stood staring for an uncertain amount of time in a state of total confusion. It was the touch of Max's cool, wet nose that brought me back to my senses.

In a stupor, I walked to my truck, and as I reached for the handle, I allowed myself a quick glance back. On the top floor, where Eric's room resided, I saw curtains close shut. Eric's silhouette was visible for only a second before disappearing behind the heavy drapes. He'd been watching.

I debated going back to the front door and demanding some answers. Eric was certainly not bed bound. But as quickly as that thought popped into my mind, Charlie's angry face overshadowed it.

Reluctantly, I got into my truck and headed out.

Over the past two years, I'd gotten to know Uncle Charlie well. Tony, Eric, and I often congregated at whichever place afforded us the least amount of parental interference. Most of the time my basement sufficed—Gram seldom bugged us—but occasionally, we'd hang out at Charlie's. He had a huge rec room with a pool table. So Charlie knew Tony. He'd seen him around on a number of occasions. That's the part that nagged at me. Why would he act so indifferent to his disappearance?

It was another layer of confusing bull-crap on an already-heaping pile of shit.

Not knowing what else to do, I stopped by work under the ruse that I needed to check the schedule. In a sense, it was a bit of the truth. I wanted to know if Tony was going to be working anytime soon.

My heart sank when I saw his name crossed out. Mr. Greenwich seemed relieved when he saw me looking it over.

"I was going to talk to you about that. Looks like the Produce Department may need you for a day. Your flaky friend came in this morning and quit. No notice, no warning; just said he wasn't coming back. Now we have to reconfigure the entire schedule to cover his shifts." He snorted and gave me a condescending look.

Mr. Greenwich reminded me of a fat turkey. His neck was thick, wobbly, and it jiggled when he talked—which fascinated and disgusted me at the same time. Whenever he clucked orders, my eyes would gravitate towards his jowls, staring in morbid curiosity as they moved in rhythm to his words. Every once in a while, if I needed some sort of deranged pick-me-up, I'd ask an unnecessary question simply to watch the fat dance. I was a sick freak.

He also had a head full of hair that he was immensely proud of. He kept it long, so he could rake his fingers through it, which he did. All. The. Time.

"He better not expect a good reference. He sure isn't getting one from me." He scratched his scalp, inadvertently touching his most prized possession. "It's this new generation," he mumbled. "They don't think there are repercussions for their actions. They don't stop to consider the consequences. Well, this one's gonna feel it. Next employer who calls about him is gonna get an earful. *Unreliable.* That's what I'm gonna tell 'em." His beady eyes rested on me. "Don't you get any ideas."

It pissed me off that he was trying to coach me, but rather than smart off, I nodded numbly. I needed that stupid job.

"No, sir," I responded with false respect.

Poultry snorted before rolling his eyes. It took him a few minutes to go over the changes to the schedule. It looked like everyone was going to have to work extra shifts to make up for Tony's absence. I was scheduled to cover the following day. I agreed eagerly, simply to show I wasn't planning on pulling a "Tony."

I was exhausted by the time I got home—and fully prepared to slip in through the basement's separate entrance—when I remembered Gram's doctor's appointment. Anxious, I took the front steps, two at a time, and barged into the living room, where Gram sat serenely with knitting needles in hand. Her eyes lit up when she saw me.

"Just the boy I wanted to talk to," she said, and patted the seat next to her.

Something about her expression triggered an alarm. All at once, I was anxious. Bad news radiated off her. She recognized my hesitation and smiled encouragingly before patting the seat again.

"You look nervous. You must know what this is about," she said as I sat down next to her.

"Of course. It's about your doctor's appointment, right?"

Gram's smile wilted. It took a moment before she returned it, only the reemerged grin had a forced edge to it, much the same as a grimace. "No," she started, "your school called. Apparently, you missed your afternoon classes."

"Oh."

"Yes. *Oh.* Want to tell me why?"

I fidgeted.

"Is it because of Sarah?" she asked gently.

I nodded. "Yeah." My face flushed. The humiliation of Alex's words still stung.

She tilted her head and looked at me curiously, "Is that all?" she asked.

I didn't want to delve into Charlie's odd behavior or the note Tony left on my car. It didn't seem like the right time. That, and how could I possibly explain a situation that I didn't understand? I nodded again, simply to end the matter. Gram narrowed her eyes doubtfully, but let the subject drop. She knew what battles to pick.

She patted my leg. "I'm sorry, Daniel. I know breakups are hard. But this is your one pass. Tomorrow, your butt better be in school."

"Promise," I said and held up three fingers. "Scout's honor. What about you? How'd your appointment go?"

Now it was Gram who shifted uncomfortably. "They don't know yet," she said honestly. "They drew some blood, and tomorrow I'm having an X-ray done."

"That serious?" I asked with a rush of fear.

Gram reached over and squeezed my hand. "I'm sure they're just getting their money's worth. That's all. Everything will be fine." I swallowed hard. Gram's health took precedence over everything else. If I lost her, I'd have no one. I'd be alone. The thought was too painful to bear.

"Promise?"

Gram held up three fingers, scout's honor, same as I'd done. "Promise," she said with a bright smile.

I hugged her tightly before excusing myself. I was precariously close to breaking down in front of her and needed to retreat to the basement before that happened.

As night closed in, I settled on the couch in my lair, too bogged down to think about homework or much else. My mind checked out as the glow of TV infomercials filled the empty space. With my phone perched on the armrest, I wrapped myself in one of Gram's afghans and let sleep blanket me, enjoying the lapse of consciousness.

Hours later, a sharp sound cracked the air and split the room, jolting me awake. It was the door. Someone was beating on it.

❧ 4 ❧

ERIC'S TALL TALE

Back before I lived with Gram, I used to sleep with headphones on. It was a necessity back then. Mom, the local bar troll, had a terrible habit of barreling home next to dusk in a graceless, inebriated state. She'd bang into furniture, slam doors, curse, hackle, and sometimes wail—all by her lonesome self. And that was on a good night.

On a bad night, she'd bring someone along for the ride.

I'd cringe from the sounds that emitted from her bedroom and take cover under my pillow. The rank fluff was all I had to muffle my ears. There were moments I came close to suffocation, which, at the time, seemed like a better alternative than listening to Mom yell "Oh, God" over and over like a sick mantra.

It lead to preemptive measures—such as taking a swig of cough syrup and putting my tunes on blast.

That was the best way to go about things, but it wasn't always foolproof. One night, after I'd sufficiently drugged myself and was lost in a state of nocturnal bliss, she brought home a nameless bastard with a bushy beard and dented head who decided mid-interlude to trash our house. He was hyped up on booze or drugs. Probably both. He tossed our only working lamp into the wall and then used Mom's face to pick up the glass. It wasn't until my door collapsed and Mom spilled onto my bedroom floor that I realized anything was going down. He'd thrown her so hard that the casing splintered, sprinkling the threadbare carpet with wood confetti.

That was a terrible way to wake up. Mom lying in the middle of my room—her blood so dark it ran black—with a stranger standing over her with balled fists. That guy and I locked eyes for only a fraction, but that was enough. He was completely vacant on the inside. He grunted in surprise—Mom must've "forgotten" to tell him about me—and without a single word, turned and walked out. When the front door rattled the house, Mom turned to me, her face in shadow from light and gore, and glared. She bared her teeth and said, "You're all the same," before rising and leaving the room.

It was the type of memory that brands you for life.

And it was that memory that blasted me awake. The side entrance to the basement shook, as an unknown person banged a leaden fist against the door. My mind reeled to that hollow place as I envisioned that same angry, charcoal-eyed dick standing outside, prepared to shred me to pieces.

I chucked the crocheted afghan to the floor and tried to make out the time. The clock above the TV was hazy, my vision blurred from sleep. It took a second to register that it was nearly three in the morning.

I froze, not knowing if I wanted to answer the door or not. As though my visitor heard my thoughts, a voice called out. It was Eric, and he sounded panicked.

"DAN! Dan, let me in!"

Thinking of Gram sleeping and the commotion Eric was making, I lunged towards the door, now fully awake.

"Coming, coming, keep it down," I said, just loud enough for him to hear. Offhandedly, I listened for noise upstairs; it was silent. Fortunately, Gram slept like the dead.

"Hurry," Eric said. The sudden burst of adrenaline caused my fingers to shake as I struggled to operate the lock, and I butterfingered the latch a few times before it clicked open.

Eric, pale and winded, stood on the other side. He crossed the threshold and hurriedly thrust his shoulder against the door, closing it behind him with the weight of his body. He turned the deadbolt with one click.

"What's going on?" I asked frantically.

Eric remained rooted as he shook his head. He rested his right hand over his heart, like he was trying to tame its beat.

I went to the couch and sat down, giving him a moment to collect himself. My eyes never left him for a second.

Three key observations were glaringly obvious. One: Eric was disheveled. He reminded me of Charlie, their appearances mirroring one another. Two: he did seem sick. His eyes were swollen and red with dark circles, and although impossible, it appeared as though he'd lost a significant amount of weight. His cheekbones protruded where his face had collapsed. But it was the third observation that concerned me the most: he had bruising on his throat. Not just any bruises, but aggressive marks. I narrowed my eyes to focus more clearly and swore I detected fingerprints. The bruises resembled a monstrous hand.

Eric, after finding some composure, left the door and paced around the room. He started to sit down—changed his mind—and stood back up. He ran his hands through his brown, greasy hair. When he finally spoke, his voice came out weak and halting. He began as though rehearsed; all arrogance evaporated.

"We're in trouble, man. Real trouble."

He pressed on without being prompted. "It was that damned double-date. Tony was eager to get going. He didn't know where you were, and he was desperate not to be late. He didn't want to disappoint Candace." Eric's wild eyes reached mine. "All I wanted was to meet Claire. That's it."

I nodded. That wasn't a secret.

Days earlier—when Candace first broached the subject, asking if I wanted to meet her sister—Eric had flown into a full-blown temper tantrum. We were all in my basement: Eric, Tony, Candace, and I. Eric, seemingly overlooked, got defensive. He insisted that Claire be allowed to choose for herself. Candace, in an attempt to de-escalate the situation, explained that Eric wasn't Claire's type—that she preferred "introspective" guys. Her argument fell on deaf ears. With his egocentric attitude and inflated confidence, Eric was certain Claire would pick him if given the choice.

He'd been vying to usurp me ever since. And he'd won.

Eric's frazzled voice tore me from my memory.

"I was at Tony's place, hoping beyond hope, I'd get the chance to go. So when you didn't show, I thought that was my golden ticket. I told him I'd be happy to take your place. You wouldn't mind, and it would be better if he didn't show up alone. I said, 'Claire will feel like a third wheel if you don't bring a date. I can come along and even out the numbers, and maybe she won't feel bad about being stood up. I'm better than nothing.'"

He stopped to look at me with hands open in a gesture of incredulity. "Can you believe that? That's what I actually said. I wanted to go so badly, I was willing to put myself down." He shook his head and sat down next to me on the couch. He rested his head in the palms of his hands before looking up. "I WISH I'D JUST LET IT GO!"

I sucked air through my teeth before hushing him. Everything was still silent above.

He continued in a quieter voice. "So I called Gramp. I was supposed to help paint the garage, and I left a message on his machine asking for a raincheck. I told him an emergency date had come up, a real beauty who liked the outdoors, an *enigma* of a woman. I said it was an opportunity that I couldn't pass up, and that Tony and I were leaving right away. I promised to help on the house later." Eric, with elbows on his knees, clasped his hands in front of his face and covered his mouth. He started to rock back and forth. "I was so excited that I didn't even stop to think. The whole situation was messed up. Everything was just weird."

Eric, as if afraid he'd lose his nerve, launched into his story. "We hauled ass to make up for lost time," he said, "and showed up almost on schedule. We decided to take my truck since the roads aren't the greatest, and Tony gave directions. He told me to watch for a strange gate with a yellow ribbon attached to an unlocked padlock. It seemed to take us forever, but we finally found it.

"It's weird how at the turnoff—almost the exact moment I found that stupid road—I started to get shaky. I kept looking at Tony, seeing if he was breaking a sweat, but he just wore this cheesy, dumbstruck grin."

Eric fidgeted with the sleeve of his shirt, tugging it over his knuckles. "When we made the clearing, I thought I was gonna blow chunks, and it wasn't because I was meeting Claire, either. It was because the place was off. Not only was it empty—Candace's car wasn't there—but it also had this bizarre feel, like there was a trigger-happy mountain man hiding in the trees with a loaded, sawed-off shotgun. Makes no sense, but it's like I knew deep down that we shouldn't have been there." Eric dropped his gaze to his lap. "I even said something to Tony, telling him we should—like, I dunno—bail and go grab a burger. That Candace wasn't even there. Tony shook his head and said Candace and Claire would be waiting at the river, that they used another route. Then he pulled out a map, pointed to where we were supposed to go, and told me to 'suck it up.'"

Eric's hands balled into tight, angry fists. "I didn't want to leave my truck," he said. "I *knew* something wasn't right, and Tony saw me hesitate. He laughed and called me a pansy before jumping out of the cab and heading towards the forest. I had to run to catch up to him.

"There was something else that bothered me." Eric paused and crinkled his forehead. "Outside the entrance to the woods, on each side of the trail, stood two humongous oak trees. They had these yellow roses growing up their trunks. It hung me up, because I know those roses; they don't bloom this time of year." Eric shook his head, as if dislodging the thought, "Dumb what your brain hones in on."

He gave me a strained, sideways glance. "The forest was unnatural. It was too dark and … *claustrophobic*. Every single cell in my body fought me." Eric gave a small, introspective grin, one that blanketed his features in cynicism. "When we reached the river, and the trees backed off, I was relieved. There was finally light. I followed Tony along the bank until the river widened. And it didn't take long before we spotted Candace and Claire."

Eric cleared his throat and touched his lips. He looked off into space.

"My first thought—jackpot. Claire was beyond gorgeous. *That* part wasn't a lie. She looked a lot like Candace, except she was taller and her hair was brown and curly. I almost busted into a smile. *Almost*. But then I noticed something was wrong.

"Two tip-offs." Eric held up a pair of fingers with nails chewed to the quick. "One, they were wearing cloaks. Like, real cloaks, the same stuff you see in plays or on Halloween. And two, they were ticked, and it was pretty obvious it was over me. I wasn't the one they wanted."

Eric turned to me. "They wanted *YOU*." His words were borderline accusatory. Quite unexpectedly, I felt the need to defend myself, against what, I didn't know. I started to shake my head, but stopped when Eric's hostile gaze flitted away. He continued without waiting for a response.

"Candace got snarky at Tony and said, 'You were supposed to bring Daniel.' Tony shrunk into himself and looked to me for help. But I didn't know what to do. Candace wasn't *my* girlfriend, so I shrugged. Tony started bumbling out excuses—groveling to her—saying stuff like, 'Daniel didn't show up,' and 'I didn't know what else to do,' you know, smearing it on thick.

"But Candace didn't care and started walking away. Claire's the one who stopped her from storming into the forest. She grabbed Candace by the arm and shook her head. Then Claire's eyes shot towards the lake. It was super fast," Eric said. "I caught it, but I'm not sure Tony did. Then they switched gears, going from all pissed to nice in a heartbeat. Candace turned around and gave us a big grin. It reminded me of the crap my ex-girlfriend pulled right before she went full-on psycho."

"Ooookaaaay." I spoke slow and long as my face twisted with confusion. *Where was he going with this?*

Eric clenched his teeth, annoyed with me. "She was baiting us," he clarified. "And it started when Candace introduced her *sister*." Eric's eyes narrowed, "Except, she didn't call her Claire; she said her name was Torture."

"Torture?" I asked, not sure that I'd heard him correctly.

Eric nodded. "Torture," he confirmed.

"That's her name?" I sputtered. *Who would name their kid Torture?*

"Yeah, that's her name." He looked down. Something was coming, and I had a feeling it was going to be big.

"I started to laugh, thinking it was a joke—albeit a stupid one—until Torture interrupted me. She asked what I found funny. Her face was flat serious, and before I could even think, I blurted out, 'You can't be serious. Torture's an act, not a name.'

"She started to smile, but it wasn't friendly. It was more like, I'd-like-to-rip-your-face-off-and-eat-it type of smile." Eric pitched his voice, "She got all sarcastic and asked me if I liked her name. When I didn't answer, she said, 'Well, if you're going to be a baby about it, I'll let you call me Torti. That's what all my friends call me.'

"She was screwing with me, and I was about to smart off when Tony yelped." Eric swallowed. "Candace had Tony's arm in a death grip." Eric clawed his hands, tensing his fingers midair as if grasping an invisible ball. He looked me square in the eyes and dropped his pose. "She punctured his skin from where she latched on. Tony's blood was pooling, man—*pooling*—under her nails. Then it trickled down, and Tony tried to stay cool, but he was all *darty*, trying to jerk his arm away and everything. Candace didn't budge, though."

"Candace was hurting him?" I asked. *What the freak?*

"It gets worse," Eric said barely above a whisper. "The blood paralyzed me. All I could do was stand there, like an idiot, while Tony tried to pull away. That's when Torti started to laugh—dumb, giddy bitch. When she caught me watching her, she winked, like it was all a big joke. She smirked and nodded towards the bank." Eric trembled as a chill flowed down his spine.

"There was a shadow in the middle of the river. At first, I couldn't tell what it was; it was too deep. Then long, brown hair floated to the top. It was attached to a woman beneath the surface. She moved so slowly, I thought she was a corpse dislodged downriver … or something; I don't know. I was stupid confused. But then her head rose out of the water, stopping at her eyes."

Sitting on my couch, Eric appeared to relive the moment. He started breathing heavily, sucking in air as if afraid it would disappear. He turned his face away, so his expression was lost in shadow.

"I … I … was speechless. I mean, what the hell? She stayed still, floating, with her nose and mouth submerged. She didn't seem to need air, but was clearly *alive*. The whites of her eyes were glowing, and she had green scales on her skin."

I cocked my head to the side. *This was getting weird.*

"I couldn't make sense of it. H-h-how could I?" Eric went on. "Tony seemed equally confused and … *horrified*. Then the lady in the river swam towards us and started to pull herself out of the water. That's when I saw the rest of her face." Eric paused and I leaned in, mesmerized. "Despite the scales, I thought she was beautiful. It was bizarre. She was a total freak of nature, but I was almost … *drawn* to her. I could tell that once upon a time she'd been gorgeous. She had that symmetry, you know?" Eric winced as if ashamed by his own admission.

"When she surfaced halfway, she stopped. She was wearing an evening gown—green sequins and all—like a prom dress. Then her eyes flashed, and she was looking directly at me. She had no irises, only black pupils. I couldn't look away. All of a sudden, I wanted to touch her and, without thinking, started walking towards the water.

"Tony yelled at me to stop. He screamed three times before it clicked. If he hadn't, I would've walked right into the river. That female lizard had me in a trance that I wasn't even aware of." A rattled breath quivered at the back of Eric's throat. His eyes started to well.

"Everything had … *fallen apart.* I felt trapped, and that's when Torti started stalking towards us, and her appearance *shifted.* She got ugly real fast. Her skin went white, and … uh…." Eric struggled to find the word, "Veins—*yes*—veins broke out all over her face. Her eyes lost their color, and she looked possessed.

"Tony lost it. He started pleading for answers, saying Candace's name over and over. It killed me to hear him beg like that." Eric grabbed his ears, as if Tony were in the living room begging for his freedom. "That's when Torti started shrieking at Tony. She screamed, 'CANDACE ISN'T HER NAME, YOU HALF-WIT! Her name is Dreams. DREAMS!'

"Tony broke into a frenzy and began slapping Candace—Dreams— whatever-her-name's hand. He was panicking and, in a last-ditch attempt, clocked her in the jaw. But her head didn't even buck. I swear I've seen steel bend more. She ignored him and instead glanced at Torti like she was waiting for a command."

Eric started rocking—the motion making me sick. I was tempted to reach out and still him, but didn't want to make him jump. He was too wired for comfort. "Torti looked at Dreams and told her it was time to get it over with. That's when Dreams' eyes flashed." Eric's voice went slushy. "She warped her features into a sick look of adoration and smiled at Tony and said, 'Hush now, darling. She's just going to drown you.'"

I gasped. *What. The. Shit?*

Eric stopped rocking, and his wide, wild eyes met mine. No words could convey what I was feeling, partly because my head was a muddled mess. Wild, unruly thoughts knotted together in a gigantic tangle. I'd been expecting a grand tale, but this was so much more than that. This was a saga rooted in pure fallacy.

Eric nodded, as if he knew where my mind had landed. "Totally nuts, right?" he said.

"Yeah," *understatement of the century.* Eric was looking at me expectantly, so I formed the most basic of questions. "So, um, what happened next?"

That's when Eric's face caved. His mouth drooped and he bent forward. "I ran," he said, "I ran. I was such a coward! I could hear Tony's screams—I could hear their laughter—and still I ran. I left him. I left him," Eric cried. "WHY WAS I SUCH A COWARD?"

I placed my hand on his arm. His skin was cold. My eyes scanned the ceiling. Gram was still asleep, but a few more outbursts like that and she wouldn't be. Eric understood.

"I went with my gut," he said, quieter. "The moment I found the path, I ran as hard as I could." He stopped for a second and twisted his hands in his lap. "I was only halfway to my truck when I heard someone running behind me. I prayed it was Tony," Eric gulped. "It wasn't him. It was some monstrous man, with red hair and claws jutting forward from closed fists. He was coming up on me fast, moving at a speed I would've thought impossible. Then it was over in less than a second." Eric gave me a shaky glance.

The look I wore must've been one of pure skepticism, and Eric didn't miss it. The lines around his mouth tightened.

"You're not buying this, are you?" Eric asked.

I snorted, but said nothing. *Well, duh.*

"I don't even know why I bother," Eric said.

"Because you need to get it out," I replied truthfully. Eric was traumatized, and I knew healing was a multifaceted process. If his journey to health consisted of telling a make-believe story, so be it. The straitjackets could wait until afterwards.

Eric gave me a disappointed look that bled into bleak resolve. "You're right. I do," he responded. The way he said it, with the manic whites of his eyes showing, made me sit up straighter. "You have no idea, Dan. None. You think I'm bullshitting you, I can tell. But there's so much more to this." Eric stood up and started pacing.

Eric mumbled under his breath, "Screw it"—as if he'd settled some argument he was having with himself—and pressed on. "The giant pounced and threw me forward, landing right on top of me. He dug is knee into my back and started taunting me. He told me I trespassed on the wrong land. That's when he stroked my face from temple to cheekbone with his claws." Eric stopped in front of me. "I think they were made of sharp, gray bone," he said as he cradled his hand, made a closed fist, and caressed the shallow divots between his knuckles.

I looked at my own hand, imagining what it would be like to have daggers sprout from my skin.

Eric threw his arms in the air, and returned to pacing. "I lost it. I started bawling like a baby. I begged him to let me go. He didn't say a word; he just dug his knee deeper into my back. Then I felt his claws scrape along my shoulders and spine." Eric twisted his mouth and made his eyes wide in an effort not to cry. "He was etching a pattern into my back, and I was forced to lie there and take it. I screamed, and screamed, and screamed. It hurt like nobody's business. I was prey, dude, *PREY*."

I leaned against the couch cushion. The image Eric described was haunting. *Unreal, but still haunting.* It took some elongated seconds before he spoke.

"Then he grabbed the back of my shirt and forced me to stand. That's when I got a good look at him. Not only did he have red hair, but he towered over me. I bet he was at least seven feet tall." Eric stopped burning tracks into the carpet, and plopped onto the couch. He fell hard, and the frame cracked. Eric didn't miss a beat. "His eyes were glowing, too, and there was no color to them—just like the girls. He leaned in, and said, 'I'm going to enjoy killing you.'"

I held my breath, eyes attached to Eric.

"He wrapped his gigantic hand around my neck and started to squeeze. My head felt like it was going to pop off my neck. My lungs got heavy, too. And I knew I was a goner.

"And oddly, I was grateful. I wanted to die. I *deserved* to die. I'd left Tony—abandoned him—and I hated myself for it. Death would be a relief. The pain in my back would go away, the shame of leaving Tony would disappear, and I would just cease to exist. I didn't have a right to live. I didn't want to.

"Then something weird happened."

"Oh, so now we're getting into the weird stuff." My sarcasm slipped out, unfiltered. I bit down on my tongue to still it, the pinch so sharp I tasted metallic blood.

Eric ignored me. "At first, I assumed it was my body shutting down." Eric struggled to get the words out. "Everything was growing cold. But then I noticed the ginger's breath: little puffs of air. It wasn't just me; everything was growing colder, and it bothered him. His eyes lost that freakish glow and he loosened his grip. Air tore through my lungs, and it burned. *Burned.* He still held on to me, so I couldn't run—but at least I could breathe. That's when I realized we weren't alone.

"Another man showed up. He was albino with chalky skin. The ginger was scared of him, I could tell, even though this guy was much smaller. He had lips that were blue and cracked, and his eyes were shining, too." Eric started to rub his forearms, up and down, over and over, as if to warm himself. "This guy was like an AC unit on legs. I didn't doubt for a second he was the reason for the dip in temperature. When he spoke he sounded powerful.

"He said, 'Let him go, Cheetoh,' and the ginger finally unleashed me. It seemed like he was subservient to the ice zombie, or something, 'cause he bowed his head in respect before stepping away. Then, the man of ice turned to me and addressed me by name. He said, 'You need to go, Eric. Leave now, before I change my mind.'

"So that's what I did. Without saying a word, I ran as hard as I could."

MYSTERY

I sat with an unhinged jaw. Eric's story was incredible—and *absurd*—in every sense of the word. Despite my doubts, I kept quiet. It was an exercise in patience for sure. I had questions, but they'd wait. First, I'd give him the courtesy of finishing.

Then I was going to destroy his asinine story with common sense.

"My back was on fire, but I didn't care. I ran hard. All I could think about was getting away. I was so freaked. When I saw light at the end of the trail, I thought I'd made it. But then I saw my truck." Eric looked at his clasped hands. "The hood was up, and cables hung everywhere. It wasn't going to start; that much was clear. I didn't even bother trying. The only option I had left was to keep running. I started down the road and hadn't gone far when I heard a vehicle coming towards me. It was my saving grace. I was going to do anything within my power to get them to stop, even if that meant throwing myself in front of their car."

He paused to look at me.

"It was Gramp!" Eric said. "I couldn't believe my eyes, but it was him."

"Charlie?" I stammered.

"Yeah." Eric's voice rose with excitement. "He knew exactly where I was. He knew exactly who I'd seen. The moment I leapt inside the cab, he turned the truck around and hauled ass outta there."

Eric continued to elaborate. His energy shifted, gaining momentum, as he described Charlie's involvement. Apparently, it was one big conspiracy, and Uncle Charlie knew all about the people in the woods.

"Gramp told me that the ice man—you know, the one who saved me—was his best friend back when they were teenagers." Eric spoke fast. "They recruited him when he was our age, and ever since then, Gramp has been helping to keep their civilization secret."

I started to shake my head, but Eric protested, "No, man! It's true. Gramp says he's been doing it for decades." Eric's voice pitched a little. "He does it to protect his friend. Gramp calls it a *tribute*."

I pinched my eyes closed. What Eric was saying was absolutely fantastical.

And imaginary.

It was insulting that Eric thought I was gullible to fall for such BS. Worse yet, Eric seemed to believe it. It was disconcerting.

"Eric," I began gently, "did you take some sort of drug before going up there?" His face crumpled.

"Dan! No! This isn't something my imagination worked up."

"Are you sure you didn't eat any mushrooms on your nature hike?"

Eric started to lose the little bit of composure he'd managed to regain. The early morning sunlight started to peak through the curtains. I needed him to see reason; this wasn't a healthy state of mind—believing in monsters and all.

"Dan. You gotta believe me. PLEASE!" Eric stood up and fell to his knees. It was a move so unexpected that I flinched. An equal mixture of shock and embarrassment rushed to my face. Kneeling before me, Eric shot out his words, "There's more. They never wanted me; they wanted you! Gramp's certain! They used Tony to get to you. You were their main target from the very beginning."

That was the final straw. Every word out of Eric's mouth was swathed in insanity. I was done listening to his delusions.

"Eric, I think you need psychiatric help," I said levelly. "Tony left yesterday. He packed up his stuff and told his mom off. He even went to work and quit. There were witnesses who saw him. Now, I don't want to point fingers, but I think you and I are to blame. Tony hasn't really had anyone in his life who's been supportive. Sunday, I failed him. I was running late, and because I left my phone at home, I wasn't able to tell him. If any part of your story is true, then that means you ditched him in the middle of a *freakin'* forest. No wonder he wants to leave. His two best friends let him down." As I said the words, I realized how accurate they were. Tony probably felt rejected.

Eric started to shake his head. I held up my hand to silence him.

"Not only that," I continued, "but your story has other holes."

Confused, Eric knitted his brows.

"You said your truck was dismantled. Well, I saw it parked in the driveway when I stopped by Charlie's yesterday. How did it get there if it wasn't drivable?"

Eric readily jumped on this.

"They brought it to the house. It was them!" He widened his eyes for emphasis. I, in turn, rolled mine.

"Okay, well what about Tony?"

"I already told you about Tony," Eric said.

"Tony made an appearance yesterday. He confronted his mom and then quit his job. How could that be possible if he were dead?"

Eric, eager, began to explain, speaking so rapidly his words nearly blended together.

"In order to transform into the monsters they are, the person needs to die first. Then they bring them back—only as something different. They come back as immortals. And that wasn't Tony they saw yesterday; at least, I doubt it. I'd bet it was one of the Doppelgänger members."

"I'm not following. ..." Where the hell had this come from? "They all knew Tony and would've known if someone was posing as him. Especially his own mother."

"Not necessarily," Eric said vehemently. "They have powers. All of them. Gramp told me. He said they all have different gifts, and Velores—that's what they call themselves—fall into seven groups. Each group has its own talents. Apparently Candace, I mean Dreams, belongs to the Doppelgänger Clan. The Doppelgängers can create illusions and screw with our minds. They can read our thoughts. They can pose as any of us, and our minds will be tricked into believing it. I'd bet money that it wasn't Tony doing the talking yesterday; I'm sure it was one of *them*."

"Wow."

"You gotta' believe me!" Eric said. "I know it sounds crazy. But look! Look at my neck. Do you think I did this to myself?" He pointed to the purple marks resting above his collarbone.

He had me there. The physical evidence seemed to corroborate one part of his story. But surely there had to be a more plausible explanation.

He could see I was beginning to waver and pushed forward. He turned his back to me and lifted his shirt. Large, white bandages covered his back. Old, brown blood, mixed with fresh, red stains, soiled the fabric.

"Look," he urged as he struggled to expose his wounds. "Look at my back. I was attacked, Dan, attacked! Not by steel, but by bone from the claws of a grown man. Look at the lines. Look at the pattern. Tell me, how could I make this up? Why would I make this up?"

My head was beginning to throb from the mystery of it all.

"Eric, I'm not saying that nothing happened. I mean, obviously something went haywire." I scanned him and clicked my tongue, all the while wondering how to explain logic to the insane. "I'm just saying that the story you're telling me is absolutely ludicrous. Yes, you're injured; I can see that with my own eyes. I can also tell you experienced some sort of mental trauma. But if you think I'm going to believe that a group of immortals attacked you—attacked you to get to me—then you have another thing coming. That's not only incredible, but impossible."

I was going to get to the bottom of this. I stood up and went to the gun safe Gram kept in the corner of the basement's living-room.

Eric froze. "Dan?" he asked. "What are you doing?"

I refused to answer; rather, I simply started dialing the combination on the safe.

"Are you even listening to me?" Eric demanded, his voice tinged with anxiety. "Dan, what are you doing?" he asked again.

I shut out his voice as the latch on the safe clicked open, pulling the heavy door towards me. Gram didn't know I knew the combination, and she'd flay me alive if she caught me getting into it. Inside, I found the rifle I used for hunting. I wasn't allowed to look at it—much less touch it—unless I was with Marie's husband, Dean, and we were out on a hunting expedition. But there was something wonky going on, and I figured it was worth the risk. I grabbed the gun and swung the strap over my shoulder. I dug deep into the safe to locate the ammo.

"DAN!" Eric shouted.

"WHAT!" I yelled back, forgetting about Gram. I paused long enough to turn around and confront him.

He flinched and meekly asked, "What are you doing?"

"What do you think I'm doing, Eric? I'm going to find answers. I don't know what happened to Tony; I don't know what happened to you. But I'm heading up there. Tony said he might camp out. Maybe that's where he ran off to."

"When did Tony say that?" Eric asked.

"I found a note," I replied, and stood a little straighter, ready to defend myself against an onslaught of questions.

Eric's lips formed into a sardonic smirk. "Well, isn't that *convenient*," he said sarcastically.

I ignored his tone. "Maybe he's laying low for a while. Regardless, I'm checking this place out for myself."

"NO!"

I narrowed my eyes. "Don't you tell me no," I hissed. I stormed past him into my bedroom to grab my jacket. I'd fallen asleep wearing the clothes from the day before, and I dipped my hand into my pocket. My fingertips grazed the note. It was still there. The paper felt warm. Reassuring, almost.

When I came out, Eric was standing by the door blocking the way.

"That's not going to work. I'm going, and there's nothing you can do, or say, that'll stop me."

"Please, Dan. Please don't go! You won't come back. *Please*. Believe me. Run away."

I scoffed. "And go where, exactly, Eric? Back home to my mom? How about to my dad? We could share a cardboard box under a bridge together." I gave him a bogus smile. "And for what? Because you think fairy tales have come to life?"

Eric squared his shoulders. "I'm not making this up," he responded through gritted teeth.

"Suuure."

"I'm not." Eric's hand flexed into fists. "Dammit, stop acting like a thickheaded fool!"

I approached him and stood nose to nose. My temper flared. Eric always had it easy compared to me. He never knew what it was like to go hungry, or how it felt to get clobbered on a daily basis. He never felt the pain of poverty. Now he was calling me a fool, and all because I wouldn't fall for his dumb-ass story.

"I'm going to find Tony," I said with an eerie calm.

Eric's shoulders fell. "They want you," he said softly. "If you go, you'll be doing just what they hoped. You won't come back."

I grabbed Eric's arm and directed him to the couch. He started to rock, and I gripped his wrist to make him sit still.

"I'll come back," I promised.

Eric shook his head and gave me an imploring look. "No," he said. "You won't."

His tone troubled me. But it didn't change anything. I needed answers, and there was only one way to get them. Retrace their steps. I took a deep breath and strengthened my resolve. I'd run out of options.

This was the only way, unless I wanted to live in ignorant limbo.

And that would be torture.

"I'm going, Eric. I need answers. All I can hope is that Tony is hanging out up there, and I can convince him to come back."

"I won't show you where it is," Eric replied defiantly.

"That's fine. You don't need to." I was tempted to pat my pocket but decided against it. The last thing I needed was for Eric to wrestle the letter away.

Understanding faded Eric's color. "Oh, that's right; I'm sure they've already told you. Silly me." The smile he gave me was laced in acid. "Did they draw you a map like they did Tony?"

I looked away, not wanting him to see how close he guessed. *No, Eric; I'm using the same map.* When I looked back, Eric's face hung with emptiness. "You've got a map, don't you?" he asked flatly.

When I didn't respond, he nodded. "You're making a mistake, Dan."

"Maybe I am," I conceded, "but I can't leave it like this." And I *couldn't* leave it like this. So help me, I would find this place—and Tony—and perhaps after a while, when time healed his wounds and Eric received some serious psychological help, things would go back to normal. "You'd better rest. Do you want to sleep here or go back to Charlie's place? I don't mind driving you."

Eric slumped over and mumbled, "I shouldn't have told you...."

"Rest, Eric," I said as I collected my ammo and went out to the garage. My bolt cutters hung from a peg board above the butcher-block workbench. I grabbed them and stowed them in my back pocket. After I was situated, I went back inside to bid Eric goodbye. He was curled into a fetal position on the couch. His eyes clamped shut.

"I'm leaving now."

Eric pressed his lids even tighter together. He moaned *"my fault,"* without looking at me.

"It's gonna be fine," I said, not knowing if I were speaking truth or not. Swayed by compassion, I grabbed Gram's afghan from the floor and tossed it over him. He didn't acknowledge the gesture.

I went through the door without another glance back.

With one friend MIA, and the other a sorry replica of his former self, my mind drifted to dark places on the drive up. I ran through every possible scenario in my head. I considered Eric on drugs, in particular, acid. Or an idiotic amount of pot. Tony must've gotten dumped and decided to save face by hiding out. Both were overreacting. I even mulled over the possibility of a health crisis. Maybe an aneurysm or seizure, with delusions as a side effect. Yet, despite it all—and I hated to admit it—a secret part of me harbored the terrible notion that Eric had been truthful. Eric clearly believed his own nonsense, but seriously, how far-fetched could one get?

Then I thought of Sarah. Her stricken image folded in on me. I pulled the truck over to catch my breath. Sarah thought something was wrong, too. She thought Candace was wrong. Everyone was leery, but Tony was still missing, and I didn't know what else to do. I couldn't go to the authorities. I'd be laughed at, and Eric would be dragged to a loony bin.

I cringed. What could I possibly say?

"Excuse me, officers. I need to report a crime. A woman covered in scales drowned my friend in a lake. Don't believe me? Well, you can ask him for yourself, since a group of immortals resurrected his corpse. If you need

further information, my cousin, Eric, will be happy to help. He looks a little worse for wear. Don't worry about that. The clawed giant that assaulted him has already been dealt with by a man who resembles a human popsicle."

No. I couldn't do that. Even sans the sarcasm, no one would buy such a story. Heck, even I didn't buy it.

Following the directions unfolded in my lap, I went east towards the Cascades. My old truck jumped at every rut in the road, making the paper hard to read. Fortunately, I was comfortable driving in the woods. All those endless days during hunting season, hiking, camping, and scouting paid off.

It was difficult to determine what road Eric and Tony had taken. I began looking for unique gates, carefully evaluating distances to determine my exact location in approximation to Candace's map. Referring to my odometer, I narrowed it down pretty well, and that's when I saw it: a gate unlike the others.

I parked alongside the road and glanced at the unlatched lock. A faint, yellow ribbon hung lifelessly. This was it.

The road was poorly maintained. I kept my eyes trained for movement. I was well aware of the dangers of traveling in the woods alone, and that the best strategy was to stay alert. The road climbed higher, and my truck groaned from overexertion. I began to second-guess my rash actions, wondering if I should've let someone other than Eric know where I was going.

Eric was in no condition to relay sensible information.

Whatever. I'm committed now. And with that thought, I pulled into the clearing. It was exactly how Eric described. In front of me stood two massive oaks with yellow roses climbing up their trunks. The pair flanked a path leading into a thick forest.

Tony's car wasn't there, but I knew there was another entrance into the woods. It was the entrance Candace usually took.

Or so she said.

Even though I'd convinced myself that Eric's story was one of fiction, I still couldn't shake the disquiet that made my pores restrict. I carefully backed up my truck so the headlights faced the road for an easy exit, allowing plenty of distance between my vehicle and the timbered forest line with its ominous trail.

I couldn't help myself.

Once parked, my stomach summersaulted. Despite logic on my side, the raw memory of a distraught Eric was hard to toss out. Something had happened, and I couldn't take that lightly.

For a split second, I considered going home, but then thought of Tony, and my resolve cemented. He could be in there, feeling broken and abandoned.

I dug around my pocket and pulled out my cellphone to check reception. Not a single bar hung out in the left-hand corner. Disappointed—but not shocked—I said a little prayer and reached for my gun. I took a heavy breath, opened the truck door, and stepped out.

As I walked to the entrance, I searched for proof that would've backed up Eric's story. I found nothing, except tracks where a car recently parked.

That meant zilch.

The morning itself was turning out to be a pleasant one. Drifting moisture hung in the air, making everything fresh and new. We were above the fog bank that hovers in the valley, so the sky was brighter. I hoped to get in and out quickly—so I could actually enjoy it—with Tony by my side.

I stalled at the oak trees. Eric was right about the roses. They were wrong and shouldn't have been blooming. It was still irrelevant. I took one last look at my truck parked on the other side of the clearing before heading inside.

It was odd how quickly daylight vanished. Limbs and trees blocked the sky, draping the forest in darkness. My skin prickled from unfamiliar sensations around me. I understood why Eric called the trees "claustrophobic." It was crowded and creepy.

The trail was well-defined. Compacted dirt from continuous tread conveyed constant use. Considering the condition of the road that led up here, it was an unexpected surprise. I walked quickly and remained keen to the environment, looking for any strange or unexpected activity. I also kept my ears open for the sound of rushing water. I would find the river and take the exact path Eric and Tony had days earlier.

That's when I caught the faintest sound.

I stopped to listen more clearly. It was a woman's voice. Had I not been listening so intently, I may not have heard it at all. She was singing. I focused on where it was coming from, far off to the right.

It was the most mesmerizing voice I'd ever heard. My mind switched to autopilot. I stepped off the path and headed in the direction of the angelic melody, not thinking for a moment that I was walking towards danger—that I was heading towards my destiny.

{ 6 }

MYTHICAL CREATURES

My muddled mind zeroed in on her magnetic music. I followed the sound of her voice without thinking. Buzzing—like a hive of bees had infested my ear canal—clouded my thoughts.

Hurriedly, I pushed through the thick brush. The walk was treacherous, since there were no trails to follow. It made my progress slow. But despite the labored hike, I started to relax. The closer I came to the singing, the louder the buzzing in my head became—and the more tranquil I felt.

The temperature change was gradual. The surrounding air chilled as the singing gained volume. The grass below my feet crunched, the dew frozen. All around me, pine needles and leaves held a fuzzy layer of frost. Yet, I saw none of it—at least not at the time. My mind registered the events, but they slipped beyond my reasoning. I'd become blind as I made my way through the crowded timber.

I quickened my pace to a trot. She was so close now that I could feel her all around me. Her voice poured into my ears, smooth and sweet as honey. The buzzing did little to detract from the yearning that consumed me.

If anything, it made it worse.

Everything was covered in ice crystals, and it made my footsteps sharper. Branches crackled and frozen grass crunched. Worried my noisy approach would startle her and she'd stop singing, I slowed.

Moving methodically, I removed my gun and rested it against a tree trunk. I didn't want her to see it and become frightened. As I inched closer, and stepped between two crisp ferns, I finally caught my first glimpse of her. Nearly ten yards away, under a large Douglas fir, she stood with her back towards me. She wore a cape of white, her hair hidden by its hood. On the back of her cloak, in a metallic sheen, was an emblem of a snowflake woven with the lightest silver. The distance could not hide the delicateness of her small frame or the gentle slope of her shoulders. Somehow, even without laying eyes on her, I knew she was beautiful.

She continued to sing her strange melody, the words foreign and unfamiliar. I didn't have to understand the language to know she was singing words of love. The urgency to bridge the gap between us overwhelmed me; it made me reckless. I misplaced my foot and landed on a frozen branch. The snap was piercing. Her shoulders stiffened and her singing ceased. Immediately, the buzzing dissipated, and silence filled the air. My mind, for a moment, was free. The tranquility evaporated. In that second, the most logical sensation swept over me, one I should have felt all along—fear.

I'd made a grave mistake, and I was unsure how to undo the damage. I remained still, rooted to the earth, as she turned around. When she faced me, I became drugged once again, falling back under her spell—only deeper than before.

Although the hood of her cape created a shadowy veil, I was still able to see pieces of her magnificence. A few strands of snowy, blonde hair escaped. The whites of her eyes provided an illuminated backdrop for clear-blue irises that shone beyond the shadows. The subtle glow of her eyes contrasted the pale flawlessness of her smooth skin. Lips of blush pink, bright and full, parted slightly as a hint of smile began to form at the corners. She may not have known it, but at that moment, I was completely and unknowingly hers.

Or maybe she did know.

Afraid of my own voice, I waited for her to speak. My skin tingled from the cold—which I mistook for exhilaration. If I'd been paying attention, I would've noticed the temperature continuing to drop, and that my breath churned out little puffs of clouds. Eric's description of the ice man had been cataloged—unwisely—to the back of my memory. No other thought existed, except the woman before me holding my mind hostage.

I attempted to smile, trying with all my might to look friendly and harmless. It must've worked because she started to walk gracefully towards me. There were only a couple of yards between us when she stopped. Now that she was close, her beauty became more clearly defined. She was indeed an earthbound angel, too perfect to be anything less.

"Are you lost?" she asked.

I pleaded with my mind to function, but all thoughts had evaporated. Her words ricocheted off the sides of my vacant skull. I was simply another stupid boy, gawking at a pretty girl, blowing it.

"Can you not speak?" she asked inquisitively.

Talk dammit! "No, I can speak." The words I found sounded all wrong—like they didn't belong to me. They were too loud, too boyish. Inadequate. I touched my throat and forced myself to continue. "I was surprised to find someone up here." There it was again, that stupid voice. Heat rose to my face in stark contrast to the cold air around me.

She gave a little laugh before asking, "What's your name?"

"Daniel Thatcher."

She ran slender fingers across her lips. A snowflake ring glittered before disappearing into her cloak.

"Well, Daniel Thatcher, I find it interesting that you've stumbled into my neck of the woods. No one ever comes up here."

"Hopefully, I'm not intruding."

She grinned. "Why are you here, Daniel Thatcher?" She said my name like it was the most tantalizing treat she'd ever tasted. My own mouth salivated at her words.

Why was I here? I'd forgotten. I clamped my mind shut in an attempt to focus, digging deep in my murky thoughts. *Concentrate, Daniel.* Then, like a picture book opened before me, Tony's image flashed before my eyes. I had all too willingly, and completely, forgotten him.

Other thoughts lingered at the surface, but I couldn't grasp them. The brief fear I'd experienced earlier had become irretrievable—as though it never existed. Eric's story drifted far away, and the more I tried to recall it, the more it evaded me. Yet, thankfully, I remembered Tony.

"I'm trying to find my friend," I blurted, fearful I'd relapse and forget. "He came up here on Sunday, and I think he may be camping out." I fidgeted uncomfortably, running my hand along the collar of my shirt. "He thinks my friend and I abandoned him, it was just a big misunderstanding. He's about my age, slender, with light brown hair. His name is Tony. Have you seen him?"

She smiled and tilted her head to the side. Silently, she took a couple of steps towards me and lifted the hood of her cape, revealing her face in all its entirety. I gasped.

I knew she was beautiful, but nothing could have prepared me for what I actually witnessed. She was breathtaking and *unusual.* Her blue eyes were too clear. Her skin, too smooth. With sculpted cheekbones and features that rested in harmony with one another, she had the essence of perfection. White-blonde hair, the texture of silk, hung to her waist. Her features embodied both youth and maturity, making her age a complete mystery. Around her neck, she wore an elaborate choker of diamonds.

Once again tongue-tied, I stood in awkward silence. She was close enough I could've easily made a few lengthy strides and touched her. And I wanted to touch her. Every fiber of my being wanted to hold her, caress her, feel her smooth, pale skin against mine.

Focus. Tony's your priority, not getting laid.

"I think I've seen Tony," she finally answered.

A momentary sense of relief swept over me. "You have?" I asked. "When did you see him? Was he okay? Do you know where I can find him?"

Her chime-like giggle rippled through the air. "You ask lots of questions," she replied coyly as she peeked at me through her lashes. "You sound genuinely concerned. That's very admirable of you. Yet, I can't help but wonder why he was even here. No one ever comes up here."

She took a few steps closer. Now I could smell her. She had the scent of vanilla.

"Maybe he was drawn here," she continued, "just like you've been drawn here. I believe everyone comes here for a reason."

Although she wouldn't answer my questions, I realized I didn't care. She had become all-consuming. She cocked her head to the side, smiled softly, and bridged the last remaining steps that distanced us. She now stood only inches away. Lifting her right hand, she softly rested it on my chest and looked up into my eyes.

"I think you came here looking for me," she whispered.

"I think so, too," I replied. The buzzing had returned—only more powerful than before, and all without notice. Tony faded to ancient history.

She tilted her head upwards, and her lips parted. An irrepressible pull to kiss her overtook me. The desire was forceful, the buzzing so loud that my skull vibrated on the base of my neck. Trancelike, I lowered my head, anticipating the touch of her lips. I wanted to kiss her. I *needed* to kiss her. My heart quickened in expectation. But before my lips met hers, our connection was destroyed.

A strong hand gripped the back of my collar and violently threw me backwards.

I landed hard on the frozen grass behind me. The thud of my body hitting the earth dissolved the buzzing in my head, and I regained control of my senses.

And now I was scared stiff.

Hovering over me, swathed from head to toe in a cloak of mismatched fabric—much like a patchwork quilt—stood the man who pulled me away. He was wearing an opaque mask, the skin underneath well-hidden behind the paper-white plastic. The mask alone was enough to terrify me, but that fear was minor—almost insignificant—compared to the woman with the snowflake cape.

She wasn't so beautiful now.

She'd transformed into a beast. Her pale skin bleached whiter, the texture fragile and powdery. Black fissures emerged on her face. The lines—like rotting cracks—sprouted over her exposed skin. The whites of her eyes glowed vibrantly, framing solid-black pupils that absorbed all traces of its former clear blue. Her kissable lips turned to the color of tinted ice, splintered and chapped. She looked like a walking corpse—a corpse that radiated a chill so intense, it froze everything around her.

The counterpart to the ice man Eric described.

A series of awful realizations surfaced simultaneously. One, the lady I was about to kiss was dangerous—*very dangerous*—and her kiss would've sent me to my untimely death. I was certain of this, although don't ask me how. Two, the person who had thrown me backwards had saved my life, and three, Eric's story was true.

My last thought prevailed above all others: RUN.

Although my limbs had grown numb from the cold, I was able to spring up on wobbly feet. It took only a fraction of a second before I bolted in the direction I'd come.

Tree limbs whipped my face and scratched my skin. Twigs and branches grabbed at me, tearing my clothing and burning slashes onto my flesh. Too frightened to look back, I pushed my legs to the extreme, exerting as much energy as possible to distance myself from the horrifying creatures behind me. I lengthened my stride—my hip joints aching from strenuous motion—and used the momentum of my arms to push forward faster, pumping them like pistons.

As the distance between myself and the woman of ice widened, the air warmed. My blood flowed freely, and adrenaline made me limber. I was starting to feel triumphant, until it dawned on me that I'd been running too long, that nothing looked familiar.

I should've made the trail, but it wasn't there.

I was lost.

Panic set in. I stopped and turned on my heel, whipping my head every which way, trying to find a point of reference to guide myself out. Impulsively, I ran to my left, hoping I was heading in the right direction. Within minutes, I realized I'd guessed wrong.

With lungs on the brink of combustion, I slowed. I needed to think logically. Running around like a madman would only make the situation worse.

I leaned behind a colossal evergreen and attempted to catch my breath. The entire scene in which I'd fled replayed in my head.

I focused on the conversation Eric and I had earlier. Now that I knew he was telling the truth, his entire tale took on a different perspective.

He said they wanted me. He told me I wouldn't come back.

How was I going to get out? My heartbeat pounded in my ears, and my temple throbbed.

A groan escaped when I remembered the gun I left behind. What the hell was I thinking? If only I had it now, I'd shoot anything that moved.

Think, think, think! I willed my mind to work.

I pushed off the tree with focus. Rebellion inflamed my blood. *I will make it out of this.* Defiance, and hope, surged through my veins. The positive thinking alone gave me newfound strength.

Yet, as soon as I found my courage, the sound of approaching foot-steps brought tragic reality crashing down around me.

Maybe I wouldn't be escaping after all.

7

FANTASIA

I'd been followed.

I pressed my body against the tree, wishing I could melt into the bark. The footsteps stopped directly behind me. Begrudgingly, I turned. Standing too close for comfort was my patchwork savior, the mask still ever present on his face.

Rationally, I knew this person had saved my life, but the mask was a distraction. Disguises such as his foretold danger. Or perhaps it was simply a disfigurement. Regardless, his anonymity frightened me.

He held out his hands, palms up, in a submissive pose. Then, in an attempt to alleviate my fear, he reached up to remove his mask. I closed my eyes, unsure if I wanted to see what lay underneath.

It took bravery, and the desire to survive, to pry my lids open.

And what stood before me defied logic.

My rescuer wasn't male at all, but female. The disfigurement I'd considered was merely a falsehood of my imagination. As impossible as it seemed, she was the most striking woman I'd seen. No one could compare. Because of her height—she was tall for a girl—and the cape that hid her figure, my initial assessment was completely misguided. She was *glorious*! She had dark, straight hair, shiny strands of onyx, with bronze skin that glistened even in the dull lighting. Her eyes, large and innocent, were shaped faultlessly and adorned with long, black lashes. Those lashes provided the perfect frame for her unusually colored irises—warm lavender. Her beautiful lips twitched slightly at the corners, hesitant to smile. She held up her hand to still me.

Her stance held tension, and I responded with sharp focus. I forced myself to look past her beauty to concentrate on the message she was trying to relay. That was no simple task, since I had the strangest compulsion to gawk at her. With concerned eyes, she held up her pointer finger to her lips in an unspoken gesture commanding my silence. She stepped lightly over to me, her footsteps now silent, as she grabbed my shoulders and urged me to crouch. She angled me so that I hovered near the base of the pine tree that I had—only moments ago—used as a refuge.

Once again, she held her finger to her lips. Her eyes held mine, the soft lavender firm, making certain I understood. I remained motionless as she stood up.

As I kneeled behind the tree, she called out a greeting. The language she used was unfamiliar. It sounded garbled, much like the words used in the tantalizing song of the female ice monster. I thought I heard, "Vagts le hungin."

Her voice fit her exquisite exterior: sweet and melodic.

The voice that returned her greeting was not. It was masculine, with a throaty gruffness. He, too, responded in the unusual language.

I inched my head to the right, moving just enough to have her in my sight.

They continued to communicate. It was incredibly frustrating not knowing what they were saying. Her voice sharpened. I could make out some movements. She was gesturing in the opposite direction of where I kneeled.

Tension was thick, and I realized once again she was protecting me. My peripheral vision picked up some grand movements as she continued to divert attention from my hiding spot. I held my breath, waiting for the conclusion of the exchange.

It seemed to take forever, but eventually her posture changed. It corresponded with the sound of retreating footsteps. The man was moving away. She relaxed her shoulders as a subtle sigh escaped.

She turned around and met my gaze. She slowly bent down to eye level and signaled with both hands that I needed to remain still. I nodded, ready to comply.

I wasn't sure how long we were like that; me, crouched low, frozen as a statue, and her, quiet and focused, looking around from time to time. Both of us made as little movement as possible. After an eternity—or perhaps minutes—she began to lip questions to me. No sound escaped, but I was able to understand by watching the formation of her perfectly shaped lips.

"Are you okay?" she mouthed.

I responded in like fashion, "Yes." My lips formed the words, but only soundless air escaped.

"They have good hearing," she motioned her ears. "You will need to be silent until I tell you it's safe."

I nodded.

"Good." She smiled, full and bright, her teeth white, straight, and blinding.

Then, unexpectedly, she reached out and grabbed my hand. A small jolt of electricity flashed through my veins. My palm tingled.

My face must've revealed surprise because she smiled even bigger, her grin reaching her eyes.

And from there on, that's how it went.

I sat there, holding her hand, in complete and utter silence. It was odd; we were hiding, in danger, yet, I was totally at peace. Being near her felt right. I felt right. When she wasn't surveying the grounds with her piercing stare, she would look at me and smile, sending sparks with each glance.

Eventually she spoke, her voice barely audible. I took it as a good sign that she was generating some noise, and not the lip formation she was forced to do earlier.

"I've got to get you out of here. We can't go back towards the trail; they'll be monitoring it pretty closely. Everyone's on high alert. They think someone came into the forest, but they have no definite proof."

She looked around again before continuing. "They found your truck and Frigid is acting strangely, although to be fair, she always acts a little strange." She gave me a bitter smile. *Frigid?* Was that the name of the woman I'd met earlier, the ice witch?

As though she knew my thoughts, she answered, "Yes, it was Frigid you saw earlier. Don't worry, she always goes a little nutty in her translucent phase; she won't remember the encounter she had with you. She gets amnesia when she turns."

Translucent phase? What on earth was that?

Once again, as though she knew what I was thinking, she responded, "I'll tell you later. Right now, we need to move deeper into the forest. I'm sorry for that. We have no choice but to lay low until everyone calms down. Your truck is our biggest obstacle. I found your gun and hid it. I don't think they'll find it. Fortunately, the way you parked your truck is a bit misleading. They are considering that whoever was driving may have gone the opposite direction and not into Narivous. Let's just hope they continue that train of thought."

She stopped again and tilted her head in deep concentration, listening for unwanted visitors.

"I need you to put this on." She took off her cape and handed it to me. We were still low to the ground, and her cloak dragged against the dirt. "Although the Animals are away, which is fortunate, the others still have a pretty good sense of smell. I'm surprised they haven't detected it yet. My scent should mask yours to an extent."

Animals? What did that have to do with anything? What was she talking about? I was sick of being confused, a common occurrence as of late. It reminded me of when I was little and my parents talked in "drug slang," using terms that I couldn't quite connect.

Obediently, I draped her cloak around my shoulders. She grabbed my elbow and pulled me up. My knees hurt from the awkward crouch I'd been stuck in. I had to kick my legs to get the blood flowing.

"What's your name?" I did my best to whisper, but it came out louder than expected. She flinched before giving me a reproving stare.

"Fantasia," she responded, after doing a prompt, visual sweep.

Now that we were both standing, her cloak removed, I was able to see her beauty in all its glory. She was dressed casually, wearing a gray t-shirt and faded blue jeans. Her laid-back attire couldn't hide her lithe figure and soft curves. I'd never seen a more perfect specimen of a woman. My thoughts must've been written all over my face because she broke out in an embarrassed blush.

"Come on." She grabbed my hand and started to lead the way, but my first step landed on a twig. The snap resounded off the timber. Fantasia's eyes broadened as her head whipped in all directions.

I mouthed the word "Sorry," but she wasn't paying attention. Rather, she continued surveying.

"Look," she began. "I don't think you'll be able to walk. I'll have to carry you."

I almost snorted in disbelief. She was tall, but I was taller—and bigger. There was no way she could manage the task. She was too small, too delicate. My skepticism was obvious.

A look of self-assurance washed over her face as she arched her brow and pulled the corner of her lip into a smirk. "You don't think I can do it?"

I shook my head, while trying to relax my features into a more respectful appearance. After all, she had saved my life.

This time *she* snorted. She bent low and stuck her shoulder in my gut. A moment later, I was held up by very capable hands as I rested on her right shoulder. She didn't even struggle, holding me like a rag doll, no burden whatsoever.

Within seconds, the air lashed past us as Fantasia broke into a run. The ground beneath her feet flashed by, making the soil and ferns blur. The overhead branches pulled at the cloak, the cool air rushing against my exposed face, the breeze fanning the perspiration on my skin.

Facing downwards, I grasped her torso, instinctively afraid of being dropped. Although she seemed to have no trouble carrying me, it still didn't erase the fact that we were moving at an alarming speed, and I was awkward to haul.

That, and I liked how she felt.

She gradually slowed. I had no idea how far we'd traveled, but it seemed like miles in a matter of minutes.

"You need to close your eyes now, and hold on as best as you can. Use all your strength," she instructed. "Don't let go of me, whatever you do. I'll tell you when it's okay to release me."

I squeezed my eyes shut as she subtly shifted me so I could wrap my legs around her waist. My head was now in an upright position. I rested my chin on her shoulder and inhaled the scent of her skin. I gripped with all the force I possessed as her pace accelerated. She was traveling much faster than before, a feat I would've thought impossible. Whatever was coming was big, and I didn't dare guess what that was.

Her pace continued to pick up momentum, her body pushing to the brink of its capacity moments before she pushed off something and leapt.

We were free-falling, I was sure. I grabbed even tighter and squeezed my eyes shut until my lids hurt from the pressure. I didn't dare let go. I didn't dare look.

Then there was a sudden jolt. The falling sensation stopped, and it seemed we now hung midair.

"Keep your eyes closed and keep holding tight," Fantasia ordered once again. Her body started to sway, first lightly and then quickening. Even with clasped eyes, I knew she was hanging from something—a rope, most likely—using it to swing us horizontally. The generated breeze was nauseating as our pendulum gathered velocity. Fantasia coiled her body before giving a final thrust. We were once again midair—I didn't doubt it—catapulted aerially before she landed with a soft thud.

"You can open your eyes now," she said as she gingerly set me on my feet. I wobbled, and she steadied me with her helping hands.

The scene before me was disorienting.

We were in a cave. A rope—still swaying—hung outside the opening. I didn't have any idea how far up or down we were, but I couldn't help myself as I carefully made my way towards the entrance. Fantasia gave me space as I inched forward.

I had to look.

Seriously?

Why did I have to look?

We were at least a hundred feet in the air, the cave a mere pocket on the side of a rock mountain. I glanced up and realized she had jumped from nearly 50 feet above. Literally, I was stuck in the middle of a giant hole.

Vertigo flipped my gut, and it brought me to my knees. It took a moment to pull myself upright and swallow back the bile that threatened to blow. I hugged the side of the cave and returned to the core of our refuge. How the hell was I going to get out of here?

Fantasia came over and grabbed my hand. That's when I noticed random household items strewn about.

Bottled water, blankets, pillows, and a couple fold-up chairs filled the dank space. Fantasia followed the direction of my gaze and explained.

"This is my private spot. My sisters sometimes come here and sit with me. It's nice having a place to hide." She blushed, and I had the strangest feeling she was sharing something intimate with me. "They won't look for you here. I'm sure of it. We'll be safe until the changing of the guards, and then I'll get you out."

"What's going on?" I asked. Fantasia waved to a chair and I sat down. She took the seat across from me and continued to hold my hand. The physical touch was comforting.

"I'm so sorry you came here," she began. "I wish Eric had the sense to keep his mouth shut."

"Eric? How'd you know about Eric? How do you know what he told me?"

She lifted her free hand and touched my forehead. Memories from Eric's earlier conversation flashed before my eyes; the revealing words filled my ears. It was as if Eric stood in front of me, retelling his tale. *The Doppelgängers can create illusions and screw with our minds. They can read our thoughts. They can pose as any of us, and our minds will be tricked into believing it.*

Fantasia nodded subtly; she closed her eyes as if in pain.

"Your thoughts are not safe from me. I can read everything." She looked into my eyes, her lavender meeting my blue. "What he told you was true. All of it. Tony is still here; he never left. I've met him…."

"You met—"

She held up her hand to quiet me.

"Yes, I met Tony. He hasn't left since Sunday. It's too late for him. He's stuck here."

"Is he okay?"

"Yes, he's … okay." She hesitated, then shook her head as though banishing some distasteful thought.

"Wait, that's impossible!" I said. "Tony went to work yesterday and quit. He told off his mom. People saw him! How could he be in two places at once?"

"You really don't pay attention, do you?"

"Sometimes I do."

"Let this be one of your *sometimes*," she said with a good-humored eye roll. She glanced at the ceiling before diving into her spiel. "They didn't see Tony. They saw a mirage created by us, created by my sisters, actually," she explained dryly. "Remember how Eric said we can alter what your mind sees? Well, that's true. It's a talent some of us possess."

I shook my head. This was just too much. Everything was too much.

"Daniel, you need to listen to me," she said urgently and gripped my hand tighter, her eyes piercing with intensity. "You're in Narivous. This is the land of the damned."

"This is impossible," I muttered.

Fantasia let out a heavy sigh. "Close your eyes, Daniel."

I did as instructed.

"Now open them."

I jumped as soon as my lids parted, nearly knocking the chair over. Fantasia was no longer in front of me; she'd been replaced by Aunt Marie. My eyes bulged. I blinked again, and the conjured image of Marie returned to Fantasia.

I finally hit the acceptance stage.

Fantasia nodded, seemingly relieved.

"Narivous has been around for many years, and our civilization consists of Velores. That's what we call ourselves. We're not human, Daniel. Some of us were created, others were born into this existence—we are immortals. It's important that you listen to me now. I need you to understand. I need you to believe wholeheartedly."

She stalled for a second, then pressed on earnestly.

"We look human, we talk like humans, and more importantly, we can trick people into thinking we are human. That's been key to our survival. We all possess gifts that make us deadly to mortals." She opened and closed her eyes slowly, before squeezing my fingers. "All Velores fit into seven groups: Earth, Water, Fire, Ice, Poison, Animal and Doppelgängers. Some of us are crossbreeds; that's the only way I know how to describe it. Every group has a primary ruler who commands us. Those rulers are the most powerful and oldest Velores ever created—they are Narivous Royalty—the Mighty Seven. We are forced to obey their orders, and disobedience of any kind is punishable with extreme force." She paused, and took a deep breath. "However, of the Mighty Seven, there is one that holds the most authority. She is our true Queen and the oldest and most powerful Velore ever created: Thorn. Thorn controls Earth, and she was the first Velore ever created. She has ultimate say."

With each revelation, more questions came to mind, but I dared not interrupt.

"I'm a Doppelgänger, and so are my sisters. Although two of us don't fit perfectly into this group, it's the most dominant, and so becomes our title. You've met one of my sisters already. Her name is Dreams, but you know her as Candace."

Candace! Hearing her name brought my anger to a boil, and I balled up my free hand. A low hiss pushed beyond my lips.

Fantasia tried to extinguish my rage.

"Don't be mad at her, Daniel. She had no choice. We were given direct orders from Thorn to recruit you. It wasn't her fault!"

Her pleading eyes calmed my temper. This woman had saved my life. I was in her debt, and I'd at least listen to her explanation.

"Once an order has been given, we must obey or face punishment. Thorn doesn't tolerate insubordinate behavior whatsoever."

"Why were you ordered to recruit me?" I asked through gritted teeth.

"You have the right aura; it's a colored light only we can see. It tells us some of the gifts you'll have once you've transformed. Most humans are transparent—over half, actually. Their aura's are clear. We call them blank-slates. The remainder typically have faint colors attached to them. But rarely, we'll find someone who is much brighter than the rest, colors bold and magnificent. We considered them destined."

"And my aura?"

She smiled. "You're a brilliant yellow, like the sun." She said it with a sense of awe.

"That's a good thing, then?"

Her grin widened. "Really, it's extraordinary. I've only heard of such brightness. I've seen many colors come through—many shades—but never has anyone shone as bright as you. I could just stare at you all day."

My cheeks heated as a strange sense of satisfaction rippled through me.

"Do they know why some people have auras of color and others don't; or why there's a difference in brightness?" Was I special? *Doubtful.* Most likely, there was something defective in my blood. Tainted, probably. It wouldn't have come as a surprise. My luck always bordered on rotten.

She shook her head. "We're not sure. We do know that it's often hereditary." Her eyes lit up as soon as the words spilled from her mouth. She appeared to remember something very important.

Her tone took on a new edge, as whatever thought popped into her head took control. "Daniel, I know a lot has happened. I can see the many questions in your mind, but I need you to take this to heart: once you join Narivous, you never leave. You will be tied to us always, forced to do the bidding of Thorn."

"And that's a bad thing?"

"It's a dangerous thing."

"This Thorn. She's deadly?"

"Oh, yes. Very. No one ever goes against Thorn. To do so is considered treason and is punishable by death."

This wasn't adding up. "I don't understand," I said. "If you're immortal, how could you possibly die?"

"It's difficult to do, but we can be destroyed." She lifted my hand and pressed my palm over her heart. "Focus, and you'll feel my heartbeat. We are living creatures, although we don't function the way you would expect."

I let my palm seek out her heart. After a few seconds, a strong thud beat against my skin. She snickered at my quizzical expression.

"Yes, my heart beats, just slowly." She smiled brightly. "Perhaps immortal is too definite of a word. We age, just very, *very*, gradually. Eventually, my heart will stop, but I'm sure it won't be for hundreds of centuries. That, and Chanticlaim is on the verge of ending the aging process altogether."

Chanticlaim? Who—or what—was that? Fantasia answered without being asked.

"Chanticlaim is our boy genius. His mother, Tipper, is equally brilliant, and together, I have no doubt that they'll stop the whole 'growing old process' altogether." She used her fingers as quotations. "Even if they don't, we have hundreds of years ahead of us. The older we get, the slower the aging process occurs. We rejuvenate so much quicker as the years move forward. That, and no one really knows what will happen once our hearts stop beating. Perhaps we will live on—forever frozen—or we may falter and die like any other mortal walking this earth. It hasn't happened yet, so it remains a mystery."

Listening to her, a sudden realization struck me. "Why are you saving me then? If Thorn ordered my recruitment, aren't you putting yourself in danger?"

Fantasia looked away, and I was certain I'd hit a sensitive subject. We were both at risk of losing our lives, and just the thought of being responsible for the death of this beautiful girl—Velore or not—would tear me apart.

She took a deep breath and said, "I don't want to be a monster."

❧ 8 ❧

UNUSUAL WORLD

"I don't know what it's like to be human. I've only caught glimpses in the memories of our recruits while they're still human. What I've seen breaks my heart. Not everyone is forced to join us; others sign up willingly. They have no idea what they're giving up. It's not an easy life being stuck here without freedom." Fantasia's chest lifted with a heavy breath. Her free hand gripped the arm of the chair.

"Dreams told me about you," she said softly. "She said some really nice things. I know you had a rough childhood." Fantasia pulled her eyes away as her cheeks brightened with color. Keeping secrets was impossible when the person sitting in front of you could pry open your mind. The lack of privacy embarrassed her, a quality that made her more endearing.

"It's okay," I reassured.

"No, it's not. Maybe you don't realize the opportunities you have before you. You have choices, you can grow old, you can live a normal life. You can travel the world on a whim, never having to ask permission, never having to control your translucent phase. That's something I've never had. It's something I've always wanted."

"Translucent phase?" Those words again. What was she talking about?

"It's when we turn, and our powers are in full effect. When you saw Frigid back there, she'd transformed. It's our response to danger, or a sudden change in environment. It makes us adaptable and helps ensure our survival. There are different levels to the transformation. The stages start off subtle, only we notice the difference. Then, as we choose, or as circumstances change, we go into deeper levels. Some of us are always in transition; others don't like the feeling and only turn when it's imperative to do so."

"What about you?"

She shook her head. "I prefer to stay as natural as possible. I guess I hover in the infant stages; just enough to give me a high and enhance my strength, but never more, if I can help it. I hate transforming all the way. You forget who you are. Your inhibitions are released, and you do things that you may regret. It makes you aggressive and angry. The hardest part is when the transformation occurs, and we're helpless to stop it. Sometimes it slips from our control."

"So you can't control it?"

"Not always."

"But sometimes?"

"It depends."

"On what?" This was beyond anything my imagination could've worked up, and I was in a desperate state to learn more. I'd stepped into a world where mystic possibilities existed. *Mind-freaking-boggling.*

"The individual. Some of us are better than others at containing it. I'd put myself in that category, but even the most disciplined have slip-ups—occasionally." She pulled her eyes away, as though she harbored some deep shame.

"So this translucent phase ... it's different for everyone?"

"Yes, depending on our specific powers. We are as unique as every human walking this earth." She gave me a crooked smile.

I was about to ask how often the transformation occurred, when she answered my unspoken question.

"The Deadbloods transform a lot; some of them struggle with keeping themselves *out* of their translucent phase. Others can be once a day, or once a year. It's all individualistic."

"The Deadbloods?"

Her smile tightened. "Yes, those are the Mighty Seven. We refer to them as Deadbloods because they're the most powerful; they were dead the longest." She let out a heavy sigh. She glanced at my face and read my confusion. "The whole conversion process consists of three factors. It's kind of difficult to explain…." She bit the side of her cheek as she pondered how to move forward. "I want you to close your eyes and envision a box of crayons."

I did as instructed.

"Now, I want you to think about your color. You are a brilliant yellow. Imagine grabbing a yellow crayon and coloring a blank piece of paper. You'll have to press hard to equal an aura as bright as yours. This will be your base. Now, every method of death has a color as well. For example, to die by water, the color is green. So now, envision if we drowned you."

I winced—unwittingly thinking of Tony.

"Sorry," she murmured. "Bad death choice."

"It's okay. Just keep going."

Fantasia, rattled, let off a breath that reached my face, all the while rubbing the back of my hand in soothing, soft circles. She continued softly, "If dying by water is green, you'll need to color over your yellow with that hue. But first, you'll need to know how hard to press and for how long. That's where the third factor comes in. The longer you're dead, the harder you push and for a longer amount of time. The final color is a mere representation of the gifts you'll possess and the clan you'll fall under. This color will be unique to you and will define your strengths once you become a Velore.

"Because of this, every Velore is incomparable. However, there is a point of no return when a body has started to decompose and is no longer viable for transformation. But if the timing is right and you wait to change them until that perfect moment, you'll have created the strongest Velore possible."

I opened my eyes. The process sounded gruesome. Fantasia nodded in agreement.

"We don't create Velores like that anymore. It's too much of a threat to Thorn. And it causes some unsettling side effects."

I snorted. "Isn't the entire result an unsettling side effect?"

She gave a grisly chuckle. "Not like you think. Remember how I told you Frigid was a bit nutty? Well, that's because she was dead for a long time. Her body didn't rot because she'd been lying in the snow. The cold temperature preserved her corpse—but not her brain—and by the time they injected her with immortality, the length of death had severely damaged her mind. Over the years, she's become more and more ... *unpredictable.*" Fantasia struggled to find the right word. "She lives in her translucent phase most of the time now, which makes her incredibly lethal *and* loony. She doesn't remember anything that happens, and it's only when she pulls out that she has moments of clarity. But lately, that's been few and far between. Despite her mental degeneration, Frigid remains one of our Seven, the leader of Ice."

"Good to know that your civilization is run by lunatics." I gave her my most absurd grin to show her I was kidding. Partially.

Fantasia repressed a smile. "Real cute."

"I was joking."

Fantasia touched my forehead. "Not entirely."

I shrugged. She was right.

"It breaks her husband's heart to watch her slip away," Fantasia went on. "Polar adores Frigid with all of his being, and he's really a wonderful man."

I lifted an eyebrow. Fantasia smiled.

"It's true, Daniel. He really is. Had it not been for him, Cheetoh would've torn Eric apart. He's fair and honest. He was a victim of circumstance, much like Tony. Like Frigid."

Tony's name brought me back to the present—her too—and I could tell she was considering our next move.

"We have longer to wait. I'm sorry."

I was in no hurry.

The rest of the afternoon passed in a blur as I sat and listened to the captivating sound of Fantasia's voice.

She told me about her sisters: Dreams and Torti. She talked of her mother, Camille. All of them held a sort of heroic adulation in her eyes. Fantasia openly admitted that she placed her family on a pedestal. She described how they looked after one another, how Torti acted more like a second mom than an older sister.

Apparently, Velores are still fertile. Fantasia and Dreams were living proof. All the sisters shared different fathers, and only Torti was born human—and remained human—for the first few months of her life. All they'd ever known was Narivous, and Fantasia hadn't realized she'd been cheated until she developed her mind-reading capabilities.

Reading minds brought a new perspective. She explained in detail the first mind she peered into and how that moment changed her. She understood then that immortality wasn't without consequences. Thorn robbed people of their freedom—and in Fantasia's mind—happiness. It was a synonymous pairing and couldn't be split.

"I went to bed that night questioning everything I knew," Fantasia said as she grabbed a lock of hair and tucked it behind her ear. She focused on the entrance of the cave with faraway eyes—lost in an old memory. "I *still* question everything," she whispered.

I leaned forward, so close that our heads nearly touched. "Even humans question everything."

She snapped to and whipped her head towards me. Her lips, now inches from mine, were almost poised to kiss. The warmth of her breath, her nearness, made me wonder how she'd taste. I couldn't help it. Fantasia, seeing my trail of thoughts, blushed scarlet and shyly looked away.

She cleared her throat and attempted to lower the energy. "Yes, you're right. Even humans question everything." She gave me an unsure smile. We both let it go. Maybe more her, than me.

I had so many questions, and because my mind was open to Fantasia, she answered them without needing to be asked. She told me Velores born into Narivous age naturally until they develop their powers. Only then does the aging process slow. She described it as a unique form of puberty—which usually occurs between the ages of 13 and 16—often mimicking human adolescents reaching their own passage into adulthood. It's celebrated as a coming of age, and all Velores gather to throw a massive party in honor of their newest adult member.

She explained that Velores born into Narivous are labeled as "Naturals," and those brought into Narivous are called "Synthetics." Unlike Naturals, all Synthetic Velores develop their powers the moment they turn—although they're weaker until their strengths have time to ferment and grow.

What muddled up the process of creating Synthetics was when they turned children. Fantasia said it was difficult to manage the little ones, especially when they held such powerful gifts. But on the flip side, as adults they were typically the most obedient subjects, having never known anything other than the life forced upon them.

I could only imagine the look of horror on my face. The thought of innocent children being pulled from their families was repulsive. Fantasia's face dimmed. Her look of sadness confirmed that she, too, disliked the practice.

She added that they rarely transform children anymore. Not because Thorn felt it was wrong, but because it attracted too much attention. Missing children were taken much more seriously than missing adults or troubled teens. According to Fantasia, the Velores had been watching me for some time but waited to recruit me. If they plucked me too young, people would notice, questions would be asked.

"Fortunately, your family life helps us," Fantasia said dryly. "They have deemed that you fall into the troubled runaway spot. That, and they simply didn't have the patience to wait any longer. They figured it was safe, since you live with your grandmother and not your mom and dad."

I whistled low. "And who said there weren't any perks to having dirt-bag parents?"

Fantasia barked a laugh so real and genuine that her voice sparkled. *Note to self: be funnier.*

"Indeed," Fantasia said as she affectionately tugged on my pants.

She said the mind-reading gift only applied to humans. Fantasia was clear that no one in Narivous could read another Velore's mind. Thorn would never permit such a person to exist. Not even Dolly—the Doppelgänger Clan leader and strongest of that breed—could read the thoughts of other Velores. She said this with conviction, but never met my eyes. Her words had the monotone drone of a line recited from memory. They felt rehearsed, although I had no proof to go on, and with so many other thoughts cluttering my head, I quickly discarded it. There wasn't any room left.

Fantasia explained that some Velores were toxic in their translucent phase, Frigid being one of them. I couldn't help but wonder if Fantasia, too, was toxic. The notion of such perfection being deadly seemed an utter tragedy. Fantasia flushed at my thoughts—for, like, the umpteenth time—and told me she wasn't poisonous. I was elated. This girl wasn't human. I shouldn't have cared, but I couldn't dismiss how my nerves tingled in her presence. Despite Frigid's terrifying image sparking in my memory,

I couldn't connect Fantasia with that immortal monster. They seemed worlds apart.

Fantasia gave me a grateful smile. "Thank you," she said, and squeezed my hand.

"The not-being-a-monster thought?" I asked.

"Yeah. Even if it's not true."

"You're not a monster," I said, my conviction strong. Fantasia looked away and shrugged her shoulders. This time I squeezed her hand.

Darkness shadowed her eyes when they met mine. Fantasia moved on, eager to let the subject drop.

Fantasia's stories seemed fantastical. She talked about the splitting of the clans, in order to cover more ground. The Poison Leader and the Fire Leader covered the south side, looking over their citizens and reporting any transgressions to Thorn.

Narivous was ever-growing as Thorn pushed for new recruits. Currently—and much to our benefit—the Animal Clan was searching the east side of the Cascade Mountains, covering thousands of acres, trying to find the most desolate regions for Narivous to put down more roots.

The Animals, Fantasia described, were the best candidates for this type of research. With superlative senses—primarily their sense of smell— they could detect human interference from miles away.

Had the Animals been nearby, I wouldn't have stood a chance. Our hideout, even encapsulated in the middle of a cliff, wouldn't have masked my scent. Narvious' desire to expand had been my saving grace. Only Frigid and Serpent were local; they were in charge until Thorn and the others returned that evening.

Although not many Velores were present, guards still roamed. She said it was lucky for Eric as well. Cheetoh was the only Animal in the area on Sunday and left after Polar intervened on Eric's behalf. Indignant over Polar's orders, he set off to participate in more "productive endeavors."

"I'm sure Thorn will be angry when she hears about that. I hope Polar doesn't get into trouble." She bit down on her bottom lip as her forehead furrowed. "But Polar is one of her favorites and can talk his way out of anything. I'm sure it'll be okay."

She never said so aloud, but I suspected she disliked Thorn. She carefully skirted around any direct description of her Queen, choosing her words wisely.

Fantasia also told me about Tony.

His transformation had gone smoothly. Serpent, the leader of Water, was the one to drown him. That's who Eric had seen emerge from the lake moments before he fled. They let Eric escape, knowing they could use him as a Protector. She explained that Protectors on the outside were essential. They helped cover the Velores' tracks, divert attention, and keep their society a secret.

Her eyes grew sad when she circled back to Tony. She reiterated he was all right, although shaken up. She claimed he was eager for a family, so much so, he accepted Narivous without a second thought. According to Fantasia, Tony's aura was clear, so his powers were easy to predict.

She also said her people preferred personality traits Tony possessed.

Lonely, neglected humans made the most pliable Velores. Often, their desire to find a home overrode any misgivings they may have over Narivous' unorthodox methods of recruitment and obedience. In addition, the years of abuse made for angry victims—angry Velores—with a general dislike of the human race.

"But Tony doesn't have a dislike for the human race," I reminded her.

She gave me a sweet smile. "I know. Tony is one of those rare creatures. He's a good spirit. It's refreshing. I'm just saying many who join our ranks don't have such an optimistic view on life—at least the ones who join us willingly." She puckered her lips, twisting them into a sour expression. "They're bitter and eager to extract revenge, if given the opportunity. It makes them *happy*."

Fantasia stated that Thorn was power hungry. Cautious to be in control, she selected her recruits carefully. She preferred wounded humans, but every once in a while would stumble across a 'prized selection'—one too irresistible to pass up. When presented with the gift of immortality, some of these coveted humans resisted, but Thorn had an effective weapon in her arsenal: love. Having come from good homes with loving families, they had no prejudice against humanity, and fiercely fought Narivous' snare. So to make these less-adaptable Velores toe the line, Thorn threatened the lives of their loved ones.

It worked well.

Despite it all, I was surprised to find comfort buried within Fantasia's words—at least in terms of Tony. Sure, Tony had been caught in the cross-hairs, used as a device to get to me, but he finally found a place to belong. No one in his family cared for him, at least not the way Gram cared for me.

Gram. Thinking of her, I instinctively reached for my cellphone. I now had reception, which baffled me. Why would the inside of a cave allow one bar to peek through when the open clearing allowed none?

I suppose it didn't matter. A number of texts, as well as a voicemail, appeared on my home screen. Three of them were from Eric, one was from Sarah, and the voicemail was from an upset Gram. No doubt she was calling about my missing school again. Trestle High had an automated notification system that alerted parents if students missed class.

To avoid her wrath, I'd have to call her immediately.

I was about to hit the callback button when Fantasia's hand covered my phone.

She looked directly into my eyes and whispered the words, "Lie. Tell her you went to the beach. That you needed time away from Sarah and your fellow classmates."

I nodded and dialed her number. It took one ring before Gram picked up. When she answered, I knew something was off. "Daniel," she breathed. "Where are you?"

"Hi, Gram." I paused. "Is everything okay?"

The line went silent. I pulled the phone from my ear to see if we were still connected.

"Gram? Are you still there?"

"I'm here," Gram's voice quivered. "I need to talk to you. When will you be home?"

"Is everything okay?" I asked again, alarmed by her defeated tone. Had missing school really upset her that much? It was only one extra day.

"It's fine. I just need to know when you'll be home."

"I'll be home in a little while...." I hesitated before diving into my apology. I sucked at excuses and knew this was going to hurt. "Gram, I'm sorry I ditched today. I just couldn't stand being in class. Alex tried to confront me again, and I didn't want to do anything rash. I decided to leave. I'm at the beach right now." Regurgitating the lie Fantasia provided was surprisingly easy. I threw in the part about Alex to make it extra believable.

"You skipped school?" she asked, surprised.

"You didn't know?"

"NO, I DIDN'T!" Here was the anger. "Listen up, young man; this stops now. I know breakups are hard, but that's no excuse to jeopardize your education. Your grades are bad enough as it is. I'm not going to tolerate this behavior. Tomorrow, your butt better be in class. Do we understand each other?"

I suppressed a chuckle before replying dutifully, "Yes, ma'am."

"This isn't funny," she countered.

"Of course not."

Gram's voice lightened. "Now, what time will you be getting home tonight?"

"Well, I've got to work this evening. I get off at seven. Now that Tony quit, I have to help cover his shifts."

"Tony quit his job?"

"Yeah, it looks like he's skipping town. He wants to start fresh else-where." I did my best to sound casual. Fantasia nodded her encouragement.

"Hmmm." I could almost see Gram's disapproving scowl. She would've never supported Tony's decision to uproot a few months before graduation. *No one would.*

"I think it's pretty rash and reckless," I added for brownie points.

"Well, I need to talk with you this evening. I'm going to see Charlie after I get off the phone. I've been meaning to visit him all week. Will you be home right after work?"

"Sure, Gram. Sure. Is everything okay?"

"It's fine, Daniel. We just need to have a talk."

"Hints?"

I sensed her smile. "Well, for starters, we're going to talk about this skipping school baloney." She paused before adding, "The rest can wait until you get here—it's nothing to fret about. Be careful heading back. You know how dangerous that highway is."

"Roger that."

"I love you."

"Love you, too, Gram."

My nerves prickled when the line disconnected. Something was plaguing Gram; I could hear it in her voice.

"Gram didn't sound normal." I flipped the phone over in my hand. "Odd, I didn't have reception earlier. Now I do."

Fantasia's eyes flickered with guilt. "Oh, well, that's Chanticlaim's work. He has a reception blocker that messes with people's electronics. It never used to be an issue. No one got reception up here, but as more cell towers go up, the more precautions we need to take." She gave me a mis-chievous grin. "My cave, ironically, interferes with his device. I'm usually able to get at least one bar in here."

I almost laughed at the irony. Here I was, sitting in a cave next to an immortal girl, holding a conversation about an undead civilization and one surviving cellphone bar. Surely, the world had gone insane. Or maybe it was just me. My lips curled into a smile from the utter madness of it all, until Fantasia's head snapped towards the cave's entrance. My blood turned to ice. The rope was moving; someone was coming down.

9

AFFAIRS IN ORDER

Fantasia—panicked—gasped loudly. We both stood up to face one another. Her grip on my hand tightened, vise-like. Trapped like caged animals, we held our breath.

That's when our unannounced visitor appeared. Hanging on the rope, like it was an everyday occurrence, was Dreams. Her eyes widened when she saw the both of us, holding hands, standing in the heart of the cave. Fantasia relaxed and approached the entrance, letting go of my hand in the process. I instantly missed her touch. Dreams began to swing back and forth, building a momentum before leaping towards us. Fantasia reached out her arms and caught her.

She landed on balanced feet and then pulled herself from Fantasia. She placed both hands on her hips and let her accusing stare sweep between Fantasia and I.

"What are you doing?" she asked Fantasia. Her blue irises turned a shade darker with poison. "Are you out of your mind?"

Fantasia held out her hands, palms up.

"He doesn't deserve this life."

Dreams arched an incredulous brow.

"That doesn't matter," Dreams hissed. "We are so far beyond that."

"Yes, it does matter."

"Not anymore! It's too late. He needs to be brought to Thorn, NOW!" Dreams spat the words.

"No! I won't let you."

"Fantasia! You have no idea what kind of trouble we're in. I have messed this up royally. They are talking about putting Romeo on this job." She pointed at me and said, "I need him. *We* need him." Fantasia shook her head. Dreams grabbed her by the hand and led her to the back of the cave. She started whispering in the garbled language that Fantasia spoke earlier. Clearly, I wasn't supposed to understand the communication between them.

They went back and forth, Fantasia and Dreams making grand gestures with their hands, every so often pointing in my direction. Dreams became more agitated as Fantasia's head continued to shake. Her whole body trembled with suppressed frustration. I decided to trace the cracks of the cave, uncomfortable with their exchange.

Eventually, Fantasia held up her hand to end the discussion. Her unwavering eyes held firm.

"NO! I WONT HAVE IT!" Fantasia shouted. Dreams stepped back.

"Be reasonable, Fantasia."

"No." She stuck her finger close to Dreams' nose. "We're done having this discussion."

Fantasia stalked over to me and with clipped words told me to hang on. Apparently, Dreams' arrival was our cue to go. Dutifully, I latched on and prepared to close my eyes. There was only one way out, and I had no desire to see it firsthand. But before I did, I couldn't help but take one last look at Dreams. She was cowering in the corner. Her knees were pulled to her chest as she cradled her head in her hands. A pang of sadness rippled through me as her shoulders quaked with sobs. She reminded me of Eric, whitewashed and shattered.

Something deeper was going on.

I kept my eyes closed as we made our way up the rope, and continued to clamp them shut as Fantasia sprinted through the forest.

It wasn't until Fantasia stopped, and I was firmly on my feet, that I opened them. We were still in the woods, but it was different. It wasn't suffocating.

"We're no longer in Narivous," she said knowingly. "I've taken you to the opposite side of the entrance." She pointed to the spot in front of me. Faint rays of sunshine dappled around the trees. "The clearing is on the other side. This is as far as I can take you. Look, a lot of things are riding on your leaving. Trust me; you don't want this life. You need to leave Oregon—and leave soon. The best I can give you is a couple of days to get your affairs in order. Dreams and I can postpone them for that long. Please, you mustn't delay. If you stay, they'll take you."

"But what about you?" This couldn't be the end. I had to see her again.

Fantasia stepped closer and ran her hand along the front of my shirt. She focused on her trailing fingers, keeping her expression hidden from my view. Then, after a beat, she looked up. Her face flickered with a series of nuances as she battled an internal struggle.

I thought I saw regret and wistfulness. I also detected longing, but that may have been wishful thinking skewing my receptors.

"You need to go now." Fantasia let out an unstable breath. "Don't worry about me, and please, don't say a word to anyone, *ever*. To do so would condemn me to death."

"I'd never put you in danger!"

The smile she gave me was marred with sadness. It never reached her eyes. She paused before wrapping me in a hug. When she spoke next, her voice broke. "Please go. Don't make this harder than it has to be." She released me and stepped away. Black tears puddled in her eyes. The unnatural liquid reaffirmed her inhuman nature and that I didn't belong.

Even still, I reached out and tucked a strand of hair behind her ear. I didn't care who, or what, she was. I liked her. A lot.

She knew it, too.

She gave off an uncomfortable smile and wiped away her tears.

"You don't deserve this life," she said.

"Neither do you."

She didn't answer and instead looked at her feet.

Reluctantly, I removed her cloak and handed it to her. She grabbed it and draped it over her shoulders.

"Please leave," she said.

My face dropped. Those were terrible words to hear. They struck a chord—a beat-up, well-abused chord. She reached out and squeezed my hand. "You know what I mean," she said. "This is just a goodbye."

"I don't want to say goodbye," I responded honestly.

"This time you do; trust me." She nodded towards the speckled light. "Your truck should be fine. They don't dismantle them unless they're certain someone's entered Narivous. Get in, and don't look back." Then, perhaps to make our departure easier, she pivoted on her heel and took off in the opposite direction.

She vanished into the crowded foliage while I stood there, wondering how someone I had just met could affect me so profoundly. My heart hurt.

And that was the moment I realized I'd never be the same again.

It wasn't just the discovery of a hidden, undead civilization that did it—although that would've been enough. It was Fantasia. My world had been irrevocably changed, and I wasn't entirely sure how I felt about that.

I was certain, however, that I wanted to see Fantasia again.

That was for damn sure.

I don't remember the drive home. One moment I was turning the key in the ignition, and the next I was parked in Gram's driveway—the truck silent, the engine pinging as it cooled. Apparently, autopilot was a well-programed feature in my internal hard drive.

The clock on my dashboard told me three things. One, I wouldn't make my afternoon classes, making the day another academic wash. *Whatever.* It's not like school mattered. Two, my shift at Mick's was scheduled to start in an hour. And three, I hadn't had anything to eat all day, although, to be perfectly honest, it wasn't really the clock that told me that. It was my stomach that rolled with wrenching hunger pains.

Stepping into the foyer, I was taken aback by how normal it seemed. So much had changed in the last few hours; I subconsciously expected the world to shift with my new reality. Instead, normalcy greeted me at the door. The scent of lavender hung heavy in the air, and the sunshine-yellow kitchen beckoned me with its food-laden cupboards.

In no time at all, I was sitting at the kitchen table with a glorious turkey sandwich. My mind wandered while eating in silence, Fantasia forever at the forefront.

She'd said that I only had a couple of days to get my affairs in order. How was I going to leave Gram? Did I even want to leave?

My eyes gravitated towards the front door, and in particular, the long, oak entry table that showcased family photographs. On it sat a picture of Dad and me on a beach in Maine. I wore a toothless grin that shone for the recipient behind the camera: Gram. Dad, sitting behind me, stared vacantly at the foamy ocean shore. Now that I was older, I recognized the pale bruising in the crook of his elbow. If I had to guess, he'd started using only months earlier.

Gram had captured the infant stages of rot in our deteriorating family without knowing it. And years later, that decay would spread over every facet of my life. It tainted my childhood and destroyed my parents. It obliterated the love I once had for them. It was killing them—and me—without us even knowing. Drugs have that type of power; they're lethal and unassuming. They not only take down the addict, but their family as well. When

I finally had enough, I did the only thing I could think of: run to the one person who still cared.

Gram.

It was right after my fourteenth birthday. Mom had met the most glorious jerk-off of all time. He even surpassed all the hosers, which is a feat, believe me. And, as luck would have it, he decided to stick around for longer than a night.

Wayne wasn't like the others; he didn't just beat up Mom, but me as well. Now let me be clear on one thing: I've never condoned the abuse Mom suffered. There were times I tried to step in and protect her, only to end up equally injured. It took a handful of deep bruises and a pair of cracked ribs before I learned that kids can't win physical fights against adult men. They just don't.

But Wayne enjoyed violence and sought me out. I couldn't do anything right. I chewed my food wrong. I used too much water. I gave him looks that his paranoid mind mistook as disrespectful. Each infraction earned me a new mark. Plum patches bloomed over my skin on a daily basis.

It was only a matter of time before self-preservation kicked in.

So, after a particularly violent bout when Wayne fractured the wall with my head, I decided to skip town.

That night, I raided Wayne's wallet and booked a bus ticket. I left the next day and traveled the 2,000 plus miles to Oregon without detection. Mom's lack of attention edged precariously close to full-blown parental neglect.

I waited until I got to the Trestle bus station to call Mom. She didn't seem to care when I told her I wasn't coming back. Gram showed up half an hour later and found me sitting on a bench, bags at my feet.

"DANIEL JEREMY THATCHER!" she barked. "What on earth do you think you're doing?" She stormed to stand in front of me, all 5 feet 3 inches.

"Well—"

"Do you know how dangerous it is to travel across the country by yourself?"

"I—"

"WHAT WERE YOU THINKING?" she bellowed, throwing her hands in the air. Her bouffant hairdo smoldered at the roots. "Running away! I can't even wrap my head around it! I CAN'T BELIEVE YOU'D BE SO RECKLESS!"

She paused to catch her breath, and I took advantage of the lull by launching into my explanation.

"I didn't know what else to do. This was my only option." I stood up and tucked my hands into my pockets. Too ashamed to meet her gaze, I spoke to my shoelaces. "I had no choice...."

Her anger extinguished a bit.

She grabbed my forearm and gave it a gentle squeeze. "What on earth possessed you to come here by yourself? Why would you run away?"

I swallowed my fear and decided to go all in. Gram needed to know the truth, so I filled her in on the big secret that'd become my life. I told her about Mom's prescription hobby, how it had gotten progressively worse over the years. That if she wasn't swallowing handfuls of pills, she was drinking pints of liquor. I told her that Dad never contacted me anymore. Most importantly, I told her about Wayne. I told her everything: every fight, every hit, every hateful word. And as I spilled out our secrets, I could see the horror of my life reflected back at me through her eyes. By the time I was done, Gram was in tears and clinging to me.

"I'm not sending you back," she whispered, and with that, it was decided. I was officially going to live with Gram, and for the first time in years, I had a little bit of peace.

But now that peace had been shattered.

Everything had changed. Gram would be disappointed if I left now, abandoning her on the home stretch.

That, and where would I go? Sure, Mom and Wayne were ancient history, but her recreational activities hadn't ceased. I didn't want to go back to that life.

But what choice did I have?

I wanted the fog back. I needed that disconnect. *Craved it.*

Everything was too overwhelming. I shoved the plate away and let my head fall to the table. It was only a matter of seconds before my eyelids closed on their own accord. I started to fight the urge and then realized I didn't want to. Darkness ensued, and everything went blank.

The creak of the front door jostled me awake. Gram stood frozen, her hand on the knob, staring at me. Her face was void of color—as if she'd seen a ghost.

It made my adrenaline pump.

I sat up and ran my hands through my hair. I gave her a tentative smile—one she didn't return. Instead, she remained rooted. My heart-beat accelerated.

"Hey," I said lightly, hoping to break the tension.

She said nothing and continued to gawk. It started to wig me out.

"What happened to you?" she finally whispered.

Ah! So that was the reason for the strange look. I gave my clothing a once-over. I was dirty and tousled. My shirt ripped. My run from the ice-catastrophe had done a number on my clothing, not to mention the faint, pink scratches that etched my forearms. She wasn't going to buy my BS story about the beach—not with the telltale evidence laying testament to the contrary. It was best to mix a little truth with fiction.

"Oh, this." I indicated my shirt. "I did some scouting in the woods near the coastline. You know how it is over there, dense as all get out." I smirked. "I saw a herd of elk, which was pretty cool. There was even a bull the size of my truck." *Smile, Daniel.* Give her the reassurance she clearly needs. "I guess I got more tore up than I thought." I lifted my shoulders and let them fall.

Gram's eyes darkened.

"So you went scouting on the coastline?" Her question came out slow, uncertain.

"Yes."

She continued to stand near the front door, unmoving. I could almost see the gears in her head move, gaining rhythm as she attempted to make sense of my appearance. My mind, on the other hand, had blown a cylinder and wasn't functioning properly at all.

"Have you seen Eric recently, or Tony?" Her eyes narrowed to reptilian slits.

It made me pause. Why was she asking about Eric and Tony? Why now?

I didn't know how to directly answer that question, either. I knew, without a doubt, I would regurgitate the story of Tony skipping town—that was simple. Eric, however, was a bit more complicated. What if she started asking questions and I slipped up? The risk was too great. I feared too much for Fantasia's safety.

So I decided to deny all. I shook my head and molded my expression into one of indifference.

"Nope. Haven't seen either of them."

"Not even Eric?" Gram asked.

I shook my head and widened my eyes. "No, I haven't seen or talked to him since Saturday."

She tilted her head to the side and intently stared. Doubt was stamped across her face. She closed the door and stepped towards me. I shifted uncomfortably in my seat.

Gram was a miner for truth—digging up nuggets of information with only her eyes. I tried to keep my face flat and unflustered. Questions could lead to slip-ups. It was time for a diversion.

"So did you see Charlie this afternoon?" I asked.

This question, apparently, wasn't a good one to ask. As though a switch had been flipped, her face transformed from suspicion to pain. She grabbed a seat across from me and sat down.

"Yes, I saw him. He seemed … distracted." Gram hung her head and stared at her lap. She sighed.

I was at a loss. Gram wouldn't look at me, and I didn't know what to do, or say. It was the oddest interaction I'd ever had with her. My eyes swam around the room, searching for something stable to land on. I couldn't take looking at Gram. I found the clock and jumped up.

Work. I was going to be late.

"Shoot! I've got to get to work!"

I bent to give Gram a prompt kiss on the cheek, but she surprised me by grabbing my hand with remarkable strength. Her knobby fingers grasped tightly. I took notice.

"Daniel?" she asked haltingly.

"Yes, Gram?"

"Daniel, I want you to know that I love you." Tears puddled in her eyes. I found myself swallowing hard and kneeling down so we were at eye level.

"What's this about?"

"I just think it's important to say it out loud."

"Is that all?"

Gram bobbed her chin subtly.

"Well, then," I said. "It's best I tell you that I love you, too."

She gave me a smile loaded with sadness as she studied my face. I had the feeling she was trying to commit my features to memory. She held out her arms, and I dove into them, letting the scent of her lavender perfume cloak me.

When I pulled away, she grabbed my head between her palms, cupping my face. She faltered for a second before kissing me on the forehead.

"I am so proud of you, young man. I can't even begin to tell you how you've impacted my life." She smiled as a single tear coursed down her cheek.

"Gram, please tell me what's wrong. Are you okay?" My voice shook as my trembling hands brushed away her tear. My throat constricted. Something was most certainly off.

She smiled tightly. "Everything's fine, darling. I'm just getting mushy in my old age. Now, you head on to work. You'll come sit with me afterwards, right?"

"Right."

Now she smiled brightly. "Good. I'll make dinner. How does that sound?"

I nodded. "That sounds great, Gram."

I was reluctant to leave, and she saw me stall. Causally, she waved her hand, dismissing me. I didn't really have to work; I wouldn't be keeping that job for long. Narivous had changed everything. But it was the struggle for normalcy—a routine—that I craved. An escape plan of the mundane.

I leaned down and kissed Gram on the cheek.

"Bye, Gram. I'll see you this evening."

"Goodbye, Daniel." She clasped her hands onto the table and gave me a sweet, forced smile.

Beneath it all, I knew I shouldn't have left.

I told myself it was paranoia—plain and simple—convinced that extreme fatigue and shock had warped my logic.

But really, I was a selfish prick and wanted a little more time to myself.

I sighed heavily and walked out the door.

Work was the distraction I hoped for, that is, until thirty minutes before my shift cut out. I was in the middle of stacking a pyramid of bananas—carefully arranging the ripe, least mangled ones along the perimeter—when an old man started to cough. He stood near the Organic section, bent over as he warred with his body. He gripped his side and tried to stop the jarring of organs as he rocked with each throaty convulsion. I started towards him with a paper towel, you know, so he had a place to set his hacked-up lung, when I stopped in my tracks.

It was his cough and the way his shoulders tensed against the thin fabric of his polyester shirt. The action was familiar; I'd seen it before. With Gram.

Lab work.

I tossed the towel onto the produce cart and sought out Turkey-Neck to tell him I was about to blow chunks. For once, he didn't challenge me—probably because it was partly true. The thought of Gram receiving bad news made me sick to my stomach.

Then I hauled serious ass home.

When I pulled into the drive, I knew something was wrong right away. Gram's house was eerily dark. All I could see was a small glow coming from the direction of her kitchen table.

Dusk landed an hour before, and the thickness of night shrouded everything in silence. The creak of my truck door was too loud for the quiet evening.

On unsteady legs, I made my way to the house—already sure of its vacancy.

The door opened to total isolation.

To my right, I spotted the source of the small light I'd seen from the driveway. It was an LED candle, and it was sitting on top of a letter.

Recognizing Gram's handwriting, I sat down and began to read.

GRANDMOTHER

My Darling Daniel,

I'm so very sorry. All I've ever wanted was for you to be happy and safe.

I went and saw Charlie this afternoon. He didn't hear me approach, since he was having a heated conversation with Eric. I overheard what Eric told you. I heard where Eric said you went. I know you weren't on the coastline this afternoon. But more importantly, I know YOU KNOW about "them." I recognized the look of despair in your eyes—the same despair I'd seen years ago by someone who resembled you in more ways than you know.

And now you have to know the truth.

When I was 16, I fell in love with Charlie's best friend, a boy named Paul Henley. He was the center of my universe, back when I was young and impressionable. I wanted to spend the rest of my life with him, but our forever was cut short.

Narivous was hunting him, and by the time he realized it, it was too late.

They took Arthur, Paul's older brother, first. After Arthur, Paul and their younger brother, Jack, soon followed. By the time I found out I was pregnant with Paul's child, they were gone. They'd been drawn into Narivous, and there they remain.

Paul came and saw me shortly after he'd transformed. They'd turned him into a man of ice, going by the name of Polar. Although outside contact was forbidden, his unwavering compassion urged him to meet with me one last time. I was grateful. I told him I was pregnant.

He told me to run.

He didn't want to put our child at risk; just the proximity to Narivous put the baby in danger. If the baby were anything like himself, or his brothers, the child would be sought out by Narivous—the recruitment eminent—and he'd be helpless to stop it.

Grandpa Dylan had been in love with me for years, and in a moment of desperation, I married him and passed off Paul's child as his. Then we moved to Maine.

Dylan deserved so much more, and I've had to live with that shame. But truthfully, Paul stole my heart years ago. He still has it. You've held it as well, Paul's carbon copy. Paul was the real reason I moved back to Oregon. Knowing he was nearby gave me comfort. I realize now what a mistake that was.

I got some bad news today. The doctors discovered lung cancer, and there's nothing they can do to save me. And since it's too late for me, I've decided to do something selfish. I'm going to Narivous to see Paul. If I'm going to die, I want to do it in his arms. I hope they won't deny an old woman that one last request.

I'll call Charlie to tell him goodbye. I'll encourage him to have Eric run, since his knowledge places him in real danger. Marie and Lacey should be safe; it's not their bloodline they're after. Regardless, I was careful to make provisions.

I don't know how you made it out of Narivous, intact and still you. I'm just grateful you were given a second chance. Treat it as a gift, Daniel, and leave Oregon. Don't ever come back.

I love you more than you'll ever know. Please forgive me.

-Gram

The letter slipped from my hands. All this time, I'd been looking at my life through a broken mirror, never knowing fragments were missing. Then, quite unexpectedly, the shards had been returned. The image left staring back at me was one I didn't recognize. I'd become my own stranger.

But none of that mattered because I was too overcome with grief. *Gram.* My wonderful, loving Gram, was gone. I'd lost two precious things: my identity and my heart. It was crippling.

Wetness sprang to my eyes, and for once, I didn't care. I dropped my head to my forearm and wept. It was horrible; Gram deserved so much more.

Then hope flared.

Maybe I could save her. For less than a nanosecond, my energy shifted. If I could beat her to the punch and stop her from walking towards her death, we could fight her illness together.

Then I realized there could be no "we." I couldn't stay.

That, and she certainly wouldn't have given me the opportunity to stop her. I'd only skipped out of work thirty minutes early—it wasn't nearly enough. My only hope was that she'd change her mind, but I doubted that. She didn't want to be saved. Her final letter was testament to her anguish— and relief. No more secrets; she was finally free.

And I was finally aware.

Now I understood why Gram never wanted me to visit. For years, I thought she was sparing my feelings—that she didn't want me to live with her, and keeping me at bay was the easiest solution.

How wrong I was.

My confession at the bus stop must've broken her. Guilt tingled tightly beneath my ribs. If only I'd known, perhaps things would've turned out differently.

Perhaps not.

Living with Mom was mental deprivation at its best—at its worst, full-on physical warfare. To try and squeak out a few more years under her roof would've been torture. Would I've stayed in Maine or run to Oregon regardless?

Sitting there with the letter laying limply on my lap, a cool hand rested on my shoulder. I jumped at the sudden touch and twisted in my seat. Behind me, with eyes shrouded in sadness, stood Fantasia. She had managed to walk in without my noticing, silent as a cat on padded paws. I wiped at my eyes and looked into her face. Her expression spoke volumes and confirmed my greatest fear. It was too late. My grandmother—my wonderful, loving grandmother—was gone. She'd willingly embraced death.

Words escaped me. So many questions ran through my mind it took a moment to grasp one. I stood up and faced her, and before I could ask, Fantasia read my thoughts. She hugged me and whispered "Polar." My grandfather had been the one to deliver the fateful blow; he was responsible for Gram's death. Despite knowing that was her last wish, I couldn't help the surge of hatred that exploded through my veins, setting my skin on fire.

She interlaced her slender fingers around my calloused ones and led me to the living room. We sat on the couch. She seemed to gather courage as her eyes searched mine.

"I'm so sorry," she began. "I never wanted this to happen, and if I'd known, I would've done my best to stop it." She looked at me with earnest. What she saw in my thoughts gave her incentive to continue.

"I didn't see what happened, but as soon as I heard, I came."

"What did you hear?" My voice wasn't my own. It was smaller, boy-ish. *Afraid.*

She deepened her grip, "Of all the bad luck, it was Thorn who found her." She inhaled sharply through her nose. "Apparently, she'd been calling out your grandfather's name. Thorn overheard and went to investigate. She was angry when she saw your grandmother. Thorn is possessive of her land and lashes out at anyone who trespasses. Even though your grandmother posed no physical threat, Thorn wasn't inclined to be merciful. It's not in her nature."

She paused, firmed her shoulders, and intently focused on our laced fingers in her lap. "Thorn used her powers to grow the blackberry briars to trap your grandmother. She didn't even have a chance to run, not that it would've made a difference. No one can outrun Thorn in the forest; she has too many weapons. Every living plant is at her disposal, and she knows just how to use them." Fantasia flexed her hand, crushing my fingers. "Thorn used the briars as shackles, trapping her where she stood."

This time, when Fantasia paused, her eyes darted with uncertainty. She was gauging my reaction, seeing if she was being too detailed. I urged her forward, both with my mind and words. "Please, don't stop. I need to hear it all."

Taking a deep breath, she continued. "She was very brave. When she found herself pinned, she refused to struggle. Calmly, she asked to see Polar." Fantasia's voice held a sense of awe. "No one ever asks anything of Thorn. Your grandma had a forceful spirit. Courageous." She stalled and cleared her throat. "Naturally, Thorn was outraged. She hates insubordinate behavior and was greatly offended that your grandmother asked a favor."

My cheeks flushed. Thorn was a cold, calculating bitch to pin a help-less, old woman down—with blackberry briars, no less. Phantom pains pierced my wrists as my imagination took hold, conjuring the hurt Gram must've felt.

"Thorn left your grandmother captive while she sought out another Velore. She located Splint and ordered him to bring Polar to her. She also demanded a Doppelgänger. She wanted a mental examination before she terminated her. Polar arrived first. When he came upon the scene, he was appalled. Thorn was beyond reason, her anger boiling as she waited for answers that should've never been kept from her. Polar pleaded with Thorn to have a moment alone with your grandmother. She agreed, but reluctantly. Then they exchanged a few hushed words before Polar kissed her."

Fantasia stopped talking and looked at me. I waited for her to continue, when it occurred to me that she'd finished her story. She was waiting to see if I understood the enormity of her words. It took a moment to register. The kiss. It was deadly. That's how she'd died, just as I would've died had I kissed his immortal wife only hours earlier.

Polar's kiss was equally deadly.

"Her blood froze in her veins," Fantasia continued. "I know that paints an awful picture, but I've been told it's actually a peaceful way to go. It was much better than the alternative. Thorn would have tortured her; she is without compassion. And…."

Fantasia hesitated.

"And?" I prompted.

"Well, had he waited for a Doppelgänger, there would've been much bigger issues to deal with. Thorn was enraged that he killed her before her mind could be read. The fact that she knew about Narivous—and we'd missed it—has caused some serious repercussions."

Fantasia's brow wrinkled in worry.

"What kind of repercussions?" Despite the shit-filled dumpster heaped on me, I found myself concerned for her well-being more so than my own.

"I'm not sure yet. I just know Mother was responsible for this area." Fantasia shook her head and pinched the bridge of her nose. "It was her job to make sure people were ignorant about Narivous. She clearly missed your grandmother."

"Does that happen often?"

"No, never!" Fantasia's voice lifted. "At least, not that I know of. Right Mother and Polar are being interrogated by Thorn. I'm not sure what's going to happen; I only know things are really bad right now. I could barely sneak away to see you. I might be making everything worse...." The last part came out in a shameful whisper.

"Will they be okay?" I asked and squeezed her hand.

She gave me a tight, sad smile.

"I hope so."

Fantasia—on edge—tore at my already-broken heart.

"Where is she now?" I asked, referring to Gram.

"She's still in Narivous. We can't let anyone know what happened to her, so they're preparing the body. They plan on returning her to her bed before the night is out. Once her blood has thawed, the authorities should rule it death by natural causes."

"What if I tell them differently?" My sorrow flipped to rage without missing a beat. For Gram's death to go unpunished would be unfair. *Wrong.* Even if she'd sought death, surely she deserved justice. And if no one else would seek it for her, I would.

Fantasia became uncomfortable. Quickly, she let go of my hands and pulled away. She lowered her gaze and twisted her fingers nervously in her lap. She knew I was serious; the benefits of mind reading left little doubt. I wanted this terrible cycle to end. Thorn would only grow stronger as she recruited more Velores. What would happen if she created an army? And what was she planning on using this army for? It was a troubling thought. If only people knew the truth....

But it was Fantasia's gaping mouth, and frightened parlor, that stopped my line of thinking. The horror I saw was real; it made my heart stop.

"You need to leave, Daniel. You remember earlier when I told you I could give you a couple of days? Well, that option is completely gone—*annihilated.* Time is up. You can't beat them. Do you think you're the first person to try?" she snorted in disdain. "If you stay here, they'll take you."

"I have nothing more to lose, so why shouldn't I stay and fight?"

"Oh, but you do! Don't you see? Just because your grandmother's gone doesn't mean there aren't others they can't destroy." She spoke her words vehemently. "Think of Sarah, Eric, Charlie, your Aunt Marie, and Lacey," she said, spouting the names in rapid succession. "Think of all your friends! Think of Tony! She has him; he's trapped in her realm. Anyone who has ever made a difference in your life is in jeopardy … think of me." The last part came out strained as she struggled to form the words. She was afraid. My close proximity put everyone in danger. I was a ticking time bomb with a defunct timer.

Her words, like bullets, made me heavier and weaker. Each name knocked me down a peg. She saw my thoughts and eagerly jumped on my train of thought. "If you stay, a fellow Doppelgänger could possibly discover my disloyalty by reading your mind. I've told you too much. This is your one chance, Daniel! Take it and run!"

"Would they really out you?"

Fantasia tipped her head. "Would they really out me?" she repeated.

"Yeah. I know they'd have to reveal how Gram knew about Narivous; that's pretty obvious. But no one has to know that you told me anything. I'm not going to expose you." I ran my tongue across my lips. "So would they rat you out? You know, after they read my mind?"

She averted her eyes. I'd found the weakness in her armor, the chink. They wouldn't betray her. When she looked back at me, she knew that no amount of lying would convince me otherwise. She tried a different strategy.

"No. I don't think they would. Not over what I've told you. They could tell by your thoughts that your knowledge is safe. They wouldn't expose me over that. But it's still a very big risk. If you ever changed your mind, if you ever told anyone, it would have to be reported." She raised her eyebrows in emphasis. "I would always be concerned that they would spill my secret. I would have to live in the shadows of their knowledge. That would be a horrible way to exist."

"Not over what you've told me?" I asked. It was the solitary slip-up from her spiel that revealed a deeper transgression, one that would have forfeited all loyalty.

She shook her head, ignoring me. "Never mind that. Staying isn't an option. Honestly, it wouldn't be beyond them to just kidnap you. They want you that badly. You'd never be safe here. You'll always be hunted."

So it appeared I had two choices: stay and become one of them, or leave and remain human. Otherwise, I'd risk the safety of everyone I cared about. If I tried to fight, it meant losing them all, and I'd already lost too much. I never had a father, my mother wasted away years ago, and my grandma—the one who loved me unconditionally—was gone.

I suppose there was a third choice, but rotting in the ground six feet under seemed more unfavorable than the other two options.

And secretly, I longed to join them. Not to become a monster as Fantasia described, but to be near her always. I hated Thorn, but privately wondered if I were capable of defying her and getting away with it.

Perhaps I could free Fantasia.

Now that Gram was gone, I didn't see much of a life ahead of me, especially not back in Maine or living out of boxcars as a teenage hobo. It was an ugly future, no matter how you looked at it.

But with Fantasia, maybe things would be okay.

She was one of them and wasn't bad. On the contrary, she was per-fection in every sense of the word. Now that I had no one, perhaps a life with her would be all I'd need. I've always felt lost. Perhaps a part of me—hidden deep in the recesses of my soul—knew I didn't belong. Maybe I'd been waiting for Fantasia all along.

Fantasia saw my thoughts and covered her mouth, but not before I spotted the happy twitch of her lips. She looked down and cleared her throat. Maybe it was wishful thinking, but I suspected she had feelings for me, too. I reached out and grabbed her hand. It was the touch of my skin that brought her back to the mission she'd come to achieve.

"Daniel, you need to leave now. Pack your bags and run to the airport before they get here."

"But I don't want to leave you." There. The words were out, and I wasn't taking them back.

"Don't worry about me. You need to keep your freedom, Daniel."

I shook my head. I hadn't realized it, but I was already forming excuses to stay. I'd made up my mind. She was worth turning into a monster. Fantasia went into damage control.

"No, Daniel! You know how I said earlier that I wouldn't be outed for my earlier revelations? That my offenses would be kept secret as long as you maintained your silence? Well, listen to this: Thorn is a tyrant. She is the most despicable person who walks this earth. She kills without mercy, and she tortures her victims." She paused, before adding, "I plan on taking her down."

And then she stopped. I tilted my head, confused as to why this last piece of information was significant. Fantasia cleared that up for me.

"I have now officially committed Narivous treason. Punishable by death. Even my fellow Doppelgängers won't keep this information from her, especially her pet, Romeo. If Romeo reads you—which, at this point, I guarantee he will—he'll tell her my treasonous words. He's too afraid of her. I know he won't like it. I know he'll feel immense guilt, but he's bound to her and won't be able to keep such a secret." My jaw dropped. She had tied my hands.

Just then, lights pulled into the drive. Was I too late? The thought made my heart race. Fantasia, too, held a dark look of fear. She went to the window and barely peeked out.

"It's Charlie," she said. "You need to pretend that I wasn't here; you need to pretend that you don't know anything."

She went to the dining room table and grabbed Gram's letter while I wiped away traces of tears.

Her probing eyes scanned my face. "I'm going to lay low." She pointed to the office. Just as she was in the doorway, she turned and said, in a desperate voice, "Please, Daniel. Don't let her death be for nothing. She tried to protect you."

{11}

REUNION

Her words threw me. Not only that, but now I was forced to put on an act.

Don't let her death be for nothing. She tried to protect you. I kept replaying her message. Something was wrong, but I couldn't put my finger on it. Anyhow, I didn't have long to dwell because, within moments, Uncle Charlie was busting through the house.

He was frantic; so much so, he didn't see me standing in the living room. He called out for Gram, going room to room, throwing doors open. A torpedo of pent-up anxiety. I hadn't turned on the lights, and the darkness allowed me a few extra seconds to compose my expression into one of innocence. I hoped that my face was dry and free from grief. I would need to put on the performance of a lifetime.

Charlie hit the light switch for the living room and jumped at my sudden appearance.

"Y-you're here," he stammered. He took a step back, creating a wider berth between us. "Why are you here?" he asked.

"Why wouldn't I be here?"

Charlie's eyes flitted to the door.

"I don't know," he replied as he ran his fingers through his hair. "I'm not thinking clearly." He shook his head and mumbled "Stupid" under his breath.

"We all have our off days," I said.

Charlie's head snapped up. He squared his jaw. "Where's Lillian?"

My mouth stretched into a rubbery smile. "I don't know. I was taking a nap on the couch, waiting for her to come home. I thought she was out to dinner with you."

His lips formed a small "o" as he nervously pulled at his sleeve. He shoved his weathered hands into his pockets.

"Not with me," he finally replied. So far, he seemed to believe me. That was a good sign.

"What's going on?" I asked with fake concern.

Charlie hesitated. He hadn't planned on my being here and struggled to come up with something to say.

Charlie no longer held a wholesome sheen—the truth had tarnished him. He'd expected me to be in the forest, a new member of the undead. My presence puzzled him. Charlie was a pro, however, and found his lies. "Nothing. I just had a message on my phone from her. I thought I'd come by and see if she needed anything." So he was putting on an act, too. Of course he would. He'd been doing it for years, and it probably came naturally to him. We were both dancing around the truth, pretending together.

This may work. Remember, you don't know she's gone. It was such a painful thought that a stabbing ache hit the pit of my stomach. *Keep it together, Daniel; this is for Fantasia.*

"Oh, well since she isn't with you, maybe she's out with Aunt Marie or Rosemary. It's Tuesday, and sometimes she goes to Bingo."

"Sure, sure," he quickly agreed, his brows turned in. "I'm sure that's all there is to it. But, if you don't mind, I'm going to check all the rooms. Leave no stone unturned." He gave a forced grin as his eyes went to the door behind me.

Crap. Gram's office, aka Fantasia's hiding spot. I couldn't risk her discovery—assuming, of course, that she hadn't already fled.

"Damn, Charlie. What's wrong with you? I've been here for over two hours." I rolled my eyes. "No one's in there."

My detachment swayed him. He swallowed hard and nodded.

The front door squeaked on its hinges. Eric stood outside the threshold. He paused when he saw me and then shuffled inside. Never had my cousin looked so small and miserable. His shoulders were hunched in as he attempted to fold into himself.

"I TOLD YOU TO STAY IN THE CAR!" Charlie barked.

Eric flinched and his eyes watered, but he held his ground.

"I know, Gramp. I thought maybe I could help."

"There is nothing to help with," Charlie said through gritted teeth. "Lillian isn't here. Daniel thinks she may be at *Bingo.*" He stressed the last word as a warning to Eric: keep your mouth shut.

Eric nodded, "Oh, good deal. Well, I'm glad everything's okay." So Eric was playing along, too. *Good.* I needed them to believe that I thought Eric's story was pure idiocy. Eric told Charlie about our earlier conversation—Gram's letter was clear about that—but since I was intact and human, they probably assumed I'd never found Narivous. I wasn't dead, after all.

I was relieved that my initial reaction to Eric's tale was disbelief and that I called him crazy. I'm sure Eric relayed that message to Charlie; I hoped he cited me verbatim. Right now, both Eric and Charlie had no idea how much I really knew. The situation was becoming more contained. I only had to keep up the charade.

But just when I thought I was starting to get things under control, we had another unexpected visitor—Dreams.

Candace. Her name was Candace. I'd have to call her that if I wanted to salvage my ignorance. I had only a glimmer of hope, but being that's all I had,

I held on to it tightly. Dreams could read minds. It would take only a single glance to know the danger Fantasia was in. Please, *please*, look my way.

Dreams—wild and frantic—was a whip of blonde hair and flashy movements. She stalled upon seeing us, but only for a moment. She met my eyes, hesitated, and then squelched my last remaining chance of salvation.

"FANTASIA!" she screamed. My hope plummeted. Dreams shoved me to the side and bolted into Gram's office. All the blood left my limbs, leaving behind cold, numb appendages. It was really over. I saw the shock on Charlie's face and the fear in Eric's. Eric looked worse than I felt—a task for sure.

"Mother's coming!" Dreams' voice drifted from the bedroom. We didn't have to strain to hear; she was loud and talking fast. "She'll be here any second!" Her panic surged through the air. Dreams tugged on Fantasia's arm as they stepped into the living room. Fantasia hugged herself and wouldn't meet my eyes; she stared shamefully at the floor. Dreams, however, caught the direction of my gaze. She pinched her face in annoyance before turning to Fantasia and leaning in close. Dreams' brushed her lips against Fantasia's ear and whispered hushed words. Fantasia softened a fractional amount.

The door was once again thrown open—with such force that the sheetrock fractured from the onslaught. The sight was paralyzing: Camille. Beautiful and perfect Camille, as lovely as her daughters, stood fuming in the threshold. It had to have been her; the likeness to Fantasia and Dreams was too strong. She was as tense as an alley cat ready to pounce. Yet, even her anger couldn't mask her grandness.

She had long, curly hair of gold. Her skin was smooth, porcelain-like, and held features that were striking and wonderfully proportioned. If Fantasia hadn't explained the Velore's aging process, I wouldn't have believed it was her. This woman was youthful, and as beautiful as any supermodel walking the runway—perhaps even more so.

Had it not been for her eyes, I would've marked her as perfect. But those glowing orbs cast a pall over her features.

The supernatural light reminded me of Frigid. I shuddered at the memory.

"DAMN YOU!" she screamed, but I wasn't sure at whom. "YOU'VE ALL MESSED UP UTTERLY AND COMPLETELY! I LEAVE FOR ONE WEEK, YOU HAVE ONE TASK, AND I COME HOME TO THIS GIGANTIC MESS!"

She stormed into the room and approached Dreams. In one swift motion, too quick to almost catch, she slammed her palm against Dreams' face. The loud *thwack* followed Dreams to the floor, where she fell in a crumpled heap. Dreams cupped her assaulted cheek and flushed with both embarrassment and pain.

Camille grabbed Fantasia by her shirt and pressed her face so close, their noses touched. Fantasia's eyes widened, mortified.

"Do you have any idea what you've done?" Camille asked ominously. It brought a chill down my spine. "We had one responsibility. JUST ONE! We were to bring the boy to Narivous." She pointed a finger at me, her face never leaving Fantasia. "Does he look like he's there?" she taunted. "Instead, we get the old one, and now they're watching us! They've put Romeo on this task. Can you think of why that might be bad?"

Fantasia started to tremble. Camille pushed her forcefully away, causing her to stumble.

"What do you mean, *old one*?" Charlie asked, but Camille ignored him. Instead, she looked around the room before settling her all-knowing gaze on me. Her face wilted as her anger slipped into horror. She saw Fantasia's treason in my thoughts, and it frightened her.

With giant, shining eyes, Camille looked back to Fantasia. She started to sway. Fantasia stepped up quickly and steadied her mother.

"What have you done?" Camille asked softly.

Fantasia bit her bottom lip as onyx tears shadowed her lavender irises. The creaminess of Camille's skin faded to ash as she searched Fantasia's face. "Why, Fantasia?" Camille whispered.

In the far back, near Gram's china hutch, Eric whimpered. Camille's sadness dissolved, turning to unbridled rage. Her eyes sparked. Color bloomed along her collarbone and spread to her cheeks. She whipped around and approached the pitiful creature hiding in the corner.

"Oh, is liwwle Eric scared?" she asked in a disdainful baby voice. "Well, that's too bad. DO YOU HAVE ANY IDEA WHAT YOU'VE DONE? Your inability to keep your mouth shut just signed your death warrant."

Charlie stepped up and cut her off. "Now you wait one minute!" he demanded, as he moved in-between her and Eric. "The boy made a mistake, and last time I checked, you *people* need us. I've covered for you countless times, and had I not, your little society would've been discovered a long time ago. The way I look at it, I think we should get a pardon for our one indiscretion."

"Oh, you think so?" she asked, her tone overflowing with sarcasm. "Well, that's not how this works." She smiled then, cold and evil. "We're in big trouble here, Charlie. Polar let Eric escape; he let him live. We gave him a second chance, thinking we could use him as a Protector. Well, now Romeo is on his way. He's coming to investigate this gigantic mess, and he's going to follow Thorn's orders to a tee. Your *grandson*"—she emphasized the word grandson—"has disclosed our secret, and he did it the first chance he got. How do you think that's going to go over?"

"It was a mistake!" Charlie reiterated.

"We can't have mistakes," Camille hissed. She bared her teeth like a rabid dog. "Mistakes could destroy us all." Her eyes flitted back to Fantasia, and she winced. "They will be our undoing," she said faintly.

Camille tucked her head, shielding her emotions from everyone in the room. She gripped the hair on both sides of her scalp and stared at the floor. Her knuckles flexed white amidst the golden curls.

She was wracking her brain; I was certain of it. I could almost see her burrowing deep, desperately seeking a solution to save Fantasia.

I willed her to find a way.

Camille's fingers relaxed, releasing the ringlets from her grasp. Her head snapped up. She turned to Dreams—still resting on the floor—and ordered eagerly, "Go get Torti. Do it now, and do it quickly." She then tossed her head in my direction, relaying an unspoken message for Dreams' knowledge alone.

Dreams sprang to her feet at the exact moment someone shouted from the doorway.

"Mother!"

Everyone jumped. A new member had joined our reunion. No one saw her approach; she'd materialized out of thin air, an apparition.

It could've only been one person by the fleeting smile that grazed Fantasia's lips and the grimace dampening Eric's. This was the third sister. Her brunette hair—the same texture and length as Camille's—was her defining glory. Unlike everyone in the room, Torture looked calm, almost triumphant, her exquisiteness on proud display.

Her short, brown dress stopped mid-thigh, revealing long, toned legs. She was barefoot and held her ivory, high-heeled shoes in one hand. She languidly placed them on her feet before taking a solitary step forward. Torti's authoritative presence filled the space.

She grinned smugly at Charlie and me, only to have her grin widen when she focused on Eric. Ever so elegantly, she sauntered into the room as though she owned it. Camille paused and narrowed her eyes at her eldest child. Something was up. We all knew it. And everyone collectively stilled, waiting to hear what that *something* was.

"Mother," she said once again as she walked over to Camille and placed her hand around her waist in an affectionate gesture. "Why are you so upset?"

Camille tilted her chin and looked at Torti. She was both cautious and intrigued.

"Why am I upset?" Camille asked, before pointedly looking at me and then at Fantasia. "I think it would be obvious."

Torti followed Camille's gaze, her eyes meeting mine as she gave me a wicked, confident smile before leaning in and whispering in her mother's ear. Camille's stance relaxed.

The same as when Dreams whispered to Fantasia.

Camille's expression still held fragments of worry—albeit considerably less. Torti continued without being prompted.

"I think this is a great success, don't you?" She asked the question, clearly not needing a response. "I think Dreams and Fantasia should be commended for their hard work."

Torti let go of Camille and began walking around the room. She gazed at everything as though it held mild interest. Her fingertips brushed the rim of a lamp, the edges of a doily. She stopped at the fireplace, plucking a photograph off the mantel. It was of Lacey.

I almost choked on my spit.

My hands knotted, and my breathing went shallow. I wanted to rip the photo from her hand. *Don't even think about it!* Torti looked me square on and smirked. She flashed the photo for Charlie and Eric.

"Such a pretty little thing," Torti said conversationally. "Hopefully, life will be kind to her." She raised her eyebrows in humor, mocking us. The threat was clear. She returned the picture, angling it for everyone to see, then continued to glide about. She stepped lightly until her eyes fixed on Eric. She halted.

"Honestly, Mother. You treat us like we're still children. I thought you'd be proud of our results." She turned with an exaggerated simper. Eric, still cowering near the hutch, could barely stand on his wobbly legs.

Torti approached him—cornered, more accurately—like a huntress with her prey.

"So, Eric. You did just as we expected, didn't you?" Torti asked the answerless question before turning brightly to Camille. "You see, Mother, if you had a little more faith in us, you would've known that we fully expected Eric to go running to Daniel. I knew it the moment I saw him. He's been spoiled and has never had to answer for his actions.

"Isn't that right, Eric?" Torti inquired.

Eric shot daggers of hatred at her. He clamped his lips and breathed heavily through his nose. He flexed his jaw, but didn't answer. Torti batted her lashes and gave him a haughty smirk. "I know it's embarrassing, Eric," Torti said. "But I imagine you've learned a very valuable lesson. Always obey your betters." Her eyes darkened as she turned and addressed Camille.

"Of course," Torti went on, "we didn't expect Eric to take Daniel's place on the double-date, but even mind readers can't predict a flat tire. That's a circumstance out of our control. But, all in all, I think it worked out in our favor."

She turned and faced Eric, giving him an artificial smile. "And Eric's going to be a good boy from now on, aren't you, Eric?" Eric melted at her jeering tone, collapsing to the ground. This delighted Torti. She squealed and was about to clap her hands when Camille stopped her with a pointed throat clearing. Torti regained focus.

I really wanted to defend Eric—to do something rather than stare—but I was frozen, absolutely mesmerized by the situation unfolding before my eyes. Torti pivoted and walked towards Dreams, who was still holding her cheek. Torti reached out her hand, and Dreams took it straightaway. "It'll be okay," Torti mouthed, before squeezing her fingers and letting go.

Dreams tentatively smiled. There was a lot of trust flowing off her. She believed in Torti.

Torti addressed the room. "We knew Eric would tell Daniel every-thing. We knew Daniel would think he was crazy. We knew he would come into the forest in search of answers. And it was awfully convenient that Fantasia was there, to find him, to help him." She looked to Fantasia and arched her perfectly sculpted eyebrow to hone in the point. Fantasia nod-ded. Torti had a plan, and Fantasia was ready to follow it.

Then it was my turn for her scrutiny. Torti turned her beautiful, green eyes on me and carefully, so no one else could see, winked. From her expression, I understood she was trying to relay a message, but I was unable to grasp what it was. She walked towards me and discreetly looked towards Fantasia and smiled. Fantasia, as well, was looking in my direc-tion, and her expression told me to focus. I understood in that moment; I knew then what they were trying to convey. Torti merely gave a half-nod. Having read my mind, she acknowledged that I'd reached the right conclu-sion. She was creating a false trail, one for Eric and Charlie to follow. It was a deception. Ironically, I knew what she was going to say before she said it.

She turned and continued, so as not to tip off Eric and Charlie.

"Simply, Mother, we knew that Daniel wouldn't come to us unless his heart was bound. You know the rules as much as I do. We prefer our recruitments to be willing, even if it's a choice they hate to make. Plus, our instructions were clear: being he's Polar's grandson, we needed to make sure he not only joined us, but that he was *eager* to join us. It was the least we could do to alleviate Polar's anxiety."

Eric looked up, surprised. He hadn't a clue I was related to the man who had spared his life. Charlie, on the other hand, didn't flinch. I won-dered how he knew. Had Gram told him? Perhaps Polar? Or was it my appearance that tipped him off?

Torti bit the inside of her cheek thoughtfully before moving on. "Dreams was sure she had Tony, but Daniel was a bit more of a challenge. Now don't get me wrong. Had his vehicle not gotten a flat and he had met us as initially planned, I think I could've seduced him to our side. I've been told that I can be very charming when I want to be." She tossed her hair and winked at me over her shoulder. "But, as they say, we were thrown a curveball. So after we let Eric leave, we worked on another game plan. We knew how useful Eric would be as a Protector; we also knew that we had to get Daniel emotionally invested. I was off the table, since we were certain Eric would paint me as a villain. So we had no choice but to use our pretty little Fantasia."

She turned to me with big, innocent eyes and said, "Not to say what she feels for you isn't real, Daniel. I had a feeling she'd fall for you, too. It's a happy benefit for us all!" She clapped her hands together in feigned happiness. "It's about time she found someone worth fighting for!"

She turned back to Camille. "But I suppose we should've filled you in on all this. I'm sorry, Mother. We thought it would be a happy surprise for you. But now I suspect we shoulder the bulk of the blame. It looks like Thorn has decided to reassign this task to Romeo. I'm hoping once he's here, we can explain this mess to him with little trouble."

"Torti, darling," Camille said as her eyes returned to their normal, non-glowing state. "This is delightful news. But I believe there are still some unanswered questions." She pointedly looked to Fantasia and me. I knew too much, and Romeo would surely see this when he arrived. Torti seemed to understand where her mother was leading. "But he now knows too much," Camille said, indicating Eric. And although her gesture took the attention from me, it was clear that I was the source of her concern.

"Oh, that!" Torti said cheerfully. "It's all well. We have so much to be grateful for. Now that we're all on the same page, we can move forward. I think Eric will make a wonderful Protector. Charlie has done such a great job over the years; it seems only natural that it's passed down to his grandson. A new start for a new generation. I'm sure Romeo will agree. Plus, isn't it wonderful having friends who will protect us."

Her gaze traveled to Charlie, who nodded enthusiastically, eager to keep Eric safe. Charlie darted a look towards Eric. Eric mumbled "Okay" and scratched his upper arm. Neither one of them were paying attention to the girls. Had Charlie kept his eyes on Torti, he would've seen her slip a packet into Camille's hand. Camille had only a split second to see what it was. Relief softened her features.

Camille gave her first authentic smile of the evening. "Well, this is wonderful!" Whatever Camille held, it fixed her attitude. She lost the razor edge. Now the textbook version of a loving mother, she went to Dreams and gave her a big hug. Dreams sniffled before latching onto her with surprising intensity.

"My darling children! Are they not the most brilliant girls?" With the package hidden within the cup of her palm, Camille placed her hands on each side of Dreams' face and kissed her forehead. "I'm so sorry I got upset. It was a big misunderstanding! Please say you forgive Mommy?"

Dreams beamed and nodded, eager to be back in her mother's good graces. Camille hugged her again and directed Dreams to sit on the couch. Looking fondly down on her daughter, she called for Fantasia.

"Fantasia, would you be a dear and help Dreams?" Her voice twinkled. Very charming—and very manipulative.

Fantasia sat down and held out her arms. Dreams went in and leaned on Fantasia. They embraced, and Fantasia cradled Dreams' head in the crook of her neck—much like a mother would a young child. Then, with her hand on Dreams' swollen cheek, Fantasia began to glow. It was utterly fascinating.

Before our eyes, the redness on Dreams' face dissipated. Fantasia's hand turned transparent as it lit up like the sun. Within seconds, Dreams' cheek was back to its regular, creamy perfection.

"Thank you," Dreams said as Fantasia released her hold and her hand lost its light.

"You're welcome," Fantasia replied as they turned into one another. Dreams rested her head on Fantasia's shoulder, and Fantasia pulled her knees onto Dreams' lap. Their familiarity spoke volumes. This was something they did often.

Everyone was in silence. Camille and Torti looked like nothing extraordinary had happened—and honestly, it probably wasn't extraordinary for them. But I was astounded. Charlie and Eric were slack-jawed, too. Fantasia could heal. *Mental note: ask about that later.*

Uncle Charlie was quickest to regain his footing. He still wasn't completely convinced by Torti's speech and of all the people here—well, the humans anyway—he'd know best whether to trust them, and the lines around his mouth said he didn't. Charlie used our respite to inquire about his most pressing concern.

"Where is Lillian?"

Camille adopted a sad air and walked over to Charlie. She gently placed her hand on his chest. "I'm sorry, Charlie. There was nothing I could do to save her."

Charlie crumpled; he went to one knee and buried his face in the cups of his hands. His body shook in waves as he sobbed. He repeated "no" over and over, as if the word could erase her death.

The grandfather clock's second hand made a full rotation before Charlie found the strength to stand up. "What happened?" he asked with a shaky breath.

Torti spoke up. "She was sick, Charlie. Terminally ill. She'd seen the doctor today, and the lab results showed she had stage-four lung cancer. She only wanted to see Paul one last time, and so she did just that. Please, rest assured, she did not suffer." I appreciated that she wasn't giving him the gruesome details, especially the part about the briars. Torti kept her tone kind. "It was the most humane death possible. We had your interests, as well as hers, in mind. Actually, had we known she was planning on doing this, we would've tried to stop her, but this damn lavender muddles us up."

Wait, what? The lavender? Gram loved lavender. What was this about lavender muddling them up? But before I could process this new sliver of information, there was a commotion outside.

Others had come to join us.

{ 12 }

THE PRETTY BOY AND
THE GENIUS

Everyone stopped talking at once as our eyes all turned to the door. Camille started to fidget. She twisted the item in her hand while looking back at me multiple times. Outside, two male voices spliced the air: one gave orders while the other complained. Torti walked over to the front door and shouted at them both.

"Hello, boys! So nice of you to show up." A muffled greeting drifted from outside. "We're all having a nice little chat in here ... we had some surprise visitors. Romeo, would you be a dear and check the perimeter?" Pieces of a response reached my ears. Torti shot her mom a quick look.

"I know, hun, I know," she replied. "Are you saying you don't trust me?" Torti paused as a faint, male voice drifted into the living room. "Then check the perimeter!" Torti shouted back. "I checked when I got here, but it's been a while. You can read minds, Chanticlaim cannot; that makes you the best candidate. Honestly, Romeo, it'll just take a moment." She smiled then. Apparently, Romeo gave her the response she was looking for. "Thank you, dear!" she shouted.

Fantasia shuffled over to me and under her breath whispered, "You can trust Chanticlaim," before drifting away. It happened so fast, I almost missed it.

Slight footsteps approached, and Torti stepped aside. In came a gangly fellow with disheveled, brown hair and intelligent, almond-shaped eyes. His olive-colored skin was flawless, and although more awkward than the girls, he, too, looked surreal and almost beautiful.

His presence wasn't threatening. He seemed honest and good. Charlie tilted his head to the side, unsure of who this man was. The newcomer appeared equally surprised by the number of people present. He hid his surprise by displaying a large, welcoming grin. Turning to Torti, he asked for introductions.

Torti quickly made a pass through the room, naming off Eric, Charlie, and I. When she landed on my name, his face lit up. He crossed the room in three assured strides and reached his hand out. I grabbed it, and we shook as though we were lifelong buddies.

"I'm Chanticlaim," he said. "It's a pleasure meeting you. Polar's grandson! What an honor!" His smile was genuine—almost infectious. Despite myself, I grinned.

"It's nice to meet you, too," I replied earnestly.

Chanticlaim turned to Eric and Charlie and greeted them with warmth as well. "Thank you so much for your service to us," he said and bowed his head in respect. "Truly, we are in your debt."

Uncle Charlie nearly smiled; he seemed to like this kid, despite his background. I tried to place where I'd heard the name Chanticlaim before. Then it struck me. This was the boy genius whom Fantasia had talked about.

"Ahem." Torti cleared her throat, commanding the attention of Chanticlaim. "I think Daniel is on board to join our family."

She was prompting him. "Oh, yes, yes," Chanticlaim agreed. "Sorry, ladies. I got distracted! Do you have the medication I gave you, Torti?"

Torti smiled, and Camille stepped forward. She opened her hand, and in her palm was the item Torti had slipped her. It was a small envelope, the size of a postage stamp. "Right here, Chanticlaim."

"Very well," Chanticlaim replied. He rubbed his hands together before grabbing the package. "Water, please," Chanticlaim instructed Torti, now all business.

He turned to me and asked, "Now, Daniel. I need to hear it from you. Unfortunately, I don't have the gift of reading minds. You'll have to grant me your permission aloud. Are you willing to join us in Narivous?"

This was happening too fast! He wanted an answer now, which should've been easy. The story Torti told—the shift in the situation—all of it would be meaningless if I didn't agree. Every person's life in this room would be affected by my decision, and worse off, many others who had no idea of the danger they were in. This was simply a prerequisite. Saying no was impossible.

Yet, I couldn't resist asking, "Isn't that question just a formality?"

Chanticlaim had the decency to look ashamed. He glanced away while his skin turned a smidgen pinker. It took only a second for him to pull it together and return his focused stare.

"Well, yes it is. But I still need to ask it. I guess if you wanted to get technical, we could propose your usage as a Protector, but at this stage in the game, you really don't have many options."

"I'm curious, Chanticlaim. What are my options?" Although I had nothing against this guy, I was irritated. Pained and horribly annoyed— with Gram's death still raw—I was past politeness. Perhaps it was because my control was already gone. Or maybe I was just an asshole.

"Well, um…." He bounced from foot to foot. "Well, you now know about us, and that's always crucial in our decision-making process. I guess you really have only three options: join us, become a Protector—if they would even allow that—or…." He paused, clearly troubled by the last option. I knew what it was and held up my hand to stop him from saying it. I didn't need to hear that death was the third.

"I'm sorry," I said truthfully. "I didn't mean to make you uncomfortable."

Chanticlaim nodded. "With all that you've been through, I can't say I blame you. It's always best to make an informed decision, especially when it's of this magnitude."

"Of course I'll join Narivous." I agreed, sparing him any more discomfort. This was truly my only option, since I didn't want to die and leave my family—or Fantasia—defenseless. Although Fantasia may not have needed my loyalty, or my protection, she still owned it.

"Well, then." Chanticlaim smiled. He removed the pills from the white slip and held them out for me. "Take these immediately." Torti stepped up and held out a glass of water.

Charlie's hard face revealed no emotion. I was collateral for keeping Eric safe, his sacrificial lamb. Eric's mouth moved, perhaps to protest, but fear stole his voice. He looked away, defeated. Fantasia cleared her throat, and I turned my gaze on her. She gave me a tight smile and nodded her encouragement. "Do it," she mouthed.

So much for wanting me to stay human.

Before I could contemplate the enormity of what I was doing, I took the small, blue pills and swallowed them in one swift motion. I didn't ask questions. I didn't want to know. It didn't matter. Keeping my family and loved ones secure was all that concerned me now.

Chanticlaim laughed and clapped his hands. Torti and Camille looked at each other and smiled. This is what they'd wanted.

And so it had begun.

I waited to feel different, for the pills to begin their transformation. Honestly, I was surprised that this was the first step. I knew my heart had to stop beating in order for the transformation to begin; maybe I'd swallowed some sort of poison.

Cyanide?

I looked inquiringly at Chanticlaim, and he started to laugh.

"Are you waiting to keel over?" he joked.

That was exactly what I was waiting for. He slapped my back in a friendly gesture. "You think I'd do that to you without warning you first? You must have me mixed-up with the girls. I could never be so cold!" He was so genial that I relaxed.

He smiled and looked at Torti. "Let's just say I'm a scientist first, and I'm always conducting experiments. You, my boy, are my newest test." He made it sound like an honor, but I was mortified. Chanticlaim read my expression and switched tactics.

"Don't worry; you won't feel different during this phase. I simply wanted to try something out. I promise," he held up one hand while placing the other over his chest, "that you won't experience anything unpleasant from the medication I gave you."

I wanted to ask how he was sure if I was his first subject, but decided against it.

"Now, why don't we all have a seat and relax? Looks like everyone's had a taxing day," Chanticlaim gave a pointed look to both Charlie and Eric, who looked worse for wear, before he went into the dining room to collect a couple of chairs. He set them up beside the recliner—where Camille sat as if on a throne—and motioned for Eric and Charlie to sit next to her.

Torti went and sat on the arm of the couch next to Fantasia. She reached out and grabbed Fantasia's spare hand. Her other was still holding on to Dreams.

I sat on the loveseat, and Chanticlaim plopped down next to me. Small, trim teeth flashed as Chanticlaim looked around the room fondly with a big grin. He ran his hand along the sofa's fabric and commented on how "Homey" the place felt.

He was kind of a neat soul.

As a whole, the room was crowded and miserable. We sat in silence, waiting for Romeo to arrive. Eric chewed his nails, Charlie picked at a hangnail, and I sat with my hands in my lap like a toddler in timeout. Gram's floral furniture was much too bright in contrast to the company we were keeping.

Chanticlaim attempted to lighten the mood. "So, um, I hear we might get a thunderstorm tomorrow."

It was so absurd—and downright out of place—I almost busted out laughing. Torti actually did.

"No, Chanticlaim. No," Torti said, in-between breaths. "We are not talking about the weather." She rolled her eyes, and the tension melted. Everyone seemed to loosen, until the door flung open. Static crackled above our heads with frenetic energy.

When Romeo walked in, I thought he more clearly resembled the male counterpart of Camille and her daughters. He was the vision I expected, and the opposite of goofy Chanticlaim. He was a pretty boy who carried himself with authority.

"Looks like you started the party without me," he remarked. His cocky grin focused on Eric, clearly the weakest of the group. He snickered and assessed the damage—via reading our thoughts. He paused at both Charlie and Eric before turning his eyes on me.

This freaked me out. Fantasia told me too much. He would see my thoughts and report her betrayal to Thorn. I searched for an image— something to mentally hold on to—to stop his mind from discovering my secrets. I concentrated hard, silently fabricating a mental barrier of thick fog with clouds so dense, they shielded every memory.

It must've been working because Romeo looked at me peculiarly. He tilted his head and took a step forward. He bent low so our gazes locked. Not once did I let the image of the thick clouds fade. He frowned and reached out to touch my head. Perhaps he hoped physical touch would transmit the images he was seeking. I stopped myself from pulling away as he tried to pry into my mind. His eyebrows drew in as his focus intensified. By the time he pulled away, he seemed absolutely mystified. He turned to Camille, then Torti, and lastly, Chanticlaim.

"I can't read his thoughts," he said, stunned. "This has never happened before. Why can't I read his thoughts?" he asked Chanticlaim.

"Can you see anything?" Chanticlaim inquired.

"No! I can't see a damn thing. Nothing! What the hell is going on?"

I exhaled heavily; I hadn't even realized I'd been holding my breath. Since he didn't mention gray fog, I figured it was okay to let the image drop.

Chanticlaim shrugged. "How should I know? I guess these things could happen naturally." Then his eyes lit up in mock surprise, like an unexpected thought occurred to him. He sniffed pointedly. "I bet it's the lavender."

"That's impossible. I can read their thoughts just fine." He pointed to Eric and Charlie.

"I don't know what to tell you. Maybe it's a combination of his bloodline and the lavender. We all know from personal experience that certain combinations have interesting results."

"They're related! They share the same blood!" Romeo angrily continued to point at Charlie and Eric.

"Tsk, tsk, not all the same blood! I think you need to pay more attention in my lessons," Chanticlaim replied coolly. "You should know better than that."

Romeo jabbed his finger towards Chanticlaim. He shook with rage. "Honestly, Chanticlaim, I think this whole lavender bit is a big ruse. Smoke and mirrors! What am I going to tell Thorn?"

Torti stood up and walked over to Romeo. She placed her hand on his chest and slowly circled him, all the while pressing the length of her body against his. When she was directly behind him, she leaned against his back and spoke softly in his ear.

"Are you saying we're lying about the lavender, my dear Romeo?" Romeo wavered under Torti's soft and sultry intensity. He placed his hand over hers.

"I think there's more to it," he retorted. Torti smiled.

"Romeo, oh, Romeo. Why would we make that up?"

He let out a deep sigh and looked guiltily towards the floor. Ever so discreetly, away from the eyes of Charlie and Eric, Torti shot Chanticlaim a conspiratorial wink.

"Wait a second!" Romeo pulled away and looked directly at Charlie. Charlie's thoughts gave him a new lead. It took only a second for him to grasp the information. He looked between Chanticlaim and myself. "You gave him something." Romeo's finger jutted in my direction. "What was it?" he demanded as he pushed Torti away and took a threatening step towards Chanticlaim.

It didn't seem to affect Chanticlaim in the least. He pretended to brush a piece of lint off his trousers before replying.

"I'm a scientist, Romeo. I have the right to test out products as I see fit. He's perfect. I can try something out while he's still human, and if it goes haywire, we just turn him all the quicker."

"Did you get the okay from Thorn?"

Chanticlaim shifted in his seat. "Well, she didn't tell me *not* to do it. And besides, we're all experiments in the game of Narivous. If we didn't take any risks, none of us would be here. I had a new solution to try, and

Daniel was kind enough to oblige. May I remind you that you, too, are an experiment of my own making. I think you owe me a little more credit." His tone turned accusatory.

"What was it supposed to do?"

"It's a pill to help with the transformation process, make it less painful. I thought it would be a nice courtesy to bestow upon him, considering he's the grandson of one of our leaders."

"Oh." Romeo slackened. "I suppose you have a point. Do you think that's maybe why I can't read his mind?"

I think that's exactly the reason why as all the pieces came together—Camille's relief when Torti slipped her the pills, and her anxiety when Romeo and Chanticlaim showed up before I'd taken them. Torti's delaying of Romeo, having him check a perimeter that I doubted needed to be checked. It all fit. Whatever I'd swallowed, it blocked Romeo from reading my thoughts. Chanticlaim had earned my gratitude.

"Very possible, but I think the lavender could have something to do with it, too." Chanticlaim kept throwing the lavender excuse out—perhaps to ingrain that thought into Romeo's mind.

"Oh, man," Romeo fretted. "What am I going to say? I have to answer to Thorn, and she's not going to be happy that I can't read his mind. She was so upset earlier. I don't want to be the bearer of bad news, especially after the old lady fiasco...." He looked up fast and stared at Charlie. He'd remembered the reason why he'd been prompted to come here.

"What about the grandmother?" Romeo asked.

"What about the grandmother?" Chanticlaim replied.

"Thorn's angry! She slipped through the cracks. She knew about Narivous!"

"How is that our issue?" Chanticlaim turned it around. "We can't be held responsible for Polar's actions. If he thought it was appropriate for her to know, that's his prerogative—not ours."

"But it was missed!"

Chanticlaim rolled his eyes. "Smell the air, Romeo! Do you think they missed that intentionally? It's the lavender. It's not their fault."

Romeo mumbled, "I think you guys are messing with me."

As if on cue, Torti returned to him and grabbed his face between her hands. She kissed him lightly on the lips. Chanticlaim winced next to me and pulled his gaze away. It seemed more than one man was infatuated with her.

"Why would we make this up?" she asked serenely. "Why, Romeo?"

Romeo struggled for words, and finding none, looked towards the floor.

Torti used her finger to lift his chin so their eyes would meet. Looking him straight on, she asked again, "Why, Romeo?"

"I don't know. Something seems off."

He struggled with his thoughts, fidgeting nervously under Torti's stare. He might've been Thorn's pet, but he was Torti's baby first. She led, he followed.

"I know this all seems very confusing," she soothed. "And that's partly our fault," she said, gesturing in the direction of Fantasia and Dreams. "Had I told Mother what we were up to, she would've been able to explain to Thorn, and you would've never been brought into this whole mess. But as you can see, everything is as it should be. You have nothing to worry about. Daniel will be joining us, and Eric will become a new Protector. He'll help Charlie until Charlie is unable to, and then he'll replace him."

Romeo stood to attention. "No, Eric's to come to Narivous. He's to be eliminated. I have orders to follow."

Charlie stood up in a fury. Eric gasped and almost collapsed from the chair. Camille had the peace of mind to grab him before he fell.

"OVER MY DEAD BODY!" Charlie bellowed. He went straight to Romeo and stabbed his finger into his chest. "No one touches the boy." Romeo didn't flinch as his cocky grin returned.

"Well, we can arrange that."

"Arrange what?" Charlie asked.

"Your dead body." Romeo smiled. Eric started sobbing, and Charlie cringed. An onslaught of pain hit, like I'd been sucker-punched. I mustered the strength to speak up.

"Wait a minute!" I shouted. "I thought if I came along, he'd be safe. Why would he be killed?"

Romeo bared his teeth into a menacing snarl. "Thorn gave me crystal-clear instructions," he hissed. "She said that if he'd told anyone—*any-one*—he would need to be brought back to Narivous and eliminated. He told you." He pointed an accusatory finger at me. I shriveled into the couch. "That's a violation; I don't care if it was planned. I will not risk disobeying Thorn to cover for that petty, weak, mortal boy!"

I looked to Torti for help. She stood with her head bowed, fingers pinching the bridge of her nose, concentrating.

"I was under the impression he'd be safe," I repeated once more.

"Who told you that?" he asked.

"I did," Torti stated, and pulled her head high, standing with ramrod posture. Her eyes zeroed in on Romeo. *Please have a plan….*

Once again, Torti used her presence to manipulate Romeo. She angled her body so he could drink her in. Subtly, she dipped her shoulders and pushed out her chest, giving him an eyeful. Romeo licked his lips as his gaze raked over her. Torti walked to him. His eyes glowed with desire as she breathed into his ear, "I'm sure once we've explained everything to Thorn, she'll be okay with having a new Protector. If I remember correctly, wasn't she just talking about trying to locate more outsiders to help us with our growing population?"

Romeo nodded. Torti placed her hands on his shoulders and flexed her fingers, massaging him with her touch and her words.

"Sooo … wouldn't this be the perfect opportunity to impress her, show her you were paying attention?" she said with a smile. Torti ran her nose along the flesh of his cheek. Romeo, the fool that he was, grew weaker with every word.

Chanticlaim did, too. His face dimmed watching Torti's performance.

"You can see for yourself that Eric will never slip up again." Torti's voice was hypnotic. "He made a one-time mistake, and we should be thankful that he did; otherwise, Daniel may not have been so willing to join us. It worked wonderfully well. Now you can convince Thorn he would be the perfect Protector. If anyone can talk her into it, it would be you."

Her flattery was working. Romeo began to nod.

"But Thorn was adamant," he said.

"She was angry when she made those orders. She didn't know the full extent of what we were dealing with. I'm sure the other Six were not even consulted. We were trying to be helpful by keeping her out of the loop. That was a rather large mistake, but it can easily be remedied."

Romeo nodded more aggressively; he liked where Torti was taking this.

"And lastly, we need to remember who Eric is and how Charlie has been working for us for years. We can't let one hasty decision—based on inadequate information—tear apart everything we've so carefully put together. We at least owe her a proper explanation before any decisions are made."

And haul in the nets, fellow fishermen. The guppy was hooked!

It was plain as day that Romeo was completely onboard. Charlie and Eric saw it, too. Each exhaled a deep breath as Romeo relented. Charlie squeezed Eric's shoulder and gave it an encouraging shake.

So far, everyone was safe, with the exception of me. My life was at play in a dangerous game with the highest stakes.

A sweat broke out along my brow, and my head started to spin. Seconds later, a gentle hand clasped on my own. I didn't see her approach. And despite her inability to read my mind, Fantasia knew how to comfort me. As our eyes made contact, my anxiety slipped away.

⊰{ 13 }⊱

GOODBYE

"So now what?" I asked. I held tightly to Fantasia's hand, my only comfort in my newly destroyed world.

"We take you to Narivous," Romeo said.

My pulse raced. I thought I had more time. Fantasia squeezed gently and whispered in my ear, "Patience."

"Do you think that's the best idea, Romeo?" Camille asked.

"Why wouldn't it be?" Romeo replied.

Camille smiled, showing perfect teeth. "Honestly, Romeo, why do you think? We will be returning Lillian to her bed before day breaks. I think it would raise red flags if Daniel disappears on the same day Lillian passes. Why, I think we should tread lightly. If I've learned anything over the years, it's that one can never be too careful."

"I didn't think of that," Romeo stated as his brows pulled in. He may have had good looks, but he was outmatched by the cunning minds in the room. He never stood a chance.

"So, when?" he asked.

"I think we should give it a week. Let him put his affairs in order. Let the poor sap recover." Camille swept her hand in Eric's direction. "He'll keep his mouth shut, and we can arrange the details after we've talked to Thorn and received her approval. I think it's best we keep her fully-informed from now on."

They all nodded, including Romeo.

Chanticlaim stood up and clapped his hands in finality. "All right then! I suppose it's time for us to bid you all farewell. We will be in touch." He looked to Charlie and Eric. "I'm sure we now have your full cooperation. Please stay local so we can relay our orders once they've been received."

"Yes, sir," Charlie responded respectfully.

Everyone prepared to leave. Charlie and Eric were the first to exit, darting out the door as soon as it swung on its hinges. The others followed behind. Fantasia and I were last. Before we stepped outside, I tugged on her hand. Fantasia reached out and grabbed Camille's blouse, stopping her from crossing the threshold.

"Please, Mother. May I stay with Daniel?"

Camille shook her head. "You'll come home with us; we have a lot of explaining to do."

Fantasia felt my alarm as my grip deepened. I didn't want to be anywhere near this place when they brought Gram home. I'd go crazy knowing they were moving her inside, staging a scene that wouldn't arouse suspicion.

Camille sensed my concerns, turned to Fantasia, and continued, "If, and only if, we get the okay, you can return after we've had our discussion with the Rulers."

"It'll be okay," Fantasia said. "I'm sure they'll let me come back. Please, just stay put. I'll come to you as soon as I can."

I nodded. I would wait for her. She gave me a warm hug as Chanticlaim bounded up the steps.

"I nearly forgot," he said and held out his hand. In his palm was a small, pink pill. "I figured you might have a hard time sleeping. This is a very strong sedative; it will take effect almost immediately. Make sure you're near your bed when you take it. You'll sleep the hardest you've ever slept in your life. It's the least I could do." He gave me a tentative smile. "We'll be in touch. Just go about business as you usually would … well … with the exception of your grandma. I'm honestly very sorry for that." His sincerity touched me.

And with that, everyone disbanded. Charlie pulled his truck out with a little too much zeal. Gravel caught in his tire's tread and splayed Gram's lawn. His taillights were ominous orbs as they receded into the night.

I stood on the porch while the others congregated near the oak grove. There were no other cars, and apparently they weren't needed. After a few words, Romeo took off with a blast. He was fast and quickly faded away. Chanticlaim followed his lead, as did Camille, Torti, and Dreams. Fantasia stalled for a second. Her eyes glittered in the moonlight as she raised her hand in farewell.

I did the same.

"I'll be back," she shouted before disappearing into the dark abyss.

I opened my palm to stare at the small, rose-colored pill. This was my only chance for peace. I went downstairs, poured a glass of water, and sat on my bed.

"Please work," I whispered to myself, and downed the pill. Within moments, I drifted into complete oblivion.

The morning light was bright and disorientating. It was also atrociously out of place, and it took me a moment to register where I was—safe in my bed. It took even longer to recall the events of the previous night. For a moment, I wondered if it had all been a dream.

Then reality hit. The tip-off was the warm presence in my bed. Her energy made my skin tingle. I turned to a sleeping Fantasia curled next to me.

Never in all my life did I think I'd wake up to such a gorgeous woman. If it weren't for the circumstances, I would've thought myself lucky. As impossible as it seemed, Fantasia was even more beautiful in her sleep. She looked damn near angelic.

I couldn't help watching her, even if it did make me a creeper. She stirred, opened her eyes, and hesitantly smiled.

"Moorninng," she said while stifling a yawn. She stretched her arms over her head, pulling her body tight. My eyes lingered appreciatively. She caught my gaze and blushed.

"Morning," I said gruffly. "Thanks for coming back."

"I'm glad I was able to."

"Me, too."

"I, um, arrived with the others," Fantasia said, placing a shroud on my glimmer of happiness. I shouldn't have been thinking of Fantasia when Gram was upstairs. Shame oozed over me; it leaked from my pores.

"Oh, so is she…." My words fell away. I didn't want to finish that sentence. *Gram. Upstairs. Dead.*

"Yeah," she answered.

I focused on her. "Looks like you're back to reading my mind again."

She shook her head. "No, it was just an easy guess." Fantasia fell back against the pillow. "I don't know what I can do to help."

"Your being here helps plenty," I replied honestly.

"Well, don't get used to it. I have to check in. Speaking of…." Fantasia glanced over my shoulder at the clock. It was almost 11. I'd slept hard and long indeed. "I should get going. As it is, I may have waited too long."

Fantasia sprang from the bed and ran her fingers through her hair. She reached for her sneakers and started to slip them on before my brain could compute.

"Wait! You're leaving?" *What kind of shit was this?* "You can't leave. Not now."

Fantasia stopped mid-tie. "I'm sorry, Daniel. They're keeping close tabs on everyone, especially me and my sisters. There's nothing I can do about it." She finished lacing her shoes and faced me.

"When will I see you again?"

"This afternoon. I won't leave you for long."

"Promise you'll come back?"

"Promise." Fantasia stepped forward and placed both hands on the side of my face. She kissed my forehead—halting my heart mid-beat. Then she walked out the door.

It took every ounce of strength to make the grueling walk upstairs. When I reached the foyer, I scanned the space, looking for inconsistencies. Nothing was out of place. They had covered their tracks well.

The living room was clean and polished—pristine—just how Gram liked it. I peeked into the kitchen. Her sheer, pastel curtains and the yellow kitchen cabinets made my chest ache. Lavender hung in the air. It permeated every single surface in her home. Not only did it perfume the hallways, but it seeped into the dimpled plaster of the walls. The smell reminded me of Gram and of the dark conversation we had the night before.

I stopped outside her door and steeled myself for what was coming next.

Gram's lifeless body.

I almost lost it. I kneeled low and took in a lungful of air. The coward in me wanted to call the police and have them pick her up, sight unseen.

The other part knew I'd never forgive myself if I didn't say goodbye. It would be a regret that I'd never live down.

I stood up and reached for the knob. I started to count.

One … Two … THREE!

With a hard grip, I twisted the handle and flung the door open.

It was what I'd expected, but that still didn't make the discovery less painful. Tucked in bed, dressed in a long-sleeve nightgown with her comforter pulled to her chest, she looked like she could've been asleep. Her hair had been combed back, the same as every other night. Except, it wasn't the same. She wasn't the one who did it. It was a methodical detail to a well-staged scene.

Gram's eyelids—the color of a day-old bruise—were the first indicator that something was wrong. The second indicator: her skin had lost its luster. It no longer had the glow of the living. That was the moment her death became real.

As the old saying goes: seeing is believing.

My throat constricted, and tears stung my eyes. I pressed a fist to my mouth and bit down hard. Teeth cut into my knuckles. Then, with one foot in front of the other, I approached her bedside.

I brushed my hand along the top of the bedspread and looked down on her.

Never again would Gram look at me with love. She would never smile, laugh, cry, or feel. We would never talk again. Her soul was gone.

I zeroed in on her face and detected a small smile resting on her lips. That gave me hope. Perhaps her death wasn't as traumatic for her as it was for me. Impulsively, I reached for her hand and cupped it within my own. Her skin was cold.

It dropped me to my knees.

I buried my face into the mattress and wailed like a freakin' baby.

"I'm sorry, Gram," I said between choked sobs. "I'm so sorry." I gripped tighter as I struggled to breathe. It took seconds—and large gasps of air—but I calmed enough to continue.

This was it.

My last opportunity to be alone with her. I needed the right words to convey what she meant to me. Gram's farewell letter came to mind. "You've nothing to be sorry for. You did what you thought was best. No matter what happens, I'll never blame you." My breathing shallowed. "All my life, you've been my greatest ally, the one person who loved me for who I was. If it weren't for you, I probably would've killed myself."

I'd never spoken those words aloud. Superstition kept them trapped within me. I had a stupid belief that once you put words out into the universe, they held more power. Still, Gram knew the truth. That's why she championed for me. I contemplated suicide countless times, back in the empty days when I was on a merry-go-round of pain and self-loathing. I believed that if my own parents didn't love me, then I must've been unloveable.

Gram showed me differently. She opened my eyes to the truth. It wasn't my fault that my parents chose the wrong path and destroyed their emotional receptors. It was theirs.

I stood up and folded her hands over her stomach. With light fingers, I touched her silver hair. This farewell was going to count. "I promise you, you'll never be forgotten. I'll do my best to make you proud. And so help me, I'll never forget what *she* did to you." The thought of Thorn dried up my tears. "She won't get away with this. I promise."

A surge of anger hit.

This was not the life Gram wanted for me, but now that I didn't have a choice, I figured it was best to make good use of it. Revenge seemed like a decent enough plan. I wouldn't be reckless; I'd take my time.

"I'll be careful," I vowed. I pushed the comforter around her stiff frame and kissed her forehead. Pivoting on my heel, I made it halfway out the door when a thought occurred to me. Two strides and I was back at her bedside. I pushed the sleeves of her nightgown up, exposing her wrists. There, thin circumference scratches marred her skin. No puncture wounds, no holes. It was as if the briar assault never happened. The faint marks could've been caused by anything and most certainly wouldn't raise alarm. They covered their tracks well, indeed.

With a heavy sigh, I pulled the sleeves back down and went to dial 911.

I sat on the bottom step of Gram's front porch and stared at the road. Within a matter of minutes, the gravel crunched under light footsteps.

"I lied," Fantasia admitted. She sat down next to me. "I couldn't leave you alone. At least not right now. Hopefully, you're not mad."

I wiped the water from my eyes and gave her my best impression of a smile.

"Why would that make me mad? I'm glad you stayed." I grabbed her hand. "That was one of the toughest things I've had to do."

She nodded and looked towards the road. There was no car parked in the driveway, same as last night.

"How did you get here? I don't see a car."

"We have to park far away, in case of complications. It helps us disappear much easier."

"How far is 'far away'?"

She gave me a half-grin. "A couple of miles, I can get to the car in no time. We run fast."

"Can all of you run fast?"

She nodded. "Some of us are faster than others—like the Animals for example—but we're all pretty speedy."

I nodded. Fantasia squeezed my hand as the wind picked up and rustled her hair. I captured the smell of Gram's lavender mixed with the scent of cinnamon: Fantasia's scent. The breeze was cold, and it made my nose run even more. She handed me a tissue that she pulled from her pocket.

"So the lavender 'muddles you up.'" I quoted Torti's speech from last night.

Fantasia looked away. "Yeah, it's this weird quirk my family's suffered. It makes our vision blurry. Mom thinks she was allergic to it before she became a Velore. She said we inherited her allergy."

"Your mom was able to read my mind last night, and Eric's, too." Camille's horrified face flashed behind my eyes. She definitely saw my thoughts.

She shrugged, "I wouldn't know. No one knows how badly it affects her sight. But I do know she wouldn't make something like that up. She always said it made her vision blurry, that it created holes." Her words came out clipped, defensive.

"You didn't have any problems earlier when you first came here," I reminded her.

She shifted uncomfortably.

"Well, when I say, 'we,' I really mean my sisters and mom. I've always been the anomaly of our family. Things don't affect me the way they do them. Actually, things don't affect me the way they do anyone in Narivous."

"What do you mean? Like what?"

Rather than answer, Fantasia shook her head. "It's complicated."

"Is it because you can heal?"

"A little—but it's more complex than that. I don't really want to talk about it." She squirmed, and I decided to let it drop. I had more pressing questions. That, and I knew time was the best form of corrosion to destroy mental guards. I'd find out soon enough.

"So lavender blocks their abilities. Do you think Gram knew that?"

"I think it was a coincidence. She probably just loved the plant, enjoyed the scent." Fantasia reached down to pluck a white crocus from the ground.

"A coincidence?" I asked dryly.

"Well, I guess it's a real possibility. She does seem to have an excessive amount of it." Fantasia looked to the lavender bushes in the planters, flanking both sides of the front door.

I nodded. "She knew," I said. When Gram visited us in Maine, never once did I smell it, except for lingering traces. Here, on the other hand, she doused herself with lavender perfume. I don't remember a single instance where she went outside without it. She also stashed lavender satchels in my backpack. I didn't want to hurt Gram's feelings, but smelling like a bouquet wasn't on my to-do list, so I chucked the packets. She replaced them on a regular basis, never one to be easily deterred. Then she progressed to lavender body wash (which I also replaced), followed by lavender laundry detergent, and then on to essential oils. That's when I gave up.

"Hmmm," she mumbled.

"You said something yesterday that bothered me."

"What was that?"

"You said don't let my grandmother's death be for nothing, that she was trying to protect me." Fantasia swallowed hard and began twirling the crocus in her hand. "But according to Gram's letter, she went to Narivous to see Polar one last time. She wanted to die in his arms. It said nothing about going there to plead for my life." I paused, gauging her reaction. She started to pull the petals off the crocus. Her long hair shielded her face. "You also said that Polar killed Gram before a mind reader—a Doppelgänger—could be found. So how could you possibly know that her death was an attempt to save me, and not to fulfill her last wish of seeing my grandfather?"

Fantasia sat there, playing with the flower, dissecting it with intense concentration. She didn't reply. I placed my hand over hers, crushing the remaining pieces of the crocus.

"Please," I begged. "Talk to me."

Her eyes briefly met mine before looking away. "I just assumed," she replied.

It was a lie. I was sure of it.

"That's a pretty big assumption," I replied. "This assumption had to come from somewhere. Fantasia, tell me, what are you hiding?"

This time when she looked up, her eyes shone with black tears—and they were starting to glow. She was slipping into her translucent phase.

"Please, don't ask me such questions," she whispered painfully.

I was hurting her, and that bothered me. I was getting ready to apologize when Fantasia stood up. Her eyes focused on the road beyond the trees. The police cruiser was approaching.

"I have to go. I can't be here when they do their inspection."

"I'm sorry, Fantasia."

She shook her head. "Don't be." She pointed to the wooded area behind the house. "I'll be hiding out there. I won't leave. I'll come out as soon as they're gone."

And with that, she took off, disappearing within seconds.

I turned as the police pulled in.

{14}

HIDDEN LIES

I sat in the living room while the police officer went about his business. He asked some basic questions: her age, health, when I found her; nothing out of the ordinary. He also asked my age. I lied and told him I was eighteen, which he accepted at face value. We had to wait for the paramedics so they could officially pronounce her death and remove the body. Meanwhile, the officer tried to make small talk.

"We have volunteers," he began, "who come out and give support in situations like this. If you'd like, I can have someone sit with you." The officer wore a nameplate engraved with A.J. Dickson on the breast-pocket of his navy uniform. It had the sheen of a well-polished broach and screamed rookie. He couldn't have been a day over thirty.

I stuffed my hands into my pockets and shook my head.

"I'm okay," I lied. Nothing could've been further from the truth, but the thought of sitting with a stranger for "support" was beyond mortifying.

"Well, if you change your mind…." Officer Dickson trailed off.

"Yeah, sure," I agreed. "I'll hit you up if I need help." *Fat chance*. I gave a halfhearted smile and sat on the couch.

A message came through on Officer Dickson's radio, and he excused himself with the tip of his head.

The moment the door latched behind him, I dropped the charade and slouched with relief. One thing was clear; I was no damn thespian. It was weary work, pretending all the time. Exhausted, my eyes circled the room and landed on Gram's grandfather clock nestled in the corner. It was an ostentatious thing, with carved cherubs in rich mahogany and a brassy pendulum that swayed with each passing second. The audible ticks broke the silence as my thoughts landed on Fantasia.

She was probably going to be all I thought about for the rest of my life which, in the human-sense, was less than a week, and in the immortal-sense, indefinitely.

So it was there, on the soft, floral-print couch surrounded by doilies and antique lamps, that my mind gravitated towards the secret Fantasia was desperate to hide. I replayed the conversation—and events—from the night before, certain the answer was hidden somewhere amongst all the BS swarming around.

Then it hit me.

Fantasia said that Velores can only read human's thoughts, that they can't read each other's. She said if one could, Thorn would have them executed—too dangerous to the group. A *threat.* Fantasia was an "anomaly" and could do things other Velores could not. She knew why Gram had gone to Narivous because she read Polar's thoughts.

Fantasia could read minds of both humans and Velores. It was the only thing that made sense!

A fleeting moment of triumph lifted my spirits, only to come crashing down in an equally grand fashion. A grim thought hit home. Could I have jeopardized her safety by stumbling onto the truth?

What would happen when the pills Chanticlaim gave me wore off? What if they already had? If Romeo saw the truth in my mind, he would relay the message to Thorn. Fantasia now had two deadly charges against her. One, she committed Narivous treason, and two, she was born with a talent no one was allowed to possess. Fantasia was a double-threat.

Both offenses I held in my vulnerable head—any Doppelgänger could discover them before my transformation. Fantasia would be executed, and it'd be my fault.

What the hell was wrong with me? I buckled over and gripped the sides of my stomach. My gut may have been sitting on empty, but that didn't stop the remnants from bubbling up. It tingled the back of my throat, and I swallowed hard to keep it down. I rocked back and forth, sucking in deep breaths of air.

I wasn't sure how long I stayed like that, groaning, rocking, with arms wrapped tight. It wasn't until someone fake-coughed that my head snapped to attention. Officer Dickson stood in the doorway with a pair of men in trim uniforms. A stretcher's metal frame with blue tie-downs was tucked behind them.

"So we're going to pop back there and make the official diagnosis," the officer said. "Is there anything I can bring you? Would you like some water?"

I forced a grin and shook my head.

"Well, then," the officer started. "This will only take a minute."

They trooped into Gram's bedroom. One of the paramedics—a beefy beast of a dude with slate hair—gave me a kind smile as he passed. A few random words wafted into the living room as they confirmed the obvious. When they reemerged, everyone's face was folded in sympathy.

Officer Dickens spoke. "I think we have everything we need. We just need your confirmation that this indeed is ..." he looked down on his clipboard, "Lillian Mae Thatcher."

I nodded, "Yes, sir."

"Thank you, son. Who should we contact to make the arrangements? Are there any family members who should be notified?"

I gave him Uncle Charlie's information, as well as Aunt Marie's. The officer made a few calls from the front porch. His voice drifted, and I heard his end of the conversation with Charlie. He attempted discretion as he described my mental state, and after a pause, gratitude molded his voice.

"That's good," he said. "I think the kid's taking it pretty hard." Another pause, before, "Agreed. I wouldn't feel right leaving him alone. I'm glad you're nearby."

Charlie must've given him the response he was hoping for. The call pretty much ended after that.

Officer Dickson stepped inside and notified me that Charlie would be out shortly to help with this "unfortunate event."

I was certain Charlie had no intentions of coming here. After the fiasco last night, I doubted he wanted to come near this place. He lied to make the process smoother.

And with that, they took Gram away.

After everyone left, I stood outside facing the wooded area behind Gram's house. I didn't shout Fantasia's name; it wasn't necessary. She emerged as graceful as ever, and I finally allowed myself to breathe.

She came running at me, so quick, I was certain she was going to barrel over me and knock me to the ground. Instead, she leapt into my arms. I held on to her for dear life as she threw her arms around my neck and buried her face in the crook of my shoulder. I stroked her hair, petting her.

Never breaking physical contact, she leaned her head back to gaze into my eyes. Fleeting indecisiveness shadowed her features before she leaned in and pressed her lips to mine.

FINALLY.

I kissed her back, crushing my lips against hers. She responded with equal fervor. My hand gripped the back of her head, pulling her closer. We melted into one another, locked by passion and pain. By the time we pulled away, we were both short of breath.

I smiled so hard my cheeks almost broke. Fantasia grinned, too.

For the record, I've never believed in love at first sight, and if someone asked me days earlier if it were possible, I would've laughed in their face. It was an irrational concept, one that I would've touted as total bull. But that was before Fantasia. Maybe it was a Velore thing; perhaps she'd put me under a spell. It didn't matter. All I knew was that what I felt for Sarah was merely a flicker of light. A small flame. Now that Fantasia had entered my world, I'd been blinded. She was the Sun I'd forever orbit. I was hers. But with that thought came the urgency of another: my revelation. I needed to talk to her. Now.

Pulling her by the hand, I took her through the basement entrance. Puzzled, she tucked her hair behind her ear and sat on the sofa.

"Are we alone?" I looked around. "No one's hiding in here, right?"

She nodded. I asked her if she was sure; she said she was.

"Can you read my thoughts?" I asked.

"No."

"Will you be able to soon?"

"Yes, well—"

"I need more of those pills," I said, cutting her off.

Fantasia tilted her head. "Is something wrong?"

I ignored her. "Just tell me you have more of those pills, the ones that block my thoughts."

She nodded slowly and reached into her pocket. "Of course. They're right here." She pulled out a small envelope. Inside, I found more than a dozen tiny, blue pills.

"Thank God."

She looked at me crookedly before giving me instructions. "Chanticlaim said two of these, taken at the same time, should last for 24 hours. You'll need to remember to take them every day until we turn you. Then your thoughts will be safe."

Something in my face must have tipped her off because she blanched.

"Why do you look like that?" she whispered. "What's going on?"

I looked around the room, still worried there might be ears eavesdropping.

"No one's here; I promise you that," she said.

I took a deep breath. "I know you can read minds."

"Yes … I already told you that."

"No, that's not what I meant. You can read everyone's minds."

She gasped. "Why would you think that?"

I leaned in to whisper. "Because you know what was said between Polar and Gram. There are only two ways for you to know that: either you read Polar's mind, or Polar told you. And considering that Thorn was with him, I doubt he had the opportunity to fill you in."

Her eyes flashed, and her beautiful skin faded.

She started to move her lips, but no sound escaped. She snapped them shut and bit down. When words failed her, she started to shake her head. I grabbed her hands and held them firmly.

"I won't say anything. *Ever.* No matter what happens. I promise you that."

She bit the inside of her cheek and nodded. She looked down at our hands, mine shielding hers, and seemed to gather strength. Color seeped back into her skin. After two deep breaths, her eyes lost that frantic look.

She lifted her chin and tightened her jaw.

"Well, then," she started, setting aside the topic, "on to more pressing matters." She trembled while indicating the envelope that now held the precious, blue tablets. "We need to make sure we guard this carefully. We can't let Romeo find it; he'll ask too many questions. Although he may not be able to read your mind, he would recognize these pills. Chanticlaim calls them 'Brain Blockers.' He was rather proud when he developed them and showed them off to a number of Velores."

She fiddled with the envelope, twisting it in her hands. "Romeo will be keeping a close eye on everything, and although Torti can persuade him in fragments, she can't get him to blatantly disobey Thorn."

"Where should we hide them?" I asked.

She stood up and went to my bedroom. When she returned, she held an old book in her hands, one I vaguely recognized from Gram's collection. It was a compilation of fairy tales. *Fitting.*

The worn cover had long since faded, the black shell having turned to gray. The binding, compromised and fragile, nearly fell apart in her hands. Fantasia grabbed the envelope and wiggled it, arranging the pills so that they laid side by side. It was enough to make the envelope almost flat. She hid the pills between the cover and the front page. The loose spine made it easy to conceal.

"He won't look here. I know him well. I'm going to put this on your bookshelf. Make sure it's in the same spot every day; keep it consistent."

"Yes," I agreed and followed in tow as she returned to my room. Fantasia placed it on the second to top shelf, off to the side. It blended with the other books. She'd chosen well. When she turned around, she bit hard on her lip and gestured to the bed.

"It's time to discuss the details," she said.

I nodded and sat down. Fantasia plopped beside me. She pulled her knees to her chest.

"I'm ready."

"I'm not," she said truthfully. "This isn't what I wanted. It shouldn't have happened this way."

"Too late now."

She snickered. "Yeah, but still...." She hesitated and licked her lips. The sight of her tongue running along her mouth made me want to kiss her. It also made me wonder if she were part of the plan; If I'd been duped by a pretty face.

"I need to ask you something important," I blurted. "Something I was afraid to ask earlier."

Her eyes looked expectantly at mine, waiting.

"Last night, a lot of things were said." My throat locked up, shutting out my words. I coughed and started to play with a loose thread on my comforter. I couldn't look at her. "Torti said some things, many I'm sure to protect everyone involved. But one of those things … I need to know…." My voice rebelled against me. "I just need to know…." I started again, only to stop short. Although she couldn't read my mind, Fantasia knew where my thoughts landed.

"You want to know if I was part of the plan? If what she said was true."

"Yeah." Splotches of heat broke out along my collar as Fantasia looked away. Her shoulder's sagged, and I braced myself for the worst.

Because, really, why would anything good happen to me?

REVELATIONS

"I was never part of the plan, Daniel," Fantasia said. "That's why Mother was so angry."

"Thank God," I dropped my head back.

"I almost messed things up really badly for her," Fantasia continued, "and for my sisters. I wasn't supposed to find you ... I wasn't supposed to ..." she grabbed my hand and squeezed, "fall for you."

My heart nearly burst from my chest. Fantasia cared for me. All the pain of earlier—all the pain to come—none of it mattered as long as Fantasia was mine.

"I couldn't help myself. I wanted to save you. Polar's always been kind to me, and I knew how much it meant to him for you to stay human."

This was news.

"Polar didn't want me to join?"

She shook her head fervently. "Not at all. He actually voted against it."

"There was a vote?" *More news.*

"Yeah. The Seven Rulers, and occasionally their spouses, vote before a decision is made." She snorted. "I think it's a formality, though. It was actually voted down—your joining us, I mean—but because Thorn has the ultimate say, they were overruled."

"They didn't want me?" *Did I not belong anywhere?*

"No! That's not it at all." Fantasia quickly attempted to amend herself. "Not even close! Polar and your uncles just wanted you to live a normal life. Trust me; you don't want this existence."

"You're there," I reminded her.

"Yes, but I was born there. Narivous is all I've ever known; I've only gotten to experience human life through the thoughts of others. Seeing their memories makes me want what they're giving up. Instead, I have to live in a land where freedom isn't a possibility. Narivous is a prison. But, in many ways, it's much worse. In Narivous, you're never done with your sentence; you'll be serving time. Indefinitely."

I pulled her tightly to me and held her. She was describing a foreign world, one I was starting to understand. I guess part of me refused to accept—or mentally absorb—a land with such confining laws. I was a child of a democratic society, born free. It wasn't that I didn't understand the gravity of the situation; it was because none of it seemed real. At least, not until that moment.

"Let's not talk about it anymore," I said and laid down—dragging her alongside me. I cupped her face and leaned in so my lips were centimeters from hers. "I can think of better things to do," I whispered.

"And that is?" she asked softly.

I brushed my lips against her mouth. "This," I said.

She sighed and wrapped her fingers in my hair. Our kiss deepened, and I pressed my body against the length of hers. My heart pounded beneath my ribs, so much so, I was certain she could feel it. When she pulled away, her eyes were swimming with desire.

I went to kiss her again, but she stopped me by placing her fingers over my lips.

"Don't, Daniel."

"Aw, but it's just starting to get good," I whined.

"You know we need to talk about the details. You can't keep stalling."

I widened my eyes, "I wasn't stalling."

Fantasia coyly looked up through her lashes. "Yeah, right. You're a horrible pretender."

"That's not fair," I argued. "I've managed to get by this long. That takes a certain amount of talent."

She snorted. "I'll give you that. Still, you know you can't keep putting this off. We have a lot to go over. Rules, transformation, cover-up." She ticked off each item on her fingers. *Stupid agenda.*

I fell against the pillow and tucked my hands behind my head. She was right, but I still wasn't ready to hear it.

"Can I ask you something?" I asked, deploying a new tactic to distract her. I had a laundry list of issues that still needed answers.

Fantasia leaned back next to me. "Shoot," she said with an exasperated flourish.

"I need to know, was it Sarah who made out with Alex?"

"No."

"Who was it?"

Fantasia winced. "It was Torti. She had to break you and Sarah up so you'd meet her on Sunday."

"How did they knock her out?"

"That sedative you took, well, it comes in a more-saturated powder version. Once inhaled, it knocks a human out almost immediately. The remnants dissolve, leaving no trace behind."

"And the drunken voicemail?"

"Dreams," she admitted.

I sighed. I'd started to suspect. "And the nasty follow-up text messages? Your sisters, too?"

Fantasia nodded guiltily, before adding, "Not all of them."

"Oh?"

Her tan skin turned a smidgen redder.

"I sent one, too," she admitted painfully.

"*What?*"

"I sent the message about not trusting pretty girls," Fantasia admitted. She moved her forearm to cover her face.

"Why would you do that?"

"To get you not to trust Dreams. I also drained your tire." She peeked at me from under her arm, gauging my reaction. "I thought if you got that message, you would connect the pretty girl with Dreams, and you wouldn't follow her into the forest. And, well, the tire was simple. If I made you late, maybe I could've spared you. Maybe everyone would've been spared." She moved her arm and looked me straight on. Her expression was difficult to decipher. She flexed her jaw, almost in anger, but her lips slackened in sorrow. "You should've trusted Sarah," she said lastly before locking her eyes onto the ceiling.

I waited for her to look back—to say something more—but Fantasia remained focused on the plaster pattern above our heads.

"Are you okay?" I asked.

Fantasia shook her head. I propped up on an elbow and looked down into her face. Her eyes were swathed in pain. It was real and raw, and it hurt to look at her.

"Fantasia, talk to me."

She pinched her mouth and nervously brought her hand to her lips. Frustration warped her pretty features. "I wish I could read your mind," she said.

"Well, since you can't, I think it's best we work on other forms of communication. And that starts with you telling me what's wrong."

She nodded. "So I'm guessing you'll want to see Sarah again before the transformation." Was I mistaken, or were her words tinted with jealousy?

I liked that sound.

But she had nothing to worry about. I was undeniably hers, and nothing could change that. Not even the truth about Friday. Just the thought of capturing Fantasia's heart would've been enough to sustain my soul and release Sarah's love in a millisecond.

And I'd be damned if I was gonna feel guilty about that.

I smiled and stroked her hair. "Why would I want to see her when I have you?"

"To make her feel better," Fantasia replied, matter-of-factly.

"But I won't if it hurts you."

"Would it be wrong of me to say that it would?" She fumbled with a button on her sweater.

"I'd understand."

"You're not just saying that?" Hope sparkled in her eyes.

"Not at all."

Fantasia's smile spread like a dawn. "That makes me so happy! Honestly, I feel bad about what happened with her. No one should have to go through that. But—and I know this is selfish of me—I'm glad you don't want to see her. I've grown a bit ... *possessive* over you." She didn't look necessarily ashamed, but more awkwardly proud of her envy. Fantasia was full of contradictions, and I was secretly elated. It meant she really did care.

"Well, you have no reason to be upset. As long as you want me, I'm yours."

"I'm going to hold you to that."

"I sure as hell hope so." I leaned in and kissed her. "I'd be pissed if you bailed on me." Fantasia flinched, and her mouth jerked at the corner. It happened so fast that I almost missed it.

"What was that about?" I asked.

Fantasia shook her head. "What do you mean?"

"That look you just gave me?"

"I didn't give you a look."

"Yes, you did."

Fantasia gave me a bewildered smile. "Well, then, I'm sorry I gave you a look." She ran her lips over the top of mine and spoke into my mouth. "I'll try and keep my facial expressions in check from here on out."

Her breath wiped away my thoughts. I kissed back and shifted so I was on top of her. She parted her lips so I could explore her mouth with my tongue. Tasting her sped up my heart. It fought violently against my ribcage. Caught in the moment, my hands roamed with a mind of their own. I grabbed her ass, while my other hand traveled under her shirt and up her side. Greed was my undoing. Fantasia stopped my curious fingers with a firm grip.

She wiggled out from underneath me.

I smiled sheepishly. "Too much?" I asked.

She was catching her breath, and nodded, "Way too much and way too soon."

"I'm not sorry."

She grinned. "That doesn't surprise me." Her smile wilted as her face shadowed over.

"We still need to talk…."

I'd run out of ways to distract her.

"Fine. Get it over with," I said.

Fantasia sat up and crossed her legs. She attempted to smooth her tousled hair. I joined her and used my fingers to comb out the unruly strands. She stopped me mid-stroke and grabbed my fingers, intertwining them with her own.

"I'm ready to hear it."

She swallowed and began. "So now that you're joining Narivous, there are a few ground rules you must follow. Perhaps the biggest rule is to never disobey Thorn. She controls everything. Never question her authority and never stand up against her."

The memory of Fantasia's treasonous words reverberated through my skull, but I wouldn't bring that up until she was ready to talk about it. Fantasia seemed like the type who would shut down if pressed too hard. I'd have to cool my heels for a while.

"Also, we need to keep our existence a secret. Now, you and I both know I broke that rule, but I have a bit more leeway since I'm friends with most of the Doppelgängers, and they won't betray me over that. But I wouldn't push your luck. If Thorn ever finds out what I've done, it's a real possibility I'd be sentenced to a public execution. Thorn likes to make examples out of her subordinates. Remember, she rules with fear. You have one advantage: your heritage. You are related to a husband of a Seven, which affords you a bit more protection.

Fantasia looked down and nibbled on her lip as she contemplated what to say next. Hesitant, she spoke the next few words barely above a whisper. "Now, as far as how they are going to change you, they are mulling it over. I only know what they won't do."

"And what is that?"

She gave me a sideways glance. "Remember how I told you they don't make Deadbloods anymore because Thorn has difficulty controlling them?"

I nodded.

"Well, there are also combinations that are forbidden. The results prove too fickle and unpredictable ... too deadly. Some combinations should've never been made. I know they won't make you into a Poison. Thorn forbids it. Scream and Plague are the only created clan members of that group. Even if Thorn wanted to, she wouldn't be able to destroy them."

"Why?"

Fantasia shook her head. "It's complicated. You'll see eventually. Now," she moved on without skipping a beat, "Chanticlaim's been thinking your transformation over. With Thorn's permission, he'll decide on how to turn you. He isn't sure yet. I wish I could tell you, but he's so excited about your aura, he's constantly changing his mind. You really have great potential."

She smiled reassuringly, but I couldn't dislodge the unease that'd settled in the core of my marrow. To know others were discussing my death the same way they'd contemplate dinner recipes was beyond insane. They were cooking up a new Velore and wanted to make sure I had enough bite. Then there was the "forbidden combinations" component. That bothered me, too.

And not for obvious reasons.

Although my recruitment was imminent, it was fear for Fantasia's safety that consumed my waking thoughts. She was my beacon of hope, and I was willing to sacrifice anything and everything to protect her. I'd annihilate my morals, and happily become a monster, if it meant we'd spend eternity together.

I cringed at the thought of harm coming to her.

Fantasia saw my grimace. She brought her hands to my face and asked, "Penny for your thoughts?"

"It's a lot to take in." I lied. I wasn't going to tell her that I was frightened. It would only amp up the tension and make matters worse.

Fantasia wiggled her nose. "Yeah, I wish there was something I could do…." Her voice trailed off as her shoulders slumped. She dropped her hands into her lap. Then, quite unexpectedly, her face brightened. Fantasia, struck by inspiration, looked at me with glowing eyes. "Oh, my God!" she said. "I have an idea."

She climbed off the bed and placed her feet silently on the floor. When she turned, her face was alive.

"I know just the thing to make you feel better!" she exclaimed.

I squinted, lost.

"Everything in your life's been turned upside down. But …" she took a deep breath, "I think I know a way to ease your anxiety."

"I'll bite," I said. "What's your quick-fix?"

"I think it's time you see Tony."

And I'd be damned; the girl sure knew how to pique my interest.

⊰ 16 ⊱

YOU'VE GOT TO BE KIDDING ME

Two days after I moved in with Gram, I started school. It was the worst equation on the planet. Not only was I new, but it was middle of the term, and the school was small enough that I could see both ends of senior hall in one visual sweep. That, in real-life mathematical terms, made me a walking pariah.

And walking pariah I was.

By mid-afternoon, I'd dubbed myself the human spotlight and was having a combative argument with myself on whether or not to skip my last class. That's when I spotted a guy standing by himself near the gym. He had a tattered backpack near his feet and a shirt permanently stained the color of coffee. He was uninterested in the herds of imbeciles that roamed past him and far more fixated on his shoes.

He wasn't staring at me either, which made me like him. I stopped shy of where he stood and asked, "Is this where the losers hang out?"

The guy snapped his head up. Greasy hair the color of dirt swept across his guarded eyes as he took me in. He couldn't tell if I was making fun of him or not, and his mouth turned down at the corners.

"Because if it is," I added, "I'd like to reserve a spot. You know, to be with my people."

The guy cracked a smile. "Nah," he said. "The losers don't have a hangout spot. We just float around."

I held out my hand. "I'm Daniel."

"Tony," he replied. "It's nice to have another floater."

That was my first impression of Tony. Awkward outcast, the pair of us cut from the same cloth. But now things were different. Tony was different. This newer version would have power and strength. He'd be deadly. I'd have to meet him all over again.

What if we didn't mesh?

I gasped. Fantasia arched an eyebrow at her lets-go-see-Tony bombshell and smugly smiled. "How's that for hitting the nail on the head?" she asked.

"Is that allowed?"

"You've committed yourself to Narivous, and it's a certainty that you'll be transformed. I don't see any issues meeting up with Tony, but just to be sure, I'll ask permission first."

I couldn't help the smile that stretched across my face. Seeing Tony—knowing he was okay—would take a load off. Fantasia hit the mark.

Her eyes lit up even more. "Oh! Maybe we can have a small party, too! I have a couple of friends I'd like you to meet. We could all gather at the *notorious* swimming hole." She winked mischievously.

"The swimming hole? Can't Tony and your friends come here?"

Fantasia whipped her head back and forth, an adamant no.

"That most certainly wouldn't be allowed. Don't worry. You'll be perfectly safe—this time." The right side of her ruby lips twitched at the corner.

I groaned. Going back into that forest gave me the heebie-jeebies. I'd hoped to postpone that trip a little longer. But I suppose she was right. As long as she was with me, I wouldn't mind tagging along.

"Just don't let any monsters get me."

She rolled her eyes. "Daniel, you'll be with a monster."

"Let me rephrase then." Her comment wasn't going to get a rise out of me. "Don't let any *scary* monsters get me."

She smiled despite herself. "Deal."

After a quick kiss, Fantasia headed to Narivous to get permission for a meeting with Tony and her "friends." While she was gone, I attempted to stay occupied.

For starters, I turned on my phone.

A ton of messages lit up the screen. News of Gram's death traveled fast. Aunt Marie had left four hysterical voicemails. Mom called, too, as well as Charlie. His weary voice contained a hint of warning as he told me to take care of myself. He needn't say the words aloud. I knew what he meant: obey diligently; don't mess this up.

Responsibility and proper etiquette urged me to call Marie back. I had time. I figured it was best to utilize it productively.

The conversation was labored. Aunt Marie was at a conference a few towns away with Dean. As soon as she wrangled him, they'd be on their way.

"Was she acting funny?" she asked sadly. "Did she seem out of sorts?"

The image of Gram sitting at the table, eyes pooled with tears, slammed into me. It took a moment to build my lie.

"She was fine," I said, hoping Marie wouldn't hear the dishonesty in my words. "Nothing was wrong—at least nothing I noticed."

Marie's voice echoed through the earpiece. "That's good," she sniffled. "I'm glad she went peacefully in her sleep. That's the best way to go."

I bit down on my tongue in an effort not to correct her.

"Daniel," she said. "Don't worry about guardianship. Dean and I will be happy to take you in."

Marie's kindness had me at a loss. I was about to say she needn't bother, but stopped myself in the nick of time. I thanked her and ended the conversation, my energy depleted.

I ran my thumb across the screen and considered calling Mom back. The voicemail she'd left was a bland affair. She rambled—doped to the hilt—and asked me to call her back. She said we needed to discuss my soon-to-be living arrangements.

I started to shove the phone into my pants pocket when it vibrated. Sarah's name flashed across the screen with the message: Will u call me?

My finger hovered over the callback button. Sarah deserved a reprieve from her guilt. After all, she hadn't done anything wrong. That, and I desperately wanted to talk with her. But Fantasia's envious eyes lingered behind my own, stopping me from pressing down.

I wouldn't hurt Fantasia—at least, not if I could help it.

"Sorry, Sarah," I whispered, and tossed the phone onto the bed. I walked out of the room without looking back.

I paced the living room, burning tracks into the carpet, while waiting for Fantasia. Marie could arrive any moment, and I wanted to vacate the premises before she got there. One less thing to explain, and one less interaction to encounter.

When the knob on the front door turned, I was already standing up and reaching for my jacket. Fantasia didn't bother to knock, and I liked that. She needn't knock because she belonged with me.

Her shining eyes crinkled at the corners as a radiant smile filled her face.

"I'm guessing you got the okay?"

She nodded.

"Well, m' lady." I held out the crook of my arm. "Shall we be on our way?"

She looped her hand around my elbow while her grin grew. We fit perfectly together.

I led her to my truck, since once again, her vehicle was nowhere in sight. When she jumped into the passenger seat, I couldn't help but notice how much better my truck looked with her in the cab.

It looked downright badass.

I hopped in, slammed the door, and with the turn of the ignition headed back to Narivous.

Our conversation was effortless on our trip into the mountains. Fantasia rattled on about her sisters, and I, in turn, talked about my family. From time to time, our eyes connected, having traveled with a mind of their own.

When there was a slight lull, Fantasia shifted subtly and tucked a lock of hair behind her ear.

"So … um … there's something I need to tell you."

On impulse, I tensed and clutched the steering wheel hard, bracing for bad news.

"Go on," I urged.

"So when we get to Narivous, I need you not to kiss and hug on me."

My heart plummeted. *She had a boyfriend.* I flushed. How dare she not tell me? I attempted to keep my rage in check by counting to ten. My jaw hurt from clamping it closed. Fantasia—rightly uneasy—scooted away and hugged the door. Her elongated fingers wrapped around the handle in a tight grip.

"It's not what you think," she said quietly.

I said nothing and stared straight ahead. My fingers ached as I pressed harder on the wheel, my knuckles bone white from taut skin.

"Will you pull over so we can talk?"

"Great idea," I growled.

Fantasia indicated a small turnoff to the right where I pulled over and cut the engine. When I turned to her, my eyes blazed with wrath. There was also fear. I didn't want to lose her. She held my heart; I couldn't imagine another man holding hers.

This was total bullshit.

She pleaded with her eyes and reached for my hand. I let her take it, despite the anger surging through my blood. I waited as she gathered strength to dive in to her explanation.

"Daniel, it's really not what you think. I know you're wondering if there's someone else, and I can assure you, that's not the case."

Instantly, my spirits lifted. I breathed a huge sigh of relief. "Oh, thank—"

"It's still pretty bad," she said sadly. "Daniel, remember the first time you saw me and how I was wearing a mask?"

I nodded. At the time, I surmised that the mask was a tool to scare people out of Narivous—a strong tactic, I might add—but from the look on Fantasia's face, I suspected that wasn't the case.

"Well, that mask is a form of punishment."

"Punishment? What did you do?"

"It's not what I did." Fantasia wiped at her nose. "It's what my mother did."

"Your mother?"

"Yeah, my mother." Fantasia's palm twitched within my own. Her acidic voice crackled. "My mom had an affair with one of the Seven's husbands. It was only one night. But still, that's all it took. She ended up pregnant."

Fantasia took a few breaths. "That pregnancy resulted in me. Amelia, the leader of the Animal clan, was outraged. Not only had Cougar strayed, but now they'd have a child to show for it—a constant reminder of his infidelity. Had it not been for the intervention of Tipper, Chanticlaim's mom, the pregnancy would've been terminated. But Tipper was eager to see what a child of those two clans would result in. She fought hard to keep me alive. Narivous is, after all, merely a collection of experiments."

Fantasia's shoulders started to shake, a motion that bled down to her trembling fingers.

"Amelia sought ways to seek revenge upon my mother. She came up with a cruel and clever punishment. I'd be born, but the bloodline would stop with me. I'm not allowed to have a relationship. I'm not allowed to marry. Most importantly, I'll never be allowed to have children. The only romantic interactions that I'm permitted are those intended to help with recruitments. Nothing more."

Her eyes petitioned mine. "Thorn agreed with Amelia and told Mother that I would spend all eternity as a spinster. This would be her punishment—to watch her child ostracized from the others. She then banished us to live underground. In a sense, we were exiled."

What. The. Hell?

Fantasia exhaled deeply. "Thankfully, we were still useful. It kept us engaged with the others. Who knows what would've happened if we didn't have valuable talents," she shuddered. "Over the years, the shock of Mother's betrayal wore off. We're treated much more civilly now. We even have close friends and allies, especially our fellow Doppelgängers. But Amelia never forgets and still harbors hatred. Just my appearance sets her off. She's the one who brought me the mask. I'm to wear it always in her presence."

Fantasia stopped and coiled a strand of hair around her finger. "I was five when she gave it to me. She came up and tossed it at my feet. I'll never forget the look on her face when she told me to put it on. It was an equal mix of rage and righteousness."

I shifted in my seat and stared at Fantasia's stoic face. Her voice seeped into the cab. "To quote Amelia, she said that my 'existence was a disgrace and that my face made her sick." Fantasia turned towards me. "I've been wearing that mask ever since."

"That's messed up."

She shrugged. "It's not that bad. I don't really have to wear it all the time, at least not anymore. But the messed-up part is that I like wearing it. It's kind of become my security blanket." She ended with a cheerless smile.

I reached out my arms, and she fervently dove into them. Holding her tight, words of comfort eluded me. I was disgusted. How could anyone be treated that badly? Apprehension swept over me as I thought about my impending enlistment, i.e., my future entrapment. The forest would serve as my cage, and the trees, my bars.

We held on to one another in the middle of my cab. I buried my face in her hair as we rocked back and forth.

"It'll be okay," I finally said. "I'll wait forever for you." When the words slipped out, I realized how true they were. No amount of time would make me give up on her. I'd wait all eternity if I had to.

She pulled away to meet my gaze and brushed away a black tear. She shook her head.

"They'll never change their mind."

"You don't know that."

"But I do! Amelia will never let me settle down. Plus…." She twitched, and scratched her cheek. "Plus … um … they probably already have a marriage arranged for you."

"*WHAT*?" I shouted. Fantasia jumped and bleakly smiled through bitter tears.

"I don't know for certain, but I suspect that it's already been set up. Or at least an ordered coupling…." She uncomfortably looked away.

"You need to elaborate, Fantasia," I said firmly.

She drew in a deep breath before explaining. "Narivous is very old-fashioned. Many of the marriages are arranged, or at least approved by Thorn and the other Six. Their mindset is very … *controlling*. Over the years, things have loosened up, but they still force their hand when it comes to procreation. In particular, the royalty of Narivous are always assigned a partner. I don't know where you fit in the scheme of things, but since your grandfather is married to a Seven, that means you may fall into the marriage-by-order category. Honestly, it can go either way. But I know, without a doubt, that I won't be an option. At the very least, they may want you to couple with a woman just to get a desirable offspring."

"You've. Got. To. Be. Kidding. Me." Each word came out slow and precise.

"I suppose Chanticlaim could do artificial insemination. I know it's been done in the past." That option clearly gave her hope, and she actually smiled. I wasn't as confident. Either way, it meant I'd have a child with someone I didn't love, while the one I did love was denied me.

In that moment, a brainless zombie would've been able to display more emotion than me. Shock rendered me frozen. I sat there, absolutely stupefied.

Fantasia worriedly reached out and grabbed my shoulder. She gave it a gentle shake.

"None of this is for certain," she reiterated. "I only suspect that's what's coming. It's what they've done in the past."

"It's a surprise," I finally said.

She nodded. "It's all I've ever known, so it doesn't come as such a shock. But I bet it's worlds different than what you're used to. The way things operate in Narivous is very one-sided." She looked sideways at me, before adding, "I tried to warn you...."

"No one likes 'I told you so's.'"

She shrugged. "Yeah, but I feel like I earned this one."

"I'll give you that. You *did* try to warn me." I threw my head back against the seat and rubbed my throbbing temples. A monster headache was starting to form. Fantasia placed her hand on my hip.

"Are you okay?" she asked.

I shook my head. "This is getting more outrageous. Are they stuck in a time portal? They know this isn't the 18th century, right?"

Fantasia pinched her mouth.

"This has gotta be a joke," I said, knowing full well it wasn't. Fantasia said nothing. "Unbelievable." I followed up, "I won't agree. They can't make me."

"Yes, Daniel, THEY can make you."

I glared at her. "This is so stupid!" I pounded my knees. "An arranged marriage?" It even sounded idiotic. "I don't get it! Why? Do they get their kicks by controlling everything?"

She rolled her eyes.

"Do I at least get a say?" I sputtered.

She shrugged her shoulders and said tersely, "That's how it's always been, and that's how it'll always be."

"Is there any way out of it?"

Fantasia softened. "It hasn't been decided. I probably shouldn't have said anything. Now you're gonna get all panicky on me."

"No, I'm not," I argued, although I did sound panicky.

"Look, Daniel. You've got a great ally on your side: your grandfather. I know he'll back any decision you make, and Thorn's fond of him. Frigid will side with Polar, so you have her support, and typically—but not always—Frigid's sisters stay united in their decisions. That—and they're married to your uncles."

"What? Frigid's sisters are married to my uncles?" Strangely, I kept forgetting about my grandfather's brothers. I'd been so focused on Fantasia and Polar that they slipped the borders of my memory.

"Oh!" Her eyes lit up. *Flashed actually.* "I can't believe I didn't tell you! How silly of me." She started rambling excitedly. "Now, as I've already told you, Frigid rules Ice. But her sisters are Narivous Royalty, too; they cover Poison and Fire. They make up three of the Mighty Seven. That's why your grandfather and uncles were so coveted before coming to Narivous. Not only did they have strong auras, but they paired perfectly with the sisters." She gave me a big cheeky grin. "Your Grand-Uncle Arthur became Ferno, and Jack became Plague."

"Ferno and Plague?"

She giggled as she covered her mouth. "Their names! Everyone gets renamed in Narivous. Did you think Paul became Polar just for the fun of it?" she smirked. "Ember is the leader of Fire, and she's married to Ferno. Scream controls Poison and is married to Plague."

"Oh."

Fantasia's smile grew bigger. I gathered she was fond of these rulers. "They're wonderful, really wonderful. You'll love them. That, and they're your family," she winked. "Ember is a bit fickle, but the others are easygoing and kind."

I recalled the image of Frigid in her translucent phase. It still gave me the chills. Literally.

Fantasia understood.

"I know you had a horrible first impression with Frigid, but when her mind is clear, she's terrific. She's sweet and nurturing, albeit we don't get to see that side of her often." She shook her head sadly. "Chanticlaim's been searching for a solution to halt her relapses. Polar is desperate to cure her insanity. But trust me, when she's lucid, she has a great disposition."

"I'll have to take your word for it," I replied dryly.

"You'll see in due time," she responded.

I arched an eyebrow, and she pressed on. "Your uncles are all great. I can't think of a single bad thing to say against them. Despite their desire for you to remain free, I know they're all excited to meet you. Now that everything's settled, they're anxious to move forward. They're doing their best to make the most out of this arrangement."

I warmed at her words.

But a more urgent matter took rank: Fantasia and this off-limits crap. She was the reason I was joining Narivous, and in doing so, perhaps dooming my soul. I didn't take that lightly.

"Fantasia, what about your father? Why does he stand by and let Amelia treat you so badly?"

Her shoulders slumped. "The women in Narivous are in charge. They rule over everything. The spouses have some pull, but not nearly as much influence as their wives. That, and he feels guilty for the betrayal. He did everything possible to get back in her good graces, which meant denying me. Only once has he actively defied Amelia when it came to me, and that ended pretty badly for him."

"What happened?"

"You'll see."

"I'm really starting to hate that answer."

"Eh," she shrugged.

"You can be kind of infuriating, you know."

She gave me a toothy smile. "I think that's why we get along. We're a good match."

"So you're not going to tell me?" I pressed.

"No," she said, before darkening. Her amused face vanished in the blink of an eye. "It's rather painful, and I'm not ready." And with that, she turned and crossed her arms over her chest. The conversation was finished.

⟨ 17 ⟩

LOST FAMILY

The sun was descending by the time we made the meadow, tinting the forest a shade of eggplant and transforming the field into a plot of shadowy grass.

I wasn't thinking when I reached for Fantasia's hand. She pulled away and scowled.

Focus.

"Sorry," I mouthed. She gave me a conspiratorial wink and led the way.

The first step beyond the threshold annihilated daylight completely. The forest was a dome of evergreens, an encapsulation of earth and foliage. It held the musky scent of dirt. I paused to let my eyes adjust to the sudden loss of light.

"Ahem." Fantasia cleared her throat. "Shall we?" She indicated the path.

"My eyes aren't as good as yours," I explained. "It's gonna take a sec to focus."

She tapped her foot with feigned impatience.

"If you held my hand, I wouldn't need my vision," I added coyly.

Fantasia snickered. "Sorry, Casanova. That's not gonna work."

"It was worth a shot," I said with a shrug. "You can't blame a guy for trying."

"You're impossible."

"Yeah, but that's why you like me."

She grinned and rolled her eyes. "Can you see now?"

I nodded, and she gave me a 'come hither' look before heading deeper into the woods. I followed, admiring the sight of her ass as she tromped ahead.

Everything was different this time. I picked up on abnormalities that I'd missed earlier. For instance, the trail was nicely trimmed and the flowers too evenly placed. Even the trees grew accordingly, the limbs covering just enough space overhead to block out all light. They, too, were spaced perfectly. I wondered if Thorn had anything to do with this. I suspected so.

I watched for movement. Last night's conversation revealed the expedition for land had halted. That meant more Velores would be local. I kept my eyes peeled on the darkness surrounding us, as well as on Fantasia. She'd spot them long before I did.

Sure enough, Fantasia stopped and held out a hand to still me. She called out, rose onto her tiptoes, and eagerly waved. Pairing the tilt of her voice with the happy gesture, I gathered it was someone she liked. Still, I nervously crossed my arms and waited for the stranger to step forward.

It was a man I didn't recognize. Unlike the others, this man could never pass for human; he more closely resembled a walking corpse. Even without the quarter-mask that concealed the right upper part of his face, there would be no mistaking he was of supernatural descent.

Fantasia went into a kneeling position as the man approached. She tugged on my pants, indicating I should follow her lead.

A masculine chuckle—surreal and chilling—broke the stillness as my knee hit the earth.

"Get up, you two," he said jovially, and we scrambled to our feet. He sported a smile, which seemed wrong since he appeared to be rotting from the inside. The visible parts of his face held traces of handsomeness, although it was hard to see past the corpse-like exterior. His skin was pale, see-through nearly, and his one visible eye dark. A good chunk of his thick, jet-black hair was covered. Unlike Fantasia—who wore a mask to hide her beauty—I had the distinct impression this man was hiding something much more gruesome.

He sensed my curiosity and pointed to his face.

"This, Daniel, is a result of a self-inflicted gunshot wound. Maybe I'll let you see it sometime."

He spoke matter-of-fact while attempting to add a bit of humor. I was horror-struck.

My expression must have said it all because he continued, not waiting for a response.

"I struggled with depression," he shrugged, as though that explained everything. Then he gave me another smile. "It's good to see you, Daniel. You look like Paul."

"Thank you."

He held out a hand enshrouded in a black, leather glove. Although it made me cringe, I reached out and grasped his palm. He gave me a hearty handshake.

"I'm Plague."

My eyes shot wide open. This was my Grand-Uncle Jack. Fantasia gave off a wide, cheery grin.

When I didn't say anything, Plague once again chuckled.

"A bit much, isn't it?" he asked sincerely.

I nodded. "That's an understatement."

But it wasn't adding up. Fantasia said that my Uncle Jack was the Poison Leader. How could he be toxic if he'd shot himself? In Narivous physics, the components didn't add up. I was baffled, and apparently it showed.

Plague let off a throaty laugh that bounced off the trees. "Boy, you look pretty confused. Don't get me wrong. I'll take confusion over horror any day, which is what I'm most accustomed to." He winked at Fantasia, "Newcomers are usually shocked by my dashing exterior." His smile widened. "But confusion; this is new. So I gotta ask—why the look?"

I gulped. How to ask such a question? Inwardly, I cursed Fantasia, wishing she'd warned me better, but now it was too late. Since he'd asked, I really didn't see any other choice. "Well, Plague—"

He cut me short. "Now, now. It's Uncle Plague to you."

"Um ... well ... Uncle Plague," the words felt all wrong. A wave of saliva swamped my mouth, drowning my tongue and unspoken question—a question I really didn't want to ask. Finally, I mustered the courage. "How is it you're the Poison Leader if you shot yourself?"

He bowed forward with a deep, stomach-wrenching laugh. It shook the air. After taking a second to catch his breath, he steadied himself. The grin he gave when he answered was full of straight, white teeth. "Ah, yes. Now I understand the mystery." He chuckled again and wiped at his one visible eye. "Of all things to ask, that was a good one. You see, son, I almost messed things up for everyone involved. They had to mix their cure with the toxin when they brought me back to life. It was a test—one they weren't sure would work. But alas, as you can see, I'm standing before you in all my breathtaking glory."

He patted me on the back before adding, "Yes, I'm just another Narivous miracle." He chortled at his own joke, and turned to Fantasia. "So it looks like we have a reunion in order. Shall we be on our way?" He waved towards the trail. Fantasia grinned and skipped ahead.

This was perhaps the most unusual experience of my life, walking next to a real-life zombie, led by a woman whose utter perfection could rival any Greek goddess. A smile of incredulity spread across my face without my even knowing.

In no time at all, we reached the river. It seemed familiar, even though I'd only envisioned it through Eric's tale. We turned left and walked in a straight line, parallel to the water. Fantasia led; Plague followed.

It wasn't long before I could make out voices up ahead.

We had arrived.

The group waiting for us was excited and ... *young*. Torti and Dreams stood off to the far left, looking almost bored. In the center was a man with buzzed hair and strong masculine features. Despite wearing a genial smile, his presence was intimidating. With stiff, corded biceps, he exuded a brawny power. Nearly hidden behind him was a woman with black, asymmetrical hair—long in front, short in back. She skittishly ducked her head when we locked eyes. The most unusual member of the group came next: a small, childlike girl with honey-colored curls. She reminded me of a porcelain doll, her features small and perfect with giant cherub-blue eyes. Chanticlaim completed the lineup and once again held his goofy, trade-mark smile. Tony wasn't there.

They all bowed and curtsied to Plague.

Fantasia nearly danced her way to stand between her sisters. She reached out and grabbed their hands. Fantasia's smile creased her whole face. Plague took the lead on introductions.

The cherub girl was Delilah, and although small, she held a power-ful mind and willful personality. Volt was the shy, spiky-haired girl, and her brother, Spark, was the beefy dude. Everyone clattered with frenzied excitement, shooting questions at me in rapid succession. They "oohed" and "awed" over my aura, causing my head to swell with a peculiar sort of pride.

When two men emerged from the shadows, their words died away as if someone had clipped their tongues.

It was my grandfather, and by the looks of the man beside him, his older brother. My grandfather looked like an older version of me—if I, too, were frozen. His eyes were a piercing blue, much like my own, only more intense. We shared the same facial symmetry, with lips and noses shaped alike. Even our hair was nearly the same, except his was lighter. He looked more like me than my own father.

To his right was my Uncle Ferno. He wore a dark-ash stalking cap. Around the brim, significant burn scars peeked out. One particularly nasty mark cupped his left, misshapen ear. Melted skin apparently didn't bounce back with immortality.

Everyone bowed and kneeled—well, everyone except me. My spine did not bend, nor knees buckle. Polar had taken the life of my grandmother. I knew it wasn't by choice, but it still didn't lessen the pain. My body stiffened.

They didn't seem the slightest bit offended as they walked towards us. Polar's blue eyes flashed with concern. He stopped a few feet in front of me. We were the same height, and our eyes hit straight on. His mouth twitched before he held out an unsteady, gloved hand. I hesitated, and despite the conflicting emotions swarming in my head, reached out and gripped his concealed fingers.

Polar's Adam's apple bobbed with a stiff swallow as a dim light formed behind his eyes. He had the look of a trapped animal. It made me sympathetic. We would discuss Gram later. *In private.*

"Hello, Daniel. I'm Polar," he said formally, and released my hand. Searching for words, he raked his fingers through his hair. "As you know, I'm your grandfather." He paused again, uncomfortable. "You have no idea how much I've looked forward to meeting you."

"It's nice to meet you," I managed.

Polar indicated the man beside him. "This," he said, "is your Uncle Ferno."

Ferno broke out into a colossal grin.

"This is incredible!" Ferno said. "Isn't this incredible?" He turned to Plague and Polar. "My word, Paulie. He's an exact replica of you at that age!

Wouldn't you agree?" Both men nodded. "My, my, my ... this brings back memories." He reached out and ruffled my hair like I was twelve years old. "I'm going to call you Paulie Jr."

I patted down my hair which caused him to snigger.

"Sorry. It came out naturally; you remind me so much of this pip-squeak." He pointed his thumb towards Polar. "I couldn't help myself."

"Hey!" Polar objected. "I'm as big as you are."

Ferno laughed even harder. "That's right. Little Paulie's all grown up." Polar rolled his eyes.

"So how about a handshake for your favorite uncle?" Ferno asked.

"That's yet to be decided," Plague retorted.

"I thought it was best to establish that now so there's no disappointment in the future," Ferno replied with a deadpan face.

Now it was Plague who rolled his eyes—or eye—since that was all that was visible.

Ferno reached out, his fingers bare and ungloved.

I grasped his palm, and the moment our skin made contact, a shock of electricity flowed through me. Reflexively, I ripped my hand away, but not before every cell in my body came alive. I was, for a blip in time, indestructible. My muscles spasmed with strength—a powerful sensation that was pure ecstasy. Everything altered: my vision sharpened, smell intensified, and hearing heightened. It was as if I'd spent my entire life living with dull senses, and for one magical moment, they'd been corrected.

And then it was gone—vanished—almost as quickly as it came.

A circle of mad chuckles brought me back to the present. Everyone rolled with hysterics.

I was the butt of an inside joke. Normally, that would get my goat, but a familiar voice distracted me. It rose above all the others.

Tony.

"His eyes lit up! Did you see that?" Tony shouted.

I moved to catch a better glimpse. He'd changed—become more beautiful somehow. But it was still him. I could barely control my excitement.

On impulse, I ran and eagerly embraced him. He responded with as much vigor as he could muster. *Too much vigor.* A loud crack, followed by a sudden warmth, swept across my ribs. That warmth exploded into heat as a torrent of pain rippled through my body.

A collection of shouts collided from behind: "WHOA," "STOP," and "CAREFUL."

Tony released me as I bent at the waist, trying hard not to breathe and make the pain worse.

"Dan, I'm sorry," Tony said. "I forget how strong I am."

"It's okay," Fantasia replied before I could assemble any words of forgiveness.

The next thing that happened was equally strange. Two hands touched my side, and a new warmth—one softer and more tender—flowed up my ribs. A nanosecond later, the pain was gone as my injury corrected itself. Fantasia, my healer, smiled upon me.

"Thanks, Fantasia," I said, grateful and a tad-bit awestruck. "That was impressive."

"She's an impressive girl," Polar commented proudly.

Remembering the handshake with Ferno, I pointed at him and asked, "What happened?"

"Ferno doesn't know how to make a good first impression," Plague said. Ferno elbowed him in the side.

"What do you know about first impressions?" Ferno teased. "You frighten the crap out of anyone nowadays."

"True," Plague said with a good-natured smirk.

Polar was the one to directly answer my question. "He sparked you."

"Sparked me?"

"Yeah, I couldn't help it," Ferno said as he gave me a look that indicated he wasn't the least bit sorry.

"Does that happen all the time?" I asked, and pointed to the other's gloves.

"No, not at all," Polar responded. "I wear gloves because the touch of my skin to yours would cause serious damage. Frostbite, actually. Plague wears gloves because any human contact would cause certain death from his exposed skin. He's extremely toxic—even to other Velores— although we have provisions to correct any accidental exposure. But still, it's a hell of a nasty sting."

"Yeah, he's pretty nasty," Ferno chimed in. Polar ignored him.

"The only ones who can tolerate his touch are Ferno and me, as well as our wives. It's an odd quirk. He's pretty lethal, as is his wife Scream."

"She's not nasty, though," Ferno added. Plague looked both incredulous and amused as he shook his head.

Polar snickered, "Fantasia, too, can tolerate his touch. They believe it's because she has healing hands." He smiled before he pointed to Spark. "Spark here, can accidentally electrocute someone if he isn't careful, especially when he's near water. So can Volt, but she's pretty shy, so she doesn't bother wearing gloves since she's unlikely to touch anyone."

Volt looked away, embarrassed. Spark rocked on his feet, pleased. He gave off a cocky nod of his head and wiggled his fingers midair.

"Now, my dear brother thought it'd be funny to spark you. It's something we're all capable of. It transmits our powers for a fleeting second. What you felt was a taste of what it's like to be us. However, I think he should've warned you first, but he has no manners," Polar said haughtily.

Ferno was completely unaffected. "Whatever, man. He loved it. I could tell." He looked at me for affirmation.

I nodded.

He was right.

It was awesome.

And this was the best reunion I could've hoped for.

Immortality was kind to Tony, both mentally and physically. Although he still possessed the same facial structure and lean frame, he looked better than before. The awkward gait and poor skin were gone. Although Ferno's scars were unfixable, Tony's pockmarks had been rectified. His complexion was faultless, and paired with vibrant eyes and brighter hair, he'd become handsome.

Or perhaps it was the sheer happiness he emitted.

We didn't talk much. Tony—now known as Sludge (ugh!)—was much too distracted by Volt. I sensed a budding romance between the two now that Dreams had withdrawn her affections.

He pulled me aside for only a moment.

"It's okay, man. Really," Tony said as we stood near the tree line. His eyes kept darting in Volt's direction. "This place isn't all that bad."

I folded my arms and pulled my shoulders up. "Still, it shouldn't have happened."

Tony smirked. "Damn, Daniel. That's the story of my life." He looked towards the lake, the place of his death, and shrugged. "We're the guys with crappy luck, but this …" he paused as his eyes glistened, "this man, this is good." He met my gaze and added, "Our luck's changing. Believe that."

"I hope you're right."

He smiled. "Trust me, I am."

It wasn't until the party thinned down that Polar asked for a moment alone. He led me into the forest for privacy. Polar walked in silence as I tromped after him. We went a significant distance before he stopped. Two stumps rested before us, illuminated by a faint ray of sunshine that broke through a small crack in the trees. A natural spotlight. He indicated I should sit.

He took his seat on the stump next to me, and began, "I know this has been quite a shock." He gave me a tight, nervous smile. "And I'm sure you have lots of questions. But first, there are a few things I need you to know."

I said nothing as he blew air past his lips and rubbed his hands together. "For starters," he said, "I've always known about you. I kept tabs on both you and your dad from the very beginning. I knew about Richard's addiction, and it disappointed me. For years, I blamed myself." His chest lifted with a heavy, contrite breath. "Hell, there are times I still do. I've often wondered if I could've stopped him, you know, if I'd been able to raise him myself. Maybe it would have made all the difference."

I snorted. "Doubt it."

"Even still, it's something I've always considered. You have no idea how much I wanted to be a part of his world and yours. I'm sorry."

He stopped suddenly and dug into his pocket. He pulled out two photographs. He handed the first to me.

It was a well-worn image of me and Dad at the zoo. I remember that day all too well; it was one of my earliest memories. I'd gotten lost amongst a sea of people. I was at an age where my head looked disproportionate to the rest of my body, and similarly, didn't reach most adult's elbows. The crowd was large, and I wanted to see the elephants—an endeavor that shouldn't have been doable—except Mom was too busy searching for Dad whom she was fairly certain was "hitting on" the clerk at the help desk. So while she fretted, I slipped off, disappearing into the crowd in an almost effortless fashion. It didn't take long before I realized that I'd messed up.

The crowd was too large, too sweaty, and full of noise. Human towers loomed over me, and I soon got dizzy. A well-intentioned, featureless woman grabbed my arm. Another lady, her companion, swooped in from behind. She smelled medicinal—like ointment you put on achy joints. They both wore the universal expression of all mothers when they encounter a child under stress.

"Little boy, are you lost?" "Do you know where your mommy and daddy are?" "What's your name?" The questions came at me from dark, empty holes where their mouths should be. Those holes—in my childish brain—weren't really mouths, but black holes waiting to swallow me up. Fear seized my voice and stole my words. The ground caved in as I curled myself into a caterpillar ball, and panic erupted in my head. I started to scream a painful, piercing shout that rattled the crowd.

It took two employees, an ice-cream bar, and a visit to the elephants before I settled down. Mom snapped the picture afterwards. Chocolate sugar clung to my shirt, and even in the photograph, it was sticky. Dad's watered-down face held a smirk as he posed on the bench next to me.

Now I was holding that image in my hands, given to me by a man who was virtually a stranger. Not even my parents packed around a photo of me. It was a hefty thought.

"I've got an album full of others," Polar explained. "This here is one of my favorites. Charlie was kind enough to keep me in full supply." He looked up and stared into the weak stream of sunlight. "I stopped asking about your dad a long time ago. It hurt too much to hear about him." He met my gaze dead-on and said sincerely, "You, on the other hand, have always made me extremely proud."

He handed me the second photograph. This one was much shabbier, almost tissue-paper thin from years of handling.

Staring back from the faded photograph was another image of me—or so, at first glance, it appeared. The resemblance was so strong, it took three bold blinks to separate myself from the picture. It was Polar as a young man, close to my age now. He stood behind a beautiful, petite brunette, his arms wrapped tightly around her shoulders. She gazed lovingly into his face with a smile I recognized. Gram.

The photo gave me chills.

Polar tapped the paper. "I want you to know that I loved her dearly. I never stopped."

I leaned back and crossed my arms.

"Yet, you killed her."

Polar shook his head. "There was nothing more I could do."

"You could've persuaded her to seek treatment. You could've given her more time."

"It's not that easy, Daniel. Other people were present."

"Yeah, but Fantasia said you're one of Thorn's favorites. You could've convinced her to let Gram go."

"No, Daniel," Polar said softly. "I couldn't have." He looked around the forest and dropped his tone. "And to be perfectly honest, it's best we keep our voices in check."

I took it down a notch. "What happens if they overhear us?"

Polar grimaced and leaned next to my ear, his breath cold as ice. "Bad things."

My shoulders fell, and he continued. "I loved her, Daniel. She was a special person, and don't you think for a second that her death won't haunt me for the rest of my life." He looked down at his feet, not willing to meet my gaze. "I didn't see any other choice, though. It was either that or torture." His voice trembled.

Instinctively, I reached out and rested my hand on his back. He tensed—shoulders frozen in both temperature and flesh—before his disturbed eyes met mine. It was that moment in which I realized I'd already forgiven him. Gram's death was not his doing, but Thorn's. If he'd been given a choice, he would've saved her. He wore his torment in the drawn lines around his lips. I understood why Gram loved him, and all my animosity drifted away. He and I shared a common deficit; we knew what it was like to have Gram in our lives, and worse, what it was like to lose her.

"I didn't want this life for you, but it'd be a lie to say I wasn't excited to have you here. I never had a chance to look after Richard, and it seems you've needed a father. Perhaps we can be that for one another."

And there it was. Someone wanting to be my father. I nodded and dared to hope.

Our party disbanded until all that remained were Fantasia, Polar, and I. We stayed until the sky turned inky-black and filled with stars.

We walked back to my truck in comfortable silence. The forest—much darker after nightfall—was infinitely more difficult to navigate. Polar and Fantasia had no issues finding their way, while I stumbled over every stupid root and divot. After my fourth fall, one that earned me bloody, crosshatched threads across my palm, Fantasia took pity and grabbed my hand to move me along.

We reached the meadow, and Polar stopped short of exiting the forest. The half-moon gave his skin a pearlescent glow. He appeared as undead as he actually was.

Tentatively, he stepped forward and then, almost impulsively, grabbed at my shirt and yanked me forward. I stumbled into him as he wrapped his arms around my shoulders in a desperate hug. His torso was hard as ice. When he pulled back, his eyes were shining bright, lighting up the black tears that were beginning to form. He was slipping into his translucent phase, brought on by intense emotion. It was because of me.

He didn't say a word as he gripped my shoulder and gave it a gentle shake. He smiled sadly, and then bowed his head and walked away. Not once did he look back. And while he wasn't watching me, I couldn't peel my eyes off him. I waited until his form vanished completely.

Fantasia and I were alone now. She walked with me across the meadow to my truck. Her demeanor indicated she wasn't coming with me.

It was how she hung her head, limp and broken. *Defeated.* I worried when I would see her again.

I asked her as much.

"I don't know," she answered honestly. "It's really up to them. They may decide that Romeo will relay all the orders." She glanced down and kicked a stone. "I may not see you until after you've turned."

"Convince them otherwise."

She smiled grimly. "I'll try, Daniel."

"I know," I said, and despite being off-limits, I pulled her to me. I tucked my face into her hair and enveloped her with my arms. She pushed her face into my chest. "I'll miss you."

"I'll miss you, too. I'll be thinking of you, every minute of every day."

"And I you."

She pulled away then, and after determining it was safe, planted a soft kiss on my lips.

"Please convince them," I whispered.

Fantasia brushed her fingertips down the length of my cheek.

"I'll try." She pulled away and took two steps back, our eyes linked with thirst and want.

"Promise?"

"I'll do my damnedest," she swore, and turned away. She walked towards the large oaks, and stopped at the forest wall. She glanced over her shoulder and lifted her hand in farewell.

I did the same.

I didn't get into my truck until she'd disappeared. As I pulled away, a dark figure stood near the entrance to the trail, tucked behind a tree. Fantasia's eyes flashed, illuminating the mask she wore on her face. She stayed to watch me leave.

❧{ 18 }❧

LAST WEEK

It turned out my concerns over not seeing Fantasia were completely unfounded. The next morning, I woke up with her beside me. She stirred as soon as I awakened.

She smiled and stretched her arms over her head.

"Seems they want me to stay close so nothing goes awry. Lucky us, huh?" Her voice dripped with satisfaction.

"Yeah, lucky us," I agreed and reached for her. "So does that mean we can be a couple for this last week? You know, to make sure I stay committed to joining Narivous and all?"

She nodded happily.

"I think that'd be best. We wouldn't want you changing your mind."

Our embrace, followed by a passionate kiss, was the best way I'd ever started a day.

So my days were numbered. I'd accepted this, and with Fantasia by my side, the ordeal was less daunting. I could manage as long as I had her support.

And I was going to need that support.

For starters, there was Gram's funeral to plan and attend. I also had explanations to give. I'd missed three days of school, and Marie was frantic with worry when she arrived at Gram's and I was nowhere to be found. My phone had a dozen messages, including an angry voicemail from Turkey-Neck when I hadn't shown up for work. A no-call, no-show would be my third strike.

I figured that I'd stop by later to pick up my pink slip for framing, if they even bothered handing out pink slips. I wasn't sure how that worked, or even if that's what employers did. I'd soon find out; and besides, maybe I'd get the opportunity to give him the middle-finger salute.

It gave me something to look forward to.

Regardless, I chose to take each day one at a time, and that Thursday—for reasons unknown even to me—I decided to go to school.

So that's what I did. After kissing Fantasia goodbye, I checked in with Marie. She was going through a stack of Gram's paperwork upstairs, sobbing gushy tears over manila file folders. It was hard to watch, and I ducked out.

First time in like—well, ever—that I wanted to go to class.

That is, until I got there. Pitying stares followed me through the halls—news of Gram's death traveled fast. First Sarah and Alex, now Gram; I was a colossal topic of gossip. Daniel the leper. Their sympathy made my skin break into hives.

Sarah was waiting for me at my locker, toying with a lock of blonde hair and chewing absentmindedly on a piece of gum. She lost her boredom when she spotted me and launched a bright smile.

It pained me. Narivous' treatment of Sarah swathed her in shadow, silhouetting her reputation with a lie. Now, confronted with the truth, my attitude shifted. I returned her smile with one of my own.

Her eyes glinted with hope.

My vow to Fantasia lingered, adding pressure to keep things platonic. I kept my tone cool.

"Hey."

"Hey," she replied warmly. "I'm sorry about your grandmother. Eric told me she'd passed away." She gingerly reached out and brushed my hand; reflex pulled it away. She winced, and I attempted to recover.

"Thanks. It was really hard yesterday." I made my voice soft, trying to emphasize that I wasn't angry anymore.

She nodded. "I can only imagine. I know how much she meant to you." She stopped and bit down on her lip. "Eric was a mess. He was hurting pretty badly, too."

"Eric was here yesterday?" I snorted, surprised. "I would've thought he'd skip."

Sarah looked at her feet before replying. "Yeah, he was here and a total wreck. Actually, I'm surprised he showed up, too. I'd never seen him like that. You know all … *broken*." She hesitated before adding, "That's how everyone knows what happened." Her eyes surveyed the hall. I didn't need to follow her gaze; I could feel their eyes boring into my back.

My hair prickled.

"She was a great woman. I honestly don't know what I'm going to do without her." Worried my voice would break, I stopped myself from saying more. I loved Gram. Plain and simple. Sarah understood.

"I loved her, too," Sarah said. Her eyes welled, and before I could stop myself, I reached for her. Sarah melted into my arms as I wrapped her shoulders into a firm embrace. Despite how right it felt to hug her, I couldn't shake Fantasia's lavender eyes from my reverie. Offering this little bit of solace brought a rush of guilt.

Sarah buried her face into my chest, and her warmth bled through my shirt. It took steely willpower to release her. It was as if Fantasia owned a remote and was able to force my hands to drop. Her pull was that powerful.

Sarah took a step back and wiped away escaped tears. The back of her hand glistened with salty liquid. She glanced down in an attempt to compose herself. I did the same.

The halls were beginning to thin as the warning bell rang overhead. I reached out and touched her arm. She looked up, panicked.

"Can we talk later?" she asked desperately. "Things have been so strange."

I was afraid of the questions she'd ask. An interrogation frightened me, especially without the aid of Fantasia. What if I accidentally revealed Narivous' secrets? The thought was too overwhelming. Too dangerous.

I shook my head.

"Please!" she begged. "Just give me one afternoon. One lunch break!" She stepped closer and looked into my eyes. "Think of all that we had together, all that we were. All I'm asking is for one afternoon. One. That's not much."

She was right, and with my brain and heart duking it out, I should've known what organ would win. I nodded. Her shoulders relaxed, and a smile surfaced across her face.

"Lunch, today? I'll meet you at your locker."

"Okay."

Sarah walked away at a hurried pace, her bag bucking in short, vertical jabs. She didn't want me changing my mind. I made my way to homeroom in a daze, wondering all the while how I was going to get out of this unscathed—and more importantly—keep my newly discovered secrets hidden.

It's stupid how time flashes by when you want it to crawl, and when you need it to speed up, it freezes. That's how my morning went. It passed too quickly. One second, I'm sitting in Bio staring at a book that might as well have been blank, and the next, the lunch bell was blaring on the overhead speakers.

The halls parted like the Red Sea, except I was a bad-luck curse and not the deliverer of the chosen people.

That's when I honed in on the excited murmur. It was localized in center hall, midway down the line, right where my locker was. There was good reason for it, too. Because waiting for me was Sarah, Eric, and … *Fantasia*. Her shoulders slouched, hands in pockets, Fantasia relaxed against the metal enclosure. She and Sarah were engrossed in deep conversation—so engrossed, Fantasia acted oblivious to the enchanting stares coming from every single student body in close proximity.

Especially the guys.

Approaching the trio, I caught only tidbits of information. I heard Tony's name, I heard Fantasia mention her sister, and I saw Fantasia shrug her shoulders with indifference. Eric stood awkwardly to the side, intently listening to the exchange. Sarah's back was facing me, so I was unable to read her expression. It wasn't until Fantasia looked over her shoulder and nodded in my direction that Sarah turned. The look on Sarah's face stopped me dead in my tracks. She wore a blended image of jealous fury and sadness.

It seemed at that exact moment, the entire school ceased talking. Their greedy eyes were glued to the four of us—Fantasia in particular—all of them eager for drama.

Not the least bit phased, Fantasia gave me a brilliant smile. She sauntered the few steps that separated us and placed her hand on my chest in a loving gesture. With her other hand, she reached to cradle my cheek in her palm. The smoldering look in her eyes was unmistakable, and I found myself being sucked in by her own gravitational pull. I was helpless to stop it. Fantasia was my life now, and I could see nothing beyond her. Blank as a black chalkboard, I reacted on impulse, letting our lips come together in a passionate kiss.

Bouncy gasps swarmed around me, followed by the chatter of gossip.

I didn't care.

When I pulled away, I reached out to stroke her cheek. Fantasia smiled as she grabbed my hand and pulled me back to the awaiting pair.

The gawking onlookers looked both impressed and astounded. *That's right, asshats; take a knee for your hero. Suck it.*

But my moment of triumph perished when I focused back on Sarah. She was holding her hand to her mouth, the strain around her lips visible. Shame blew color into my cheeks, just as Alex and his posse walked by. His eyes bulged as he stared unabashedly at Fantasia, and then at her hand holding mine. He scowled and, in an attempt to salvage his pride, smirked and winked at Sarah. He mimed a two-handed finger point, as if to say, "Hey, baby."

Laughter trailed behind them as the pack made their way through the hall.

Fantasia's hand tightened around my own. I squeezed back.

"I see you've moved on ... and quickly," Sarah's voice quivered. "I suppose I deserve it." Tears started to develop. Fantasia let go of my hand and went to Sarah.

"Everyone makes mistakes," she said calmly. "It was pure chance that we met when we did." Fantasia rested her hand on Sarah's upper arm. Whatever she was doing, it was calming Sarah. "If it makes you feel better, he didn't even want to date me because he was still upset over you. I pursued him."

Sarah's eyes brightened. I could only imagine the thoughts running through her mind. Seeing Fantasia, and the effect she had on, well, *everyone*, it must've made her feel better knowing I was the hunted—no pun intended—and attempted to stay loyal to the memory of our past relationship. I was no match for the striking energy of the tall, lithe brunette.

That, and I think Fantasia was using some sort of Velore power to calm her. But I wasn't a hundred percent sure on that. I still had a lot to learn.

A loud commotion snapped the calm as blood-curdling screams resounded off the walls. It came from behind.

"EEK!" came one frantic voice, another yelled "RUN!" But it was the last two shouts that really got my blood pumping. Someone shrieked "SNAKES!" then another, "SPIDERS!"

The place erupted. Warm bodies fled, and I was forced to pancake against the lockers to avoid the stampede. It was either that or be trampled by a herd of hysterical bodies. Eric, who'd remained quiet this entire time, met my eyes with wide-eyed wonder. Sarah, too, had an edge of panic. Meanwhile, Fantasia was cool as a cucumber and did her best to suppress a smile. She winked when our eyes met.

I could see why. As the hall cleared, dozens of snakes slithered around the buffed, ivory floor. They were coming from Alex's open locker. Across the hall, another metal door hung open. It, too, was oozing its unpleasant contents: spiders—tarantulas included. I shivered at the nasty little buggers. I was fairly certain I knew who owned that locker. I would've bet money it was Alex's little minion, Steve.

I took in the scene appreciatively.

Sarah began to hyperventilate as the snakes traveled towards us and excused herself with the exiting crowd.

Only a few stragglers stayed behind, mostly goth and emo kids. But they weren't paying attention to us. For the most part, we were alone.

"I think he deserved that," Fantasia said with satisfaction. "You can thank Tony for the snakes. He rounded them up this morning."

For the first time since our ordeal, I watched Eric's face fill into a brilliant smile. He looked at Fantasia with certain awe. I leaned down to kiss her on the lips.

"And the spiders?" I asked.

"You can thank your aunt."

"My aunt?"

"Scream can control arachnids, in particular, spiders. I thought about throwing some scorpions into the mix, but I didn't have enough time." She puffed out her bottom lip in a pout. "I figured this was good enough—for now."

"Well, I'll be damned," Eric voiced. He sounded somewhat like his old self. "That's impressive."

Fantasia winked at him. "You're family now, and your enemies are our enemies. Now, if you'll excuse me, I promised Scream I would bring back the tarantulas."

She walked towards the chaos. The principal, and a few teachers, gathered in a huddle near the exit doors. They kept their distance as they watched the creepy crawlers invade their hallways. Eric and I stood closer to the action than they did. They eyed Fantasia—the principal in particular—and I wondered how I'd explain my girlfriend hunting down spiders.

They would surely pin me as the planter.

Eric whispered in my ear. "That's incredible. She turned herself into an old woman." I looked at Eric. He cocked his head to the side and added, "It's crazy."

My head whipped in her direction, but I only saw Fantasia. Then I remembered the "Brain Blockers." Apparently, it not only hindered their mind reading, but mirages as well. No one could possibly confuse the beauty who had been at my side with an old grandma tossing bugs into a knapsack. No one objected to the helpful Samaritan collecting the nasty pests, even though she must have looked preposterously out of place.

Grandmas are an unthreatening bunch, after all.

After school, I went by my work and received confirmation that I no longer had a job. I was in high spirits, though, because I still got to flip off Turkey-Neck. His eyes bulged over my colorful use of language, and he sputtered when I told him to go 'suck an egg.'

Fantasia apologized that evening for her behavior in front of Sarah. She was curled on my lap, knees pulled up, as she leaned into my chest and whispered her apology. Her fingers walked along my arm, trickling power with each touch.

"I'm sorry," she mumbled, her lips tracing a path from my jaw to my ear. "I got jealous. I was waiting in the shadows and read Sarah's mind. She was gonna ask too many questions, and I thought it would be easier on you." She tucked her nose behind my lobe. "I can answer questions before they're even asked. Draw their attention away. It's better to bulk-up the offense, rather than to rely on the defense."

I gave her a halfhearted smirk. "Well, thanks for that. I didn't trust myself to not screw up." I intertwined my fingers at the base of her neck, grabbing a fistful of hair and pulling her to my mouth. I kissed her and added, "I don't ever want to hurt you."

"Speaking of that." Fantasia unfolded her legs and crawled off my lap. She crossed her arms and stood in front of me. She pinched her face in an effort not to cry. "Why did you agree to talk to her? You promised me you wouldn't."

I ran my hands through my hair. "Yeah, well, she caught me in a vulnerable moment."

She bit her bottom lip and turned her head. "Are you that easily swayed?" she asked under her breath.

She might as well have slapped me. "That's a little harsh, Fantasia. I think I deserve more credit than that."

She tilted her head and pursed her mouth. "I've given you plenty of credit. I trusted you to keep your word."

"Look, Fantasia. I wasn't planning on talking with her. It just kind of happened."

She gave me a sideways glance, and her eyes flashed. *What the hell?* How could she switch emotions so damn quickly?

"Jealous much?" I asked sarcastically.

"Yes, Daniel! I AM jealous!" She jabbed her finger into my chest and glared, "When you make a promise, I expect you to keep it. That's what upsets me the most. I hate being lied to."

I swatted her hand away and made my voice crisp. "You've got to calm down. I haven't lied to you, nor do I ever plan to. I fully intended NOT to talk with her, but she cornered me."

Fantasia snorted and looked down. I stood in a rush and grabbed her chin, forcing her to look me straight on. Her eyes dripped with hostility. "Don't you get it?" I asked before crushing my lips against hers. I pulled away and said, "You are my everything."

Her eyes darted over my face as she tried to read me. I kissed her again. And again. Over and over I tasted her, until she lost her sharpness.

"I don't get how you can be jealous," I said. "You're the most beautiful person on the planet."

"Beauty isn't everything."

"No, it's not." I leaned in and nibbled on her ear. "But you happen to have a mesmerizing heart, too," I murmured. "Now stop acting a fool."

She snickered.

"Sorry," she said.

"No, you're not."

She arched an eyebrow and shrugged. *That's what I thought.*

The next major obstacle was Gram's funeral. Aunt Marie had it scheduled for Saturday, for which I was thankful. Fantasia didn't know it, but I was planning on joining Narivous sooner than arranged. As soon as the reading of the will was over, I would make my intentions known. I couldn't handle any more days pretending. The risk of slipping some forbidden knowledge was too ominous.

Friday passed in like fashion as the day before. I greeted Fantasia in the morning and then headed off to school. I was now an idol in the eyes of my peers for landing the most stunning woman on the face of the planet.

But the day was empty, primarily because Sarah was absent. I wanted the opportunity to tell her goodbye—even if she didn't know that's what I was doing.

After school, I drove out to Sarah's house. Fantasia would be ticked, but I needed closure. I needed to know she was all right. Mrs. Adams answered the door. Her mouth dipped at the sight of me, and she pulled her chin high so I was forced to meet her eyes from a level that was far beneath her. With a haughtiness I didn't think she possessed, she told me Sarah wasn't home and shut the door with a solitary flick of the wrist.

Perhaps the display Fantasia and I had put on caused more damage than I thought.

I had to make peace with the possibility that I'd never see Sarah again. Another hard reality—one of many I'd been forced to deal with.

Saturday, the day of Gram's funeral, passed in a blur. One moment, I'm getting dressed into the suit Fantasia had selected and pressed for me, and the next, I'm standing next to a white coffin, shiny and reflective off the early morning sun. Lavender and yellow roses adorned the top, her favorite flowers. Curious gazes looked at Fantasia in wonderment. I introduced her as my new girlfriend, and she played the role beautifully, never letting go of my hand.

Most of the attendees were from Gram's church and bingo group. Mom couldn't afford the plane ticket, and I would've bet money that Dad was high as a kite somewhere in Maine.

He was a total disappointment.

Eric and his mom were there and, of course, Charlie. Aunt Marie, Lacey, and Dean completed the family lineup. Everyone wore their love on proud display.

Charlie, with his face hanging from grief, kept looking at Fantasia and me. His expression was hard to dissect. It was a blend of sorrow, anger, and fear. Perhaps even a hint of guilt.

It was really anyone's guess.

Lacey came and held my free hand. For a five-year-old, she displayed an impressive amount of stoicism. I spotted her ogling Fantasia with a look of awe.

I leaned down and whispered, "It's not polite to stare."

"I know. But I can't help it, Danny. She's the most beautiful person I've ever seen." She cupped her hand and spoke into my ear. Her warm breath tickled. "She looks like a princess."

"She does look like a princess," I agreed softly.

She leaned in and added, "I think Grandma would've liked her."

The kid sure knew my soft spots. I nodded because my voice had gotten trapped under the lump in my throat. I stood up and tried to regain my composure. Fantasia rested her head on my shoulder and said under her breath, "I would've liked her, too."

It was the little things that mattered the most.

Off in the distance, a spot of white hair ducked behind a tree. Polar, too, had come to pay his last respects.

Afterwards, Aunt Marie, Dean, Charlie, and I sat around Gram's dining room table with her attorney to go over the details of her estate.

Gram had given Dad's share to me. All assets were to be sold and split equally between Aunt Marie and myself, once I reached the age of eighteen. But there was one contingency: the property had to be liquidated—sold in all its entirety—and those monies reinvested into real estate outside of Oregon. Otherwise, all profits would be forfeited to charitable organizations.

Gram's precaution.

The lawyer was clearly perplexed by this unique detail of the will, and said he had inquired about her motives before he'd implemented them into the agreement. Aunt Marie was particularly interested in knowing what these motives were. She was confounded.

"Why would she do that?" she asked. "Are you saying that I can't keep this house? That Daniel can't keep this house?"

"That would be correct. She was very clear with her instructions. When I inquired why, she stated she wanted this done for personal reasons. She refused to give further details."

"That doesn't make any sense. This house is a part of her heritage. It's a part of our history, and now you're saying she wanted it sold and the proceeds split?" She snorted and threw her hands in the air. "You've got to be kidding me!"

Marie looked at me with turbulent eyes.

"Did she say anything to you about this?" she asked me. My tongue contorted, tangled in shock. Aunt Marie never had outbursts. I shook my head, and she turned back to the lawyer.

"We have to sell the house?" she inquired again.

"Yes, that's what she wanted." He cleared his throat.

"And I can only keep that money if I reinvest in real estate outside of Oregon?"

"That's correct," he replied neutrally.

"This is insane!" Dean angrily chimed in. "Surely, we can undo this. This has to be some sort of mistake."

The attorney shifted in his seat as he readjusted his glasses. He looked indignant over his credibility being questioned.

"I understand, Mr. and Mrs. Sullivan, that this information is shocking and a little unorthodox, but I can assure you, this will is binding. Her final wishes are to be followed as requested. I'm confident that this document will hold up in court. Of course, it is well within your rights to take it to a judge—see if it can be revoked—but I doubt you'll have much luck. I can attest that Mrs. Thatcher was in able body and mind when this will was drawn up. I take the drafting of my legal documents very seriously."

Marie and Dean leaned back in their seats, stunned. They collectively sighed and stared at one another. The news was devastating for them.

Gram had indeed done her best to keep her family safe, long before I discovered Narivous' existence. This was her provision. She wanted us to leave.

The attorney went over a few details, much more insignificant now that the bulk of the estate was locked up awaiting a real estate venture outside of Oregon. Charlie was left with family heirlooms, as was Lacey. I didn't care about any of it and left as soon as possible.

Fantasia was waiting for me in the basement. Eagerly, I dove into her arms. She stroked the back of my hair lovingly. As I nuzzled my head into her neck, I spoke with lips pressed against sweetly scented skin.

"Tomorrow," I said.

She pulled away. "What?" she asked.

"I don't want to wait a week. I want to join Narivous tomorrow."

"Are you sure?"

"I've never been more sure of anything in my entire life."

She leaned against my chest to hide the fear in her eyes. "If that's what you want, I'll notify them of your decision."

I nodded. I was ready.

19

SINGLE ACT OF DEFIANCE

So the end had come. When light peeked through the curtains the following day, I instinctively reached for Fantasia. She was there, her body providing comfort in a multitude of ways impossible to define with words.

The hug I pulled her into was strong and firm, yet she stayed rigid as a board. Her gaze locked onto the ceiling. The telltale signs of black tears brimmed at the corners of her eyes.

"What's wrong?" I asked softly.

"This is wrong."

"I need you to be more specific." I reached out and stroked her hair.

She shook her head.

"Talk to me."

The tears that threatened to spill over a moment ago had made a break for it and now flowed freely down her cheeks; I used the back of my hand to wipe them away. She finally looked at me.

"Fantasia, you've got to tell me what you're thinking."

"I'm thinking about you," she said. "I'm thinking this is wrong."

"I've made my decision. There's nothing you can do to change it." And there was nothing I could do to change it. Too many lives were at stake, and I wasn't sure I would've chosen another path had I been given the choice. Fantasia absorbed all my thoughts; she was my world now, and I would take any existence over a life without her.

"I haven't told you everything...."

My heart hammered.

"What?" I asked.

She tucked her pained face in the crook of my shoulder and shook with silent sobs. I held on tighter.

"Thorn's going to use you. She's going to try and turn you against me."

"Fat chance of that."

Fantasia shook her head against my skin.

"Don't underestimate her," she replied. "She has a way of getting people to do what she wants."

"Why would she want me to turn against you?"

"She thinks I was responsible—" she stopped and shivered.

"Responsible for what?"

She sighed deeply while her face was lost against my skin. I wanted to look at her, to gauge her reaction, but Fantasia kept her expression hidden. "A few years back, we recruited a teenager with a strong aura. Thorn was beside herself with excitement. His aura was bright, although not as bright as yours. We became really close. He was in love with me."

I held my breath.

"Were you in love with him?" I whispered.

"I loved him. But I wasn't *in* love with him." She finally unburied her face to meet my eyes. "He hated Thorn. She wanted to make him her pet. He was determined to destroy her. He once told me he thought she was the vilest creature in existence. Thorn found out about his plans and made an example out of him."

"What did she do?"

"What do you think?" she asked. "She killed him after she tortured him."

She bit her lip as dark water hung off her lashes.

"What was his name?"

Fantasia searched my eyes. "What?" she asked.

"What was his name?" *Who was this man, Fantasia, who died for you?*

"Chugknot."

"Chugknot?"

She nodded, and her bottom lip trembled. She bit down to keep it from shaking. She sat up and crossed her legs and started to pick at her pale fingernails.

I sat up and rubbed her back. I wanted to know more about this Chugknot, in particular his relationship with Fantasia. I also wanted to know what he'd been planning to do.

Fantasia sniffled. "Thorn suspected I was in on the treason. She never got the validation she needed and has been keeping a closer eye on me ever since. I think the only reason I'm still alive is I've proven myself valuable. I can heal the injured, and Thorn finds that talent irreplaceable, especially since I'm able to heal the toxin released by the Poison Clan. I know she's requested for Chanticlaim to make another like me—and I think once he does, I'm a goner—but for now, my individuality keeps me safe. Chanticlaim told her he doesn't know how to mimic my qualities. I'm not sure if that's true or not," Fantasia mused. "Either way, my life is completely contingent upon her mood, and I'm certain if she found any evidence against me, I'd be dead in a heartbeat."

A sickening revelation hit me. Fantasia made a lofty gamble when we'd first met. Literally, she'd risked her life for mine.

"I can't believe you'd be so reckless!" I nearly shouted. "Why'd you put yourself in such a position when you found me in the forest? You could've been discovered any time! Not only that, but others know what you did.

Your sisters … your mother … and I'm fairly certain, Chanticlaim. Any of them could expose you or slip up. Do you want to commit suicide?"

"I'm not a coward!" she declared vehemently. "If I die doing the right thing, then I would consider that a noble death. It's a much better alternative than living life as a weasel, committing acts against humanity." Her eyes sparked. "And I know for a fact they wouldn't *expose* me. I'd bet money they'd all die to save me. Plus, I was expecting you to leave, but you're the most bullheaded person I've ever met."

"Daniel," she continued, "she's going to try to collect you, to make you one of her spies. Everyone in Narivous is under her rule, but things are changing. She's noticed, too. She knows her subjects are becoming less tolerant of her domineering ways. She's fearful of an uprising. When she killed Chugknot, she did it to strike fear into everyone who loved him. It was awful."

Fantasia was fully capable of heading an uprising. I recalled all too vividly her treasonous words about destroying Thorn and bringing her evil reign to an end. I highly suspected she was behind Chugknot's death and wondered if she felt guilt for her role. He must've been susceptible to her charms. *No different than me.* Maybe she did hypnotize people.

Perhaps I was her dog on a leash. *Maybe I didn't care.*

"She'll never turn me against you," I said with certainty. "I'll die to protect you."

Fantasia wasn't as sure. "She's very charming and beautiful," she countered. "She'll try and persuade you, or trick you. She's intelligent and cunning, and her questions are often double-sided. She likes to corner people using their own words. Don't be surprised if she requests a private audience for that purpose alone. She'll try to get information from you about me. Trust me, she'll grasp on to a single slip-up in a snap."

"Don't say that!" I groaned. I had no faith in myself. "Tell me what I need to do. What I need to say."

"Flattery. She loves flattery. Agree with every theory she has. Most importantly, don't say a word about anything I've told you—especially anything I've told you about *her*."

My head began to ache. I wrapped my arms tighter around her. "Don't worry, Fantasia," I vowed. "I won't betray you." I was determined to make those words true. Fantasia's life depended on it.

I left a note for Aunt Marie telling her I needed some time to myself. Following my first set of official orders, I grabbed only a few necessities, making it appear as if I fled in a hurry. The overall packing took less than twenty minutes. I remembered to grab a photo album of Gram's. It was the only sentimental item I took.

I had just become a teen runaway—another sad statistic.

Fantasia was incredibly quiet on our trip to Narivous. She had me drive past the gated entrance to another turnoff a mile away. The newer road was narrower and better maintained. We'd been driving for a few minutes when Fantasia turned her penetrating gaze in my direction.

"Remember how I told you my dad committed only one single act of defiance?"

I nodded, intrigued.

"Wanna see what that was?" Her voice rose an octave. "Stop the truck."

I hit the brakes, and my truck groaned to a halt. I turned expectantly towards Fantasia as she reached for the handle. Following her lead, I stepped out.

She stood in the road and stared intently into the surrounding forest. She whistled lightly. Her eyes darted over the heavy timber until they focused on a specific area. Faintly, the sound of rustling foliage crinkled the air. The noise drew nearer.

Her smile was dazzling as she looked at me in triumph.

"I forgot to tell you … there is another great love in my life. He stole my heart the moment I met him."

My brows pulled to the center. She laughed and skipped over to the edge of the road.

"Come on, baby," she said softly. "There's someone I want you to meet."

Movement formed in her line of sight. Trees rustled and limbs snapped. Whatever was coming was monstrous. A shape of a large creature emerged from the shadows.

It was the biggest, darkest horse I'd ever seen—a stallion on steroids. His mane and coat were shiny and lustrous. He had black eyes, as dark as his fur, and they brightened with recognition. He whinnied and quickened his pace to meet Fantasia. I watched in awe as this beast of a horse gently rested his muzzle into Fantasia's waiting hand.

"This is Barney." Fantasia tossed her head over her shoulder. "Single-handedly the most precious gift anyone's ever given me." She stroked the horse's muscular neck and rested her forehead against the bridge of his face. Barney snorted in contentment. His eyes grew soft and lazy.

"He was supposed to go to Amelia's oldest son, bred especially for him. But Cougar saw my affection for him. I remember the day he was born; I fell in love instantly. I hung out at the corral just to be near him, spending every waking moment with this brute." She continued to pet him. "One day, Cougar came up and told me I could have him. It was the greatest thing to ever happen to me."

She paused. "I hadn't realized he'd given him to me without Amelia's permission first. She was livid when she found out and scarred Cougar's face. He has two mirror slashes across each cheek: one for my conception, and the other for this priceless gift." Barney snorted as he nibbled on her hair. Fantasia giggled.

"I was terrified Amelia would take him back and give him to her son. But she never did. She let me keep him. I'll always be eternally grateful for that."

Her eyes shone with love. I approached slowly, intimidated by the large horse. The closer I came, the bigger he grew. The horse had to have been over eight feet tall; my head didn't even reach his shoulder.

"He's very gentle." Fantasia pulled a sugar cube out of her pocket and placed it in my palm. Barney eagerly bent his head and nibbled at the treat. He nuzzled my other hand, looking for more.

"Don't be a pig, Barney," Fantasia chastised as she stroked behind his ear. The laughter that escaped my lips seemed out of place. He was impressive, to say the least. When would this place cease to amaze me?

"All right, buddy. Mommy's got to go now. You run off," Fantasia cooed. Barney didn't budge. "Don't be a stinker. Go now." She made a clicking noise, and Barney finally obeyed. He languishingly walked back into the forest. Evergreens swallowed up his massive frame as he disappeared into the darkness.

"No more stalling," she said after releasing a heavy sigh. "Let's get you to Narivous."

I took my place behind the wheel, and it wasn't long before I hit another clearing, although this one was significantly smaller than the other. Three narrow roads—all evenly spaced—built a trident off the meadow. Fantasia directed me towards the one on the left. I entered cautiously. Heavily packed trees brushed and grazed the body of my truck. It was dark, and I had to turn my lights on.

About two hundred feet in, Fantasia told me to stop. She stepped out and walked to a large Douglas fir. She lifted a square section of bark. It was a façade. Resting beneath the hinged cover sat a keypad. With blurry fingers, she punched in a code and returned to the passenger seat. Movement captured my attention as the road in front of me pulled away. The trap door opened to an underground concrete drive. Dim lights shone from beneath the earth. The road was camouflaged perfectly; my naked eye had detected nothing unusual about it. Now it had vanished, and in its place stood a large, consuming hole, waiting to devour us.

"Do you need me to drive?" Fantasia asked.

"I think I got it," I said and tried to balance my nerves.

"Impressive, huh?"

I nodded.

"You have no idea," she said smugly.

"I can't even imagine."

"We aim to impress."

I exhaled a huge breath of air. "Okay, let's get this show on the road." I carefully pressed on the gas and directed my old truck below the surface.

My hands, strongly compressed, gripped the steering wheel. I was surrounded by concrete as the tunnel descended on a steep decline. I wondered how far below we were going. Eventually, the road widened and led to a parking garage. As I pulled my car into a vacant spot, I stared in wonder. The lot was loaded with vehicles.

The variety was remarkable. New, high-end vehicles sat next to lower-end, beat-up clunkers. I even spotted a few pricey collectables. I let out a low whistle in appreciation. Fantasia rolled her eyes.

"Boys and their cars," she said in disgust. "I don't get it." She grew serious. "Look, from here on out, you need to watch everything you say. There are cameras everywhere. Someone's always listening."

I nodded grimly and stepped out.

"Leave your stuff in the truck. We'll get it later," Fantasia said tersely. I followed unhurriedly in an attempt to admire the surrounding collection. My eyes flickered from one vehicle to the next.

I wasn't paying attention to where we were going until a hand grabbed the sleeve of my jacket and tugged.

"Would you stop gawking?" Fantasia hissed. She was on edge, and it showed.

"Sorry," I mumbled, not wanting to summon Fantasia's wrath.

My apology softened her a bit.

"Look, Daniel. I don't mean to be short. But I need you to focus. Remember...." She let her voice drift off. I understood and composed myself, just as a door chimed open.

We'd been standing in front of an elevator.

Steel doors trapped us inside a mobile casing with warm decor. Three walls were wallpapered, and classic music played overhead.

Fantasia gave me a tight smile.

We came to a stop, and the doors separated. Two people were waiting for us: Torti and Chanticlaim. They stood uncomfortably in a sterile sitting room. The windowless reception area had plants growing from every corner—thriving despite the lack of sunlight. Generic paintings adorned the walls, and two tan, leather couches with colorful pillows sat angled near the far corner. I wasn't sure, but I thought I heard the sound of rushing water.

"She's in a bad mood," Torti said immediately.

Fantasia looked to the corner of the room where a camera was mounted. Its optical lens pointed towards the elevator entrance. Fantasia raised her eyebrows.

"It's shut off for maintenance," Chanticlaim replied. "It's safe to talk here."

Torti turned to me. "Daniel, you'll need to be on your best behavior. Things are really bad right now. Thorn's in a sour mood." For the first time, I saw real fear in Torti's eyes.

"If they ask about the pills I gave you, tell them they were big, round, and yellow—the size and shape of an aspirin," Chanticlaim said uneasily.

My head started to spin.

Fantasia glanced worriedly at me before turning to Torti. "How bad is she?" she asked.

Before Torti could answer, a door to the left flung open.

Two men stepped into the room. One was tall and slender, just shy of a giant. He had shocking red hair that fell across his forehead. The other was blocky and thick like a bulldog, with a military-style haircut.

"What's going on in here?" the red giant demanded, a scowl etched across his face.

"I just came to greet my sister," Torti replied innocently.

The man sneered at her, baring his teeth. He reminded me of a snarling wolf.

Fantasia stiffened. Torti threw me a warning look before taking charge.

"Now, where are your manners?" Torti chastised. She waved in my direction. "Are you not going to introduce yourselves?"

"He hasn't joined Narivous yet," the giant responded. "Introductions may not be necessary."

I tensed up. *Why would he say that?* My nerves fired in alarm, especially after I glanced at the three beside me. They all wore wide-eyed shock on their faces; Fantasia even blanched.

This was bad.

Very, very bad.

"What's that supposed to mean?" Chanticlaim asked.

"Thorn's upset. I wouldn't be surprised to see this go south very fast. And when I say south, I mean six feet under."

My feet turned to gelatin. Chanticlaim and Fantasia steadied me.

"This is Polar's grandson!" Fantasia barked. "You need to show some respect! You shouldn't mess with us, Cheetoh."

So this was the infamous Cheetoh, the man who attacked Eric. I took an instant disliking to him.

Cheetoh shrugged his shoulders as though my life meant little to him.

"We need to get a move on," the Bulldog finally spoke up. "The longer we wait, the more upset she's going to become."

Everyone concurred, and we walked towards the exit. Cheetoh led the way, while the Bulldog trailed behind. Fantasia lagged to talk to the stocky guard.

"Be honest, Splint. Is it really as bad as Cheetoh says?" Her whisper barely reached my ears.

I looked behind me as a worried expression flickered across Splint's face. He tried to recover, but Fantasia didn't miss a beat. I assumed she'd read his mind, but maybe her gifts were limited to the individual—or the level of her translucent phase.

"It's bad, Fancy. I think she's planning something, but no one knows what. She's been hiding out since his grandmother came to Narivous." He pointed at me. "No one has seen or spoken with her, except for the other Sevens."

"Shut up back there!" Cheetoh shouted. "I don't want to hear your gossip."

Splint quieted as we stepped into a hallway made of stone. There was one door directly in front of us. It reminded me of a holding cell. Fantasia patted my back and turned to Torti with an inquiring look. Torti met her gaze and subtly shook her head. It amazed me how intuitive they were towards each other. Subconsciously, I began preparing for the worst. Cheetoh reached the door in front of us. Before he turned the knob, he looked directly at me.

"We have a short walk ahead of us. When we get there, you'll need to bow to Thorn. Go as low as you can. Don't speak unless spoken to, and keep your responses short and respectful."

I nodded.

"I'm telling you this now because I'm not sure I'll get another chance." His ambivalent attitude altered into something that resembled empathy.

"Um, thank you," I said.

He continued. "Don't rise from your bow until she directs you to, and keep your wits about you." He paused before reluctantly adding, "I wish you luck. You're going to need it."

Cheetoh pulled the door open and we stepped out.

20

TRANSFORMATION

We exited out of a giant rock mountain. It caught me off guard, and it took a moment to gather my bearings. The door was lost amongst the ivy and ridged planes of stone. Another beautifully crafted façade. The sound of rushing water rumbled overhead. I craned my neck and spotted a majestic waterfall pouring over a cliff, landing into a river thirty feet away. Droplets of mist reached my skin, the coolness providing relief for my frayed nerves.

"This way," Cheetoh directed as he ushered us along.

We walked on a well-preserved path fabricated of gray paver stones. The trail was elegant against the backdrop of the forest with its lush greenery and emerald hues. The farther we walked, the more unusual the woods became. Trees grew impossibly large, unnatural, and tightly together, blocking all exposure to the sky. Towering ferns sprouted well above my head. By the time we reached two wrought-iron gates flanking a stone fence, the supernatural force was obviously clear. Even the soil was bunched into miniature hills from super-sized roots. Enchantment forced their overgrowth. Thorn's magic was everywhere.

Two giant men with identical images stood on each side of the gate. In their hands, they held spears. Those ridiculous weapons seemed downright barbaric, and almost made me laugh. But my impending death stifled any humor. Funny how that works. The guards were blond, blue-eyed, and extremely tall. Much like Cheetoh.

Their expressions were friendly as they nodded hello.

"This is Chaze and Taze," Fantasia introduced.

"S'up," they greeted in unison. Mischievous smiles spread across their faces. Their appearances were indistinguishable. *Identical twins.*

"This is Daniel," Fantasia continued.

One of them—Chaze, I think—rolled his eyes.

"Of course that's Daniel," he said. "Who else would it be?"

They both smirked as they opened the gate.

As we walked through, one of them said, "Welcome to Narivous" before closing the door and locking us in. I'd just walked through the gates of Hell, sealed in by a duo of blue-eyed devils.

And Thorn was Satan.

The thought of eternal torment was bold—but nothing compared to the city of Hades. The vision before me rendered me dumb.

I had stepped into a fairy tale.

To describe it as beautiful would be an insult. It was so much more than that.

It was perhaps the most picturesque town I'd ever seen. Buildings of cobblestone, with roofs tailored in copper, laced throughout the village. The bronzy metal held a fuzzy layer of mossy patina. Plants and ivy rose along the siding, creeping over shutters and enclosing webbed windows. Each structure varied slightly—some simplistic, others more elaborate—but all consistent with the same design pattern. The same as an old European village.

With the exception of a few sparse areas, the entire city was shrouded in darkness, as no sunlight escaped beyond the aerial leaves and needles. I understood the purpose: complete and utter concealment. No planes overhead would detect anything out of place, as the evergreens provided the necessary camouflage to keep the city undetected. It was quite remarkable. Flowers of every variety bloomed throughout. It didn't matter the season. Combinations that would've never grown together in a natural setting germinated in Narivous. Climbing roses clambered up homes and sprouted around window-boxes with exotic orchids in full bloom. Tulips, daffodils, hydrangeas, irises, and lilies—along with others that I'd never seen before with names I couldn't begin to guess—offset the blinding greenery.

The paver path interlaced between all the homes, connecting them with a cohesive unity. In the center of it all stood a gigantic stone fountain. An angelic woman wearing a crown of thorns stood frozen in unyielding splendor. Water flowed from behind her granite exterior, emerging from a broken tree stump made of rock. Her hands, arched open, had roses blooming upwards from exposed palms.

My thunderstruck eyes tried to absorb the scene. It was almost too much for my weak senses.

But it was the building to our left that was by far the most breathtaking. A castle of medieval multitude stood tall and overshadowing. Bits of gray slate peeked through the ivy that wound its way up the walls. Windows, with intricate crosshatched diamonds, flanked the wood door that domed at the peak. An organic scaffolding of roses framed the threshold where above it all was an "N" erected of stained glass. Without a doubt, it was the most intimidating building I'd ever seen. It was beautiful, frightening, and fit for royalty.

The grandeur of Narivous was formidable, but it was the silence of the town—and the lack of inhabitants—that made my stomach curdle. It concerned the others as well. They warily peered around the vacant city.

Silently, we all approached the stone fortress with subdued resolve. Even Cheetoh's arrogance evaporated. Chanticlaim's face was a mix of hardened focus and unease. His jaw flexed, and his eyes flashed.

Chanticlaim was worried.

A desperate hand tugged at my sleeve. Fantasia stood close and whispered in my ear, "Don't look up in the hallway."

"Why?"

"Just don't. Please."

A feathered smirk crossed Cheetoh's face, his sharp ears amused by Fantasia's warning.

When we got to the large door, it swung open without prompt. We were expected.

Once again, I was taken by surprise. The entrance to the castle was a lot cozier than I anticipated. A spiral staircase descended from above with an ornate newel post transitioning into an elegant curvature of polished oak. A chandelier hung from the vaulted ceiling. It dripped with moss and hovered over creamy, leather couches. And, like everywhere else in Narivous, plants thrived.

I was so focused on the architecture, I barely noticed a frazzled Dreams and Camille waiting for us. Dreams went directly to Fantasia and gave her an eager hug.

Dreams whispered something in her ear as Camille stepped forward and handed Fantasia her mask. I cringed as she placed it over her face, hiding her beauty in such an unnatural way.

A jab stung the center of my back and nearly knocked me off my feet—Cheetoh's special way of capturing my attention.

"Come on, mouth-breather," he grumbled. "Let's get this show on the road."

We stepped through an exit beneath the staircase and entered a windowless, stone corridor. Three doors, evenly spaced, rested on each side of the hall. They led up to a pair of french doors. The telltale emblems revealed their owners: a snake, an eye, claw marks, a spider, flames, and a snowflake. The last held a rose with prominent thorns.

Lighted sconces of cast iron illuminated the dank hallway. Shadows loomed in every corner, out of reach of the insufficient lighting. My eyes gravitated upwards, despite Fantasia's warning.

I froze in absolute revulsion.

Lined up neatly, on shelves of concrete, were human skulls. Hundreds of them—all various sizes—including skulls of children. My adrenaline pumped as my stomach revolted against its will. Bile crept into my throat, the acidy taste repugnant and sour. I couldn't pull my gaze from the sinister image. Sheer terror seized my muscles. It wasn't until Fantasia's hand gripped my own that I broke from my paralysis.

I didn't ask about the skulls. It was too late anyhow. Together, we approached the door with the rose emblem. We halted in front of it. A sense of doom shadowed my core. Cheetoh turned towards me.

"You ready?" he asked and then turned the knob.

A series of events happened at once. I was herded into a large, open room. Before my eyes could focus, a hand forcefully pushed me to my knees. Fantasia was directly behind me, and I suspected she was the culprit. It was a good move on her part.

Everyone was on their knees. I thought I was to bow, but apparently that level of respect wouldn't suffice. The room was overflowing with Velores, their bodies pressed to the floor. The tension was palpable. I even detected a few whimpers. We'd stepped into a war zone instigated by an all-powerful, tyrant ruler.

From my peripheral view, I spotted Cheetoh on the floor next to Splint. He wore a look of irritation as he crushed his body against the smooth marble.

That's when I saw her. She was standing before me, regal in her dark, purple cape with a crown of golden thorns resting on her head. Her probing gaze focused in my direction. I vaguely made out others sitting in thrones behind her, but all of my attention was captivated by her fearsome presence. She didn't have to say a word. I could feel her anger; it resonated off her like a black aura.

My mouth grew dry as I held my breath awaiting her command.

Thorn leaned down next to me, so close that her breath warmed my cheek. I could smell her scent of earth and roses, and I hated myself for liking it.

"I've been waiting for you, Daniel," she whispered into my ear. Her voice, too, was intoxicating. A buzzing sound resonated in my ears—similar to my encounter with Frigid. I worried that I'd lose my mental faculties and become a victim of this magic. What if she was able to trick me, and as a result, I spilled some deleterious information about Fantasia? The thought took me beyond terror; I'd entered a new paradox of fear.

I was bewildered by her appearance. Her outwardly shell was as Fantasia had said: beautiful. It didn't match her horrid personality. Her heart-shaped face was framed with auburn hair that hung in soft waves. Bright, hazel irises, flawless skin of ivory satin, and lips pink with health twitched with amusement. Yet, unlike Fantasia's warm and open eyes, Thorn's held the distinct look of cunning. This woman's life-force was strong and distinctly *lethal*. With an undecipherable age and obvious allure, Thorn's look presented a conundrum of information.

Evil was supposed to look evil, not angelic.

But her beauty quickly dissipated as she progressed into her translucent phase. Her eyes started to shine like beacons, while her pupils devoured the hazel of her irises, leaving behind black, inky pools. Her skin turned green and shattered with cracks.

Instinctively, I closed my eyes.

Behind me, Fantasia's hand rested against my calf, providing comfort in my moment of terror.

"Open your eyes," Thorn whispered. "Look at your future. This is what you'll become."

I couldn't manage the task. My lids had fused together. It wasn't until Fantasia squeezed my leg that I found the strength to pry them apart.

Thorn sensed my fear from the whites of my eyes and grinned with malice. Her entire presence looked grotesquely absurd. "Get up," she ordered.

With disobliging legs, I stumbled ungracefully to my feet. She smirked.

"Look around you," she said.

I let my eyes roam. Behind her, the other six rulers sat. All of them were daydream beautiful. I recognized Frigid—now in a more natural state—as well as my grandfather and uncles. Frigid's sisters, and my aunts by marriage, sat in thrones lined to the right of Thorn's. Ember was positioned closest, with Scream tiered behind her and Frigid completing the lineup. Scream, Plague's wife, had midnight hair and smooth, powdery skin. Her eyes, dark and insightful, flickered nervously between Plague and me. Plague reached out and gave her shoulder a squeeze.

Whereas Scream's hair was black, Ember's was red as light. All the males stood slightly behind their royal wives.

I was able to determine who was who, simply by the elaborate jewelry adorning their person. Aside from Scream's spider earrings, Ember wore a tiara fashioned in flames. To the left of Thorn's empty throne rested Amelia, followed by Serpent and Dolly. Dolly's collar was dressed with an eye necklace, while Serpent's cobra cuff coiled up her arm.

Of all the rulers, Amelia was the least feminine. With short, spiky hair and slender sharp features, she had an animalistic look that—at the moment—was frosted over with boredom. She wore a broach of claw marks on her black jumpsuit, and tapped her fingers with impatience on the arm of her chair.

That's when Thorn coached my eyes away with a sweeping gesture of her arms to the other Velores resting in submission.

I gaped at the image of tightly packed bodies nearly kissing the ground. Thorn, once again, moved closer to my ear. She leaned in and breathed, "I rule here. No one goes against my authority."

I nodded, while keeping my eyes trained on the motionless figures. Climbing roses burgeoned around the room, growing at an impossible speed. As though the plants were alive and limber as snakes, they flowed fluidly, moving with a mind of their own. The vines slithered through tense bodies, interweaving under and over them. Rapidly, the scene turned greener and browner as the branches—with unnaturally large and threatening thorns—reached out to cover all vacant space. Within mere seconds, every area was covered.

Thorn grasped my arm firmly, her grip intrusive and volatile. I stepped back, despite myself.

That was a bad move.

Vines latched on to all my appendages. The strength of their starchy flesh collapsed me to my knees as the creepers, acting like fingers, wrapped tighter around my wrists, ankles, torso, and most worriedly, my neck. Warm, sticky blood oozed from wounds where thorns had violated my skin. My ribs tightened as air was blocked off by the deepened grip. The pain tore through nerve endings, spiking my adrenaline and forcing my heart into a faster rhythm. A trotting tempo.

Faint words of protest drifted from where the other rulers sat. But the buzzing in my head had grown stronger, and combined with the lack of oxygen, I was unable to dissect what was being said. Black orbs darted across my vision. The vines continued to tighten. My death was imminent, and I longed for it. I wanted the pain to stop.

My thoughts drifted to Gram, her image dancing before my splotchy sight. This is what she must've experienced before Polar interceded. I felt gratitude for Polar's compassionate intervention and pure, raw hatred for the woman who had caused her such pain.

And then I thought of Fantasia. She'd be the last image I resurrected before my death. Her lavender eyes, her skin, her scent—all memories of her flowed through my fibrous being. Her warmth intermingled with my deadening senses as darkness descended over my consciousness.

Then it all went away.

The vines retreated, their release so sudden, I hit the ground with a dull thud. The air that pervaded my lungs burned on arrival. I choked and gasped. The cool marble was soothing against my irritated skin. I laid like a dead fish atop the sterile floor.

That's when I heard snippets of an argument. Polar, Plague, and Ferno, along with their wives, were protesting adamantly. My vision, out of focus, saw Plague's wife approach Thorn. Her dark, lovely eyes were wide with alarm as she held her palms up, submissively trying to persuade. Her lips moved, but my swelled brain couldn't pick up any sounds. Thorn's eyes whipped back to me, and she started to shout.

Scream retreated back to her place amongst the others, while I tried to focus on the words escaping Thorn's lips.

"GET UP! GET UP NOW!" she was yelling at me. Every muscle protested, but I managed to stagger to my feet.

Thorn's alighted gaze glided over her cowering citizens.

"THIS IS MY KINGDOM!" she shouted at no one in particular. "I DEMAND OBEDIENCE!" her voice boomed. She slammed tightly folded fists into her thighs, beating herself in anger. Then, in a snap, she loosened, relaxing her fingers to bring them to her lips. Her cheek bunched where a smile started to bloom. She began walking in circles around me, her eyes scanning the room before her.

"It seems you've all forgotten your loyalty." Her voice transitioned from loud and demanding, to soft and menacing. Even with my blurry vision, I noticed backs go ridged. I looked behind me, just as shiver flowed through Fantasia's shoulders. She remained so low, her stomach rested against the ground.

"I think a reminder is needed," Thorn said quietly, causing some to look up in alarm. Everyone remained dead silent.

Thorn stopped pacing as her eyes penetrated on a back I recognized.

"Everyone, please. May I have your attention." Thorn's order came out silky. Still kneeling, everyone lifted their heads. Countless eyes pivoted between Thorn and me, all expectant and wary.

"Reminders are an unfortunate necessity. This is not an easy decision for me." Her glowing eyes softened. A sweeping chill froze my marrow as she reached out for Tony. Confusion flitted across his face as he met her grasp. Behind me, most of the remaining Seven fidgeted with uncertainty.

Thorn had not included them in her plans.

I knew, almost instantly, what she was going to do and readied myself to try and stop it. But as I was preparing to shout "No," the buzzing in my head hit a pinnacle, snapping my mind shut and completely hindering my ability to speak. Unfamiliar images flashed through my head. I saw Fantasia and Barney, Polar and my uncles; I saw Gram's body lying amongst the briars. Someone in the room had hijacked my brain, paralyzing my body and controlling my mind. Apparently, Chanticlaim's "Brain Blockers" didn't work on the Doppelgänger clan leader. I was certain she was the only one capable of such power.

So I remained frozen as I was forced to watch, in silent horror, the destruction of my friend. The vines that had recently restricted me now climbed up Tony's torso. I saw the exact moment when he knew what was coming. It created a memory that would haunt me forever.

Thorn forced the vines into his mouth and ears. Tony struggled against the sharp vises and tried to call out, but his screams were silenced by the briars as they dug deep into his body. The prodding continued until the light in his eyes faded. We locked gazes as the last flicker of life left. The vines exited through his nose and eye sockets; they even pushed past the skin of his stomach. Tony's body was destroyed from the inside. Thorn, with a tasteless sense of morbid humor, forced the roses into bloom, creating color beyond his exit wounds. His now lifeless corpse looked like a flower garden of the richest rosebuds.

She walked over and looked down on his lifeless form. "Cheetoh," she barked.

Cheetoh sprang to his feet and approached Thorn. She reached behind her cloak and produced a knife. "Do the honors," she ordered as she placed the blade in his hand.

With methodical precision, Cheetoh reached down and grabbed his hair—now sticky with purplish blood—and began to cut away at the fleshy remnants of Tony's neck, decapitating him. Thorn reached out and collected the severed head, holding Tony by his brown locks for everyone to see.

"THIS IS YOUR REMINDER," she shouted. "THIS IS PUNISH-MENT FOR THE TRANSGRESSIONS OF OTHERS." She turned to face Polar and gave him a tight smile. Gram's face flashed before my vision, a clear indication that Polar was being punished for her knowledge. Without saying a word, my hijacker was doing an efficient job translating informa-tion to me.

She returned the head to Cheetoh.

"Would you be a dear and place this on my mantel with the others." Her voice sweet, her beauty returned. She ordered Splint to stand. "And Splint, please remove the remains. See to it that he receives a proper burial." Splint grabbed Tony's body and threw the headless corpse over his shoul-der. Cheetoh, holding the head in the crook of his arm, performed a per-functory bow. Splint tipped his head in respect as well before they exited out the door.

"Please, leave now, my darlings. This has been a hard day for us all. Remember, we are a family, and the rules are set to protect us. Everything I do is a direct result of my love for you." Thorn waved her dismissal. People flocked away in a hurry, exiting out a number of doors.

She once again focused her attention on me.

"I didn't want to do that, Daniel. He was turned without my permission, and I don't think he was the right fit. Do you understand?" She reached out to cup my face. I wanted to spit and curse, but my body was still held hostage. Outsiders would've never known that I found her touch repulsive.

Without my permission, my hand reached up and rested atop Thorn's. I pushed my head lightly against her palm. It disgusted me, but the drone in my head refused to relinquish its hold.

"It hurts, but I'll make it my duty to understand. I want you to like me. I don't want to be the source of any trouble." The words I spoke were not my own; the culprit had stolen my voice. Thorn's eyebrows shot up in surprise. This clearly wasn't the reaction she was expecting, but it was a reaction that pleased her. Rightfully so, she remained skeptical and continued to test me.

"So do you not care that I just killed your friend?" she asked. I sensed a trap, and apparently, so did my mental captor.

"I do. But I know what's at stake," my voice replied. It sounded weak and docile. *Scared.*

"And what's at stake?"

"Everything," I said humbly. She arched her eyebrow, as my controller continued forcing words from my mouth that did not belong to me. "My family, for example. My friends. I know you have the final say and that you're in charge. I also know what you're offering me. I don't want to jeopardize that."

Thorn's eyes lit up. She smiled with satisfaction. "Ah! So you choose self-preservation over self-sacrifice. Wise, Daniel. Wise." She chewed on her lip thoughtfully and yanked her hand away. "I don't know if I trust you, though." She leaned in and examined my expression. The gold in her hazel eyes shimmered. "But I suppose it doesn't matter. If you upset me, I'll make sure you pay the ultimate price. Do you understand?"

My head bobbed, and my voice leaked out. "Yes, your Majesty." My subservient tone earned me a tentative smile. I felt my face pinch and lips pull into a line—a look that would've resembled sorrow. Any outsider would have assumed I was broken.

"I hope so, Daniel." Thorn softened a fraction. "I hate having to perform executions." A flicker of regret washed over her features. It almost seemed genuine. She turned her head and pushed back a lock of hair. When she glanced back, her eyes were warm. "I'm sure this event will hurt for many years to come. But time will lessen your pain," she nodded, convinced of her own statement.

Thorn took a step towards me and cupped my face. She pressed her forehead against my own. "Follow me loyally, Daniel, and I will forever treat you with the greatest love. And ..." she leaned in to my ear and whispered, "I promise that if you behave yourself, I'll keep your family protected."

Her warning was clear.

I nodded without my consent. I was simply a living robot in the control of a gamer.

"Now, let's get you transformed. I can't wait to see the Velore you'll become. It'll be wonderful to have you added to our family. Dolly?" She turned around to meet the gaze of the Doppelgänger clan leader. Dolly, a porcelain doll come to life, stood up. She possessed golden curls and vibrant, blue eyes. Her cloak—the color of a cloudless sky—was draped over an elaborate lace gown. She reminded me of Delilah, except more intimidating. Locking eyes with her confirmed my suspicion: she was my puppet master. There was an invisible thread linking her mind with my own.

"Yes, Thorn," she said sweetly.

"Read his mind, please."

Dolly widened her eyes and tipped the corners of her mouth down remorsefully. "I'm sorry, Thorn, but his mind is blocked."

Thorn groaned. She looked to Chanticlaim, who was waiting beside Fantasia and her sisters.

"When does that stupid medication wear off?" she asked tersely, her masquerade of friendliness gone.

Chanticlaim held up his hands in innocence. "I don't know. That was the first time I'd tried it."

Thorn's face pinched in disgust. She grabbed the bridge of her nose in irritation.

"FINE! Just get him out of here. If this turns out badly, Chanticlaim, I'm holding you responsible." Her finger jutted in his direction.

She turned on her heel and began to walk towards an exit door in the back.

"What clan should we make him?" Chanticlaim yelled behind her.

"I DON'T CARE!" she shouted as the door slammed closed.

As soon as she was out of sight, the buzzing in my head quieted to a hum. I could now move but was fearful to do so.

Plague, irate, stepped past Polar and Ferno and grabbed my sleeve. He started to drag me out of the room. Scream followed closely behind.

Everything happened quickly after that.

"What are you doing?" Polar asked.

Plague didn't respond and continued to tug me along. We spilled into the hallway, and he rushed me towards the door with the spider emblem. He pushed me inside, the force so sudden, I lost my footing and fell to my knees.

A troupe of people trailed in afterwards. Plague stopped to stand over me. Polar and Ferno, alarmed, stood back with the others, which included Chanticlaim and Fantasia—her mask freshly removed. I heard a lock clamp shut and spotted Ember pressing against the door. She and Scream held knowing smiles, while everyone else wore veils of confusion. Scream stepped forward, creating a toxic barrier between myself and the others.

My instincts told me to run, but my body seized up.

"What are you doing?" Polar repeated.

Plague turned around and glared at his brother from his one visible eye, and then removed his glove.

"NO!" Polar shouted. He lunged towards Plague, but it was too late. Plague reached down and touched my cheek. Everything went dark as the toxin quickly penetrated my skin. The excruciating pain was beyond measure.

He'd chosen my death. He had selected the forbidden combination.

I started to slip away.

EPILOGUE

The next few hours passed in a haze. Only snippets of information pervaded through my distressed consciousness.

I recalled hearing an argument, the voices heated. The symphony of sounds made my ears ring, as one voice shouted out at another.

"This is forbidden!"

"What will she do when she finds out?"

"She will not let him live."

"He will be indestructible. How will she kill him?"

The voices faded in and out as my veins exploded with heat. I heard a loud scream and realized it was me. Someone reached over my face and covered my mouth. A rotting hand held me down as I withered in agony and tried to call out.

My struggle was futile as I slipped into unconsciousness again, the darkness a welcomed relief to my pain.

When I awoke a second time, everything was infinitely different.

I had transformed.

My first breath as an immortal was the most intense of my existence. The air was unnatural in my lungs. It burned as it exploded through my airways.

When my eyes shot open, I discovered newly refined vision, every image enhanced. I could easily identify dust particles dancing midair. The dim light held prisms of color.

Sitting up, dead vines fell off my skin; the starchy branches turned to dust as I picked them away. They were black against my newly transformed hand, which I held up for inspection. It looked much the same as before, except the color of my nails had turned ashen. My skin had paled, too, and was almost pearlescent.

I marveled at my new flesh and started to look around for a mirror. That's when I realized I had an audience.

Standing off to the side stood Polar, Plague, Scream, Chanticlaim, and Fantasia. They stood motionless as they surveyed me with wary eyes.

I jolted at their reflections. Their auras now visible, each held a color that tinted their skin. It was a subtlety that my sharpened sight was unable to miss. My face froze in shock while they watched me with concerned expressions.

"Thorn is angry," Plague spoke first. He pointed to the black, dead vines. "She tried to kill you before the transformation had taken full effect. She was too late."

Instantly, my eyes went to Fantasia, worried she would somehow suffer the consequences of this forbidden alteration. Polar understood my train of thought.

"I don't think you have much to worry about now," Polar said. "You are perhaps the most dangerous Velore ever created." He looked to Plague, his expression pleased. Plague gave him a satisfied smile. "I've never seen her so shaken up. She won't do anything to rile you, at least not yet."

"Not yet?" My voice came out gritty, the words like sandpaper on the back of my throat.

Chanticlaim stepped forward. "She has no way to go against you. She can't use her vines to devour you, she can't puncture your skin without releasing toxic gas, she can't even touch you without causing herself extreme pain. The antidote to your toxin rests in the touch of your blood relatives and their wives." Chanticlaim's voice came out smooth and assured. He looked at Fantasia. "And it rests in the healing powers of Fantasia, all of which I've been unsuccessful in duplicating."

My gut told me Chanticlaim was intentionally unsuccessful. I remained hopeful that his brilliance would remain blocked.

"With that said, you need to be exceptionally careful. Your touch is dangerous. Some of us can survive it, all of the Deadbloods for example; others, it will destroy. It depends on the Velore. Only the antidotes can touch you without pain." Chanticlaim's voice was somber as he went over the specifics.

My mind leapt to Fantasia. As long as my touch didn't harm her, I figured I could cope with losing the physical touch of others.

"Also, when you turn into your translucent phase, you will be much like your aunt." Chanticlaim's hand waved to Scream. Her smile was utterly smug as her gaze rested on me. "This, too, warrants caution. When she has fully transformed, the toxins try and escape any route they can. That's why we call her Scream. Her voice is deadly. She can let out a wail that will kill every living thing in its path. Your uncle doesn't possess this gift; he only holds the toxin, since the toxin wasn't what killed him."

Plague formed a gun with his index finger and thumb and mimed a shooting action towards his covered face. *Thanks for the visual, bud.*

"You live how you die," Scream spoke up, her voice harmonious. She walked over to me and grabbed my hand. Bare skin to bare skin, there was warmth in her flesh. She wasn't rotting like my uncle, and I wasn't sure why.

But now I had all the time in the world to find out.

She leaned down and pressed her ruby red lips to my forehead in a motherly gesture. I closed my eyes.

"Welcome to Narivous," she whispered as her eyes gave a brilliant flash.

I was home.

❧ THE LEGEND ☙

Many years ago, a small boy mastered the powers of invisibility. He learned that when his father came home angry to hide in the farthest corner of their shack, where light from their candles lost its reach. If his father was irritated with his mother, he'd take cover under their table to obstruct the sight of flailing fists and inky blood. He used his hands, tightly pressed to each ear, to block out malicious outbursts spewed in fits of temper. And when his father was upset with him, he'd run to the fields under the cover of night and let the hollow of an oak tree shield him.

One particular bout—when the boy was barely taller than a blade of wheat grass—his father came home and stirred a storm. The boy had spilled a pail of milk, and it brought on a rage that forced him to take refuge outdoors. He didn't return home until the light of dawn had blanketed the earth in shades of gold.

His father was sitting in a rocking chair when the door creaked open.

"There you are, boy," his father said. The child took a tentative step inside. His father's eyes were maddeningly red from lack of sleep. "You think it's okay to run out on your whoopin'?"

The boy hugged himself and looked to the floor, too frightened to meet his father's accusing stare.

"Come here," the father beckoned.

When the child didn't budge, his father sprang from his chair and grabbed him with angry hands. "When I tell you to come to me, you COME! You ran, and now you'll pay the consequences." He dragged the boy to their lone bedroom, a volatile grip digging deep into his arm. He flung back the curtain with a theatrical flair.

"This is what you did," he whispered as the boy stared with horrified eyes. The bedding of straw had transformed into needles of reddish gore. His mother lay atop—her face caved and misshapen—with one leg bent unnaturally at the knee. Her chocolate hair was a stiff helmet of dried blood.

"She took your punishment," the father leaned down and spoke in his ear. "And I made her suffer twice for it. Now, if you'd been a good boy and taken it like a man, I would've been kinder. Now go give your mommy a kiss and tell her 'thank you.'"

He gave him a push. The boy shuffled forward while his eyes washed over the broken figure. He was relieved to see her face held color. She wasn't dead.

He rested his small hands along the lines of her cheekbones and hesitated.

"Go on," his father ordered. "Give her a kiss."

The boy leaned in and pressed his lips to her lukewarm cheek. A wheeze from deep in her throat clambered out.

"Tell her thank you," his father barked, with a smile tugging on his lips.

The boy whispered "Thank you," while tears threatened to dart down his face. He couldn't cry in front of his father; that would earn him a trail of bruises.

His father took two hefty steps and rested his hand on the child's shoulder. "This is your fault," he said. "And mark my words: you'll wish you'd taken the beating." He flexed his fingers, dimpling the skin above the boy's collarbone before stomping out of the room.

His father was a man of his word.

The boy's childhood became infinitely harder—it was filled with abuse and haunting memories. He forgot how to smile. His mother never walked without a limp. She dissolved until she was nothing more than a breathing vessel, void of emotion. Empty.

Then came the day she surrendered to death. She walked into the river—her arms stretched towards the heavens—and let the water wash over her. She resurfaced downstream a few days later, her body bloated and swollen, her eyes truly vacant.

Time slipped painfully by as the boy grew from a small child into a young man. His heart hardened with each passing year. The cruelty intensified, the abject torture teaching him sinister values of the darkest curriculum. He learned many things from his father. He learned that fear was an effective weapon. He learned that control brought power. He learned how to hate.

Most importantly, he learned the value of self-preservation.

By the time the boy reached adulthood—motherless and unloved—he'd become a true product of his environment. *Diabolical.* Despite the decay in his heart and his decrepit foundation, he possessed handsome looks and used them to his advantage. Women fought for his attention, certain they could bring a smile to the handsome man with the foreboding scowl. Combined with superior intelligence and his talent of adaptability, he held all the tools to manipulate others. This gave him an edge, and he wielded this edge like a weapon.

Simply, if he inflicted pain on others—broke them with his powerful spirit—then he'd no longer be a target. He'd become untouchable. This brought great satisfaction and his first sense of peace.

It was addictive.

And it was then that he understood his father's unconventional methods. Now he appreciated them.

Time—the one aspect of his life he couldn't control—began to take its toll. His small hometown was overrun with inferior humans with weak intellect and simplistic beliefs. They were his subordinates, fated to live as sheep, content to achieve nothing. That was their future, not his. Determined to accomplish more, he set out to travel the world and discover his destiny.

Years abroad groomed him and enhanced his manipulative strategies. It made him stronger, smarter, more dangerous.

Then, one fateful night, a miracle happened. He stumbled across a glorious secret—an ingredient so powerful, he was certain it would cheat death by stopping the effects of time altogether.

Immortality.

He'd conquer death, and then the world. He made a solemn vow that he would build an empire, one in which he held total control. This would right the wrongs that had been bestowed upon him as a small child. He would be king in a world of his own making.

Grandeur of a better life—now so closely at hand—was withheld by one major obstacle: he didn't know how to use the ingredient.

That's when his mind went into overdrive.

First and foremost, he decided to treat his cure using a scientific process, testing it on subjects and perfecting the formula before turning it on himself. Anonymity was crucial. He created a new identity, reinventing himself as "Urrel," and setting up camp in the nether regions of Arizona.

Then it was hunting time.

Life lessons taught him to look for the susceptible—lost, crestfallen women. He was successful in his endeavors; within a short amount of time, he'd collected more than half a dozen followers.

Transforming himself into what they needed him to be, his chameleon adaptability took center stage. Some wanted father figures, others desired lovers. And for each woman he recruited, he molded his personality to fit their individual needs.

He called them his lambs—a mockery to the "sheep" of his hometown—and made many oaths for their loyalty. He promised them love and safety, a retirement of tranquility with no turmoil. A life of Zen.

Never disclosing the toxicity of his cure, he downplayed the danger. Urrel understood death was likely imminent, but did not care.

And so it began. Just as expected, deaths followed. The women, deliriously spellbound, allowed their bodies to be tested—and disposed of—for his cure. With each victim, Urrel recruited another. The abundance of women starved of positive male affection made the plucking easy.

With each failed attempt, Urrel became more frantic. He couldn't comprehend why his solution wasn't working. It began to drive him mad as his desire for immortality molded into an obsession. This cycle of failure repeated until a glorious recruit broke the abhorrent pattern of destruction.

She was of substantial beauty, edging precariously close to surreal. It was her outwardly appearance that first claimed his attention. But it was what lay beneath her perfect exterior that stole his heart. A mind equal to his own.

He called her his Rose.

She had charm and grace with a backbone of steel. Rose was not the weakling his mother was. It was this trait that fascinated him the most. Unaccustomed to such qualities belonging to a female, his brilliant mind was captivated.

His desire for immortality waned as he grew more transfixed by Rose. Urrel never considered testing his cure on her. In his mind, that would be an abomination against nature. She was superior—much like himself—and the solution required ultimate perfection before they turned it on themselves.

But that time never came, and Urrel eventually grew tired of the endless sequence of dereliction. He stopped replacing the women he'd lost and even let a few escape. Urrel no longer cared. Rose had plucked him off his current path and unknowingly placed him on another.

After the last recruit fled, Urrel was left with an empty compound and a thinning supply of his cure. He'd also grown careless and suspected he was being watched. Fleeing became their only option.

So under a veil of onyx sky, Urrel and Rose took his remaining ingredient and ran. They sought refuge in Oregon. He'd heard of its beauty, of its many mountains with heavily timbered forests. Ideal to hide—if the need ever so arose.

The pair set up house on the outskirts of a small town. He once again chose a new name, and Rose took her rightful place beside him as his loving wife.

They lived in poverty, renting a dilapidated, choppy farmhouse. Hobbled together from years of additions, the ceilings hung low above mismatched walkways. The hard Oregon rain wore away the white exterior paint, exposing siding in the infant stages of rot. With a sloped front porch and a lean-to garage on the verge of collapse, the entire structure looked precariously unstable to the outward eye.

The property itself held a bit more charm. Located far from the road, the ample acreage had a picturesque barn painted a rich red, a cedar-shingled woodshed, and an oak grove with timber that filled the sky. Evergreens thrived along the perimeter, their needled branches creating an organic fence that afforded them plenty of privacy.

And so, a new chapter unfolded in Urrel's life, one he'd never expected to experience: domestic bliss. He welcomed the break. Although his cure never wandered far from his thoughts, he relished in his moment of serenity.

Life was strangely perfect—calm almost—until Rose tore asunder all they'd carefully erected.

Urrel was near the oak grove chopping wood when Rose approached, wearing a blue, cotton dress that danced along the gentle planes of her body. She held in her hand a glass of iced tea.

"Thank you, my sweet." He grabbed the cup from her hand, sloshing the lemon against the brim.

Rose smiled softly as she bashfully looked down and smoothed her dress over her slim stomach. When she looked up and met Urrel's eyes, they conveyed a secret he sensed immediately. His back stiffened.

"I have some happy news." She gave off a smile that lit up her entire face. "You're going to be a father."

The moment the words slipped from her lips, Urrel clenched with anger before plastering on a false smile. Rose didn't miss the heated flash of his eyes.

"My darling, what wonderful news," he lied. He set the glass on the ground and pulled her into his embrace. "We must celebrate."

His arms wrapped around her shoulders with the strength of a python, crushing her body against his rigid chest. Rose squirmed, suffocated by his touch. Her heart hitched higher as she managed to free herself and take a modest step away. She bid him farewell—meeting his fake grin with one of her own—and started towards their house. When her foot landed on the porch, she stopped as the whistle of the axe sliced through the air near the timber pile. Phantom bugs crawled up her neck as the sound of splintering wood chilled her blood. Rose turned to watch Urrel lift the axe above his head and bring it crashing down on a narrow log. His aim was accurate. The wood cracked down the center, shooting slivers onto the ground. He'd resumed his task with a vengeance, a dark scowl marring his handsome features.

Whack, whack, whack. She flinched with each swing. When he looked up and caught her stare, he bared his teeth in a grotesque smile. Rose dashed into the house and slammed the door. She pressed her body against the wooden barrier and attempted to calm her terror.

Her fear was not without warrant. She knew what Urrel was capable of; she'd witnessed it at the compound. The midnight burials, the scent of burning flesh, the unmarked graves—cruel memories that trailed like shadows, blanketing her in times of stress.

She thought a child would bring them closer together; now she realized that was a mistake. Instinctively, she rested her hand over her stomach, trying to press her protection onto her unborn child.

"I'll keep you safe, my love," she whispered.

It was a stormy evening when Rose went into labor. At first, she mistook her pains for false labor. When the crippling contractions strengthened—stealing her breath—she realized delivery was at hand. With all her effort, she made it to their marital bed and called for Urrel.

Out in the garage, Urrel was hunched over his cure when Rose's cries reached him. Pain added a new tenor to her voice; it made him smile. He opened a drawer and selected two cotton balls, shoving one into each ear. With Rose's pleas sufficiently blocked, Urrel returned to his task.

Alone, Rose withered in torture as the baby pressed down. Minutes passed slowly, until her body gave way and she was able to deliver the child she'd so desperately wanted: a beautiful, perfect girl she named Flora.

Rose's love was instantaneous.

When Urrel removed the cotton, he was disappointed to hear the wail of a child. Reluctantly, he went inside to see Rose—and the parasite—and was disgusted at the sight that greeted him.

Blood stained the room; it was on the sheets, the floor, the pillow. And in the middle of it all, resting on the bed, was Rose, her baby suckling greedily from her breast. He stood in the doorway, too detested to enter, and gaped at the two of them. When Rose met his eyes, he saw her suspicion, and he knew he was losing her.

"Why didn't you help me?" she asked with darkness in her voice.

Urrel leaned against the doorframe and crossed his arms. He jutted his chin forward and replied, "How could I? You never called for me."

"I screamed for you!"

"I heard nothing." Urrel's voice was cold. "And it seems you've done quite well on your own." He bowed his head, feigning respect, before pivoting on his heel and leaving Rose with the abomination he hoped would die.

The days following Flora's birth were trying. Urrel retreated to the garage—locking himself away to work. Rose, meanwhile, tended to Flora alone. Despite the overwhelming responsibility, Rose's love grew stronger every day. But the care of a newborn is weary, time-consuming work, and lack of sleep bogged her mind. She missed crucial keys and the transformation occurring before her eyes.

Urrel's hatred had grown. It was overtaking him.

She missed the moments when Urrel would look over at the child and call her is little "Thorn." She missed the moment he leaned in to pinch her, causing her to wail, waking Rose from the nap she'd just settled in to take. She missed the looks, the dismissive behavior, and the cold, calculating stares. She'd missed it all.

And while Rose missed it all, Urrel meticulously planned the death of his only child.

Three months after Flora's birth, Rose's fatigue caught up with her. Urrel was ready and sprang into action.

Out back, near the shed next to the oak grove concealed by two large chopping blocks, Urrel had dug a hole. It sat empty for over a week. As Rose slept, he crept in and swept up Flora. He was gentle with the infant for fear she would scream and wake her sleeping mother. Gingerly, he carried her outside. With no remorse for the heinous act he was about to commit, Urrel placed the child—alive—into the pit he'd created specifically for her.

Justifying his actions, he told himself it was Rose's fault. It was the child's. She should've never been born, and the blame rested on Rose's shoulders for not taking the proper precautions. Surely, he couldn't be held accountable.

No, this is necessary. He wanted Rose back—he needed her—and this child was a barrier. This child had stolen from him. She had stolen Rose's love, and this was the only way he could get it back. He would not share. He shouldn't have to share, and he hated the baby for taking the one good thing in his life.

No, he wouldn't be blamed.

No, he didn't ask for this.

No, this was not his fault.

No. No. No.

He was the victim. He shouldn't have been put in such a position. This was the only way. He picked up the shovel and started scooping dirt.

When Rose woke from her nap, she immediately sensed something was wrong. She went to Flora's crib, and her heart skipped when she saw it was empty. She touched the bedding and found it cold. Her feet dashed through the house as she called out Urrel's name.

When she ran into the kitchen, she spotted Urrel through the window. He was planting a rose bush; next to him in a piled heap was Flora's blanket. Her blood ran cold as she knew with maternal instinct the horrific crime he'd committed. She grabbed a knife and ran out the door.

"WHAT HAVE YOU DONE?" she shouted.

Urrel sneered and turned to face her. His grip deepened around the wooden handle of the shovel.

"WHAT HAVE I DONE?" he shouted back. "WHAT HAVE I DONE? I'll tell you what I have done, my darling wife. I have spared you!"

Rose wasn't listening. She had dropped the knife in order to reach for the shovel Urrel held. He forcibly pulled it away. Rose got on her knees and started tearing at the dirt with her bare hands. She sobbed with each fistful of soil.

"YOU'RE A MONSTER!" she screamed through her tears.

"ME?" he yelled. "This was you! You neglected her. You brought this on yourself!"

Rose hesitated. "What are you talking about?"

"I go in to check on you two, and what do I find? I find a mother asleep and a child dead in her crib. YOU," he said, jutting his finger at her horror-struck face, "killed her with your neglect. You have no one to blame but yourself."

"No," she whispered, her face the color of cotton.

"Yes," Urrel responded firmly. "I couldn't have you see her like that; I didn't want you to bear such guilt. She succumbed to crib death, and it's your fault! But then you come at me like I'm the villain. How could you? I acted out of compassion, and this is how you repay me?" he snorted. "You're just like all the others." Urrel turned and threw the shovel to the side.

"You disgust me," he said over his shoulder as he stalked away. Rose would come to understand that he wasn't the bad guy, that she'd made the mistake. She owned this guilt. This was on her conscience, not his.

He expected Rose to follow, to beg his forgiveness, but instead she stayed near the grave. He turned just as Rose unearthed Flora. She laid the child down and attempted to resuscitate her. Rose pumped her chest and prepared to breathe into her mouth, but froze when she spotted a film of soil on Flora's tongue.

Rose covered her lips, appalled. *She'd been buried alive!* A nightmarish awakening spread over her.

"Please, no," she whispered to herself. "Please. Please." She fell on top of Flora, her hands cradling the child's lifeless head. Flora's hair, baby soft, tickled her palms. Tears gushed down Rose's face, streaking it with liquid sorrow.

Then an explosive idea came to her—one that filled her with a spark of hope.

Rose ran towards the garage. Urrel, for once in his life, was unsure of what to do. He hadn't expected her to dig up the child, and he didn't know how to explain away the dirt impacted in her orifices. He watched in a stupor as Rose emerged from the lab with his vile. It was his cure.

Every. Last. Drop.

She sprinted to the small body and cradled Flora in her arms. He watched as she cleared her mouth of dirt and poured the last of his solution down her throat. Rose worked the child's jaw, forcing the liquid down.

Flora remained still, her body cool. Defeated, Rose wailed and cradled Flora in her arms. She rocked her lifeless baby and gasped between screams. Her heart was crumbling. She was choking on grief.

"You wasted it," Urrel whispered, looking at the empty tube on the ground.

Urrel's words snapped Rose to. Gently, she laid Flora down on the dewy grass and kissed the tender skin on the bridge of her nose. Rose grabbed the knife and stood on shaky legs.

"I wasted it?" she began. "I WASTED IT? Our daughter is dead—at your hands—and all you have to say is that I wasted it?"

Urrel had regained his bearings, his mental gears rotating with ease.

"What do you mean at my hands?" Urrel hissed. "I told you this was your fault!"

"Explain how the dirt made it into her mouth if she died in her crib?"

He sneered. "You know nothing of the decomposition process. The body releases gases, and as it does, the organs compress in, easily sucking dirt into a corpse." The lie slipped easily from his lips. He could see the fresh doubt in Rose's eyes. She was confounded. He continued, "This is YOUR FAULT!"

Rose blanched as Urrel did his best to suppress a smile.

Then, unexpectedly, Rose disregarded his explanation. She narrowed her eyes before lunging at him, the knife poised to puncture. Urrel was too quick. He clutched her arm before she had a chance to stab at his flesh.

"You're being a FOOL!" he shouted as they struggled. Rose managed to maintain her grasp on the knife, eventually wrenching it away. Breathing hard, she stepped back. She knew then she'd be unable to inflict the harm she so desperately craved.

At least not on Urrel.

"You can't handle not having control, can you?" she asked with eerie calm. Urrel tilted his head in bewilderment. Rose continued, "I know you think of me as a possession. I've been nothing more than a pretty ornament to adorn your ego. Well, hear this now: you've lost. I don't want you. You can't control me anymore, you piece of FILTH!"

Rose raised the weapon and prepared to plunge it into her heart. She was taking away Urrel's control, and she knew the rage it would evoke. Her will to live vanished with her daughter's death.

He sensed what she was going to do a second before she could commit the act. Urrel charged at her and knocked the weapon away. Rose fell to the ground, and he leapt towards the blade. He reached it easily, and with a triumphant smile, tucked it into the waistband of his pants.

"Tsk, tsk, tsk." He wagged his finger while approaching her. "Now that's not a good girl." He crouched low and clenched her jaw between his fingers, forcing her to meet his eyes.

"How dare you?" he asked softly. "You don't want me? Well, guess what, princess. That's not for you to decide." He released her harshly and then smacked his palm hard across her cheek. Rose watched in anger as he pulled the knife out and ran his finger along the blade. He smirked. "Looks like you chose a rather dull edge. This won't work at all." He chucked the knife as far as he could.

Without looking, he jutted his finger towards Flora. "Give her a proper burial," he spat, and then sauntered towards the woodshed as though he hadn't a care in the world.

Rose, aching from Urrel's assault, found her feet. She started towards the knife once more, so focused, so determined, she didn't see Urrel return.

She didn't see the axe in his hand.

She didn't realize what Urrel had planned until it was too late.

Just as she grasped the cool bone handle of the knife, a shadow loomed over her. Rose turned to see Urrel with the axe lifted high above his head. He grinned a mad smile and poised the weapon to strike. Rose, in a feeble attempt to shield herself, held out her hand. Urrel's shoulders tensed a second before he swung.

It whistled on its way down.

Thud! The axe slammed into Rose's skull. It splintered along the crease of her hair, splicing bone. Rose's face registered shock. Remarkably, it didn't kill her. She dropped to the soggy earth as a stream of spittle pushed passed her lips. Blood pulsated, staining the ground a shade of crimson. Rendered helpless, pain seared through her body.

"You are mine to take. You failed your daughter and you failed me." He paused to admire the sight of Rose fading before him. "This is all your fault." He wiped his brow. "She should've never been born."

Rose gargled beneath his feet. She reached out her slender fingers—searching blindly—until Urrel forced his foot down, stepping hard, taking pleasure in the crunch of breaking bones. Then, almost as an afterthought, he added, "No one takes away my control."

Urrel positioned his foot on Rose's back and yanked the axe from her skull. She groaned, and spat blood on the wet grass. Then, in one swift motion, he hit her again, slicing through her delicate neck, killing her instantly.

Standing over her lifeless body, he worked up a wad of spit that he shot onto her decapitated torso. With the back of his hand, he wiped away droplets of sweat. A deviant smile crept across his lips, that is, until a commotion from behind wiped it away.

He froze, axe in fist, as he tried to make sense of the noise. *Impossible.* Slowly, Urrel turned to face the source of his fear.

Flora had returned from the dead. Her wailing mouth was a vat of darkness as her eyes shone with a supernatural glow. Her soft, pink skin had lost its health. Cracks seeped over her exposed, freshly green flesh. Next to her, the now supplanted rosebush faintly moved with a life of its own.

Urrel watched with eyes of splendor. He had done it. His cure had worked.

"Well, well, well," he said and began to smile. "Come to Daddy, my little Thorn."

☙ ACKNOWLEDGEMENTS ❧

I started writing this book in complete secrecy with no intentions of sharing it with another living soul. That was the safest way to write; no expectations, hence no failure. But midway through, I realized that I wanted readers to know my characters, to love them the way I love them. It was a daunting process, a long journey riddled with self-doubt and worrisome thoughts that I'd never measure up.

That's where my support system comes into play and leads to my first big thank you. Thank you to my husband, Chris. You are my greatest ally and champion. I don't know what I did to deserve you, but I thank God for you every day. When I've been plagued with self-doubt, you've helped me out of my funk. You are a huge reason why this book made it to print. When I wanted to give up, you wouldn't let me. Thank you for believing in me when I didn't even believe in myself.

Thank you to my best friend, CJ. You were the first person I told about this crazy, whacked-out venture I was partaking in. Thank you for listening to hours of excited talk and for being the first person to read my manuscript. You are one of my greatest confidants. Sorry it took me so long to share it with you.

To Kate, I owe you one of the biggest thank you's of all. Singlehandedly, you are my greatest cheerleader. You talked me off the ledge, made me believe in myself, and pretty much make my life better for being in it. I've told you this before, and I'll tell you again: you are one of my most favorite humans. That, and having someone with your writing strengths cheer me on, is the biggest compliment of all. Have I told you how wonderful you are? How much I love your book? Thanks for putting up with me and all my paranoid, quirky oddities.

Amanda—my awesome cover model—thank you for trumping around the cemetery in a cloak. Not just anyone will do that. I snapped 800 pictures, and not once did you wig out. Thanks for being a great sport (and see, no one can tell it's you).

To Joyce Mochrie, my fabulous copy editor and proofreader. Thank you for making this beast shine. You, too, have shown a tremendous amount of encouragement and patience and were able to turn my manuscript into a polished novel. I know I was the "Queen of Indecision," but you walked me through the final cleanup with ease. You're amazing, and I look forward to working with you for many years to come.

And to all the other lovelies who have stood by and given me their support. You know who you are. Thanks for everything.

J.M. MULLER lives in Oregon with her husband, twin boys, and her darling fur babies. She has a plethora of skills (okay, that's a lie), but does enjoy writing and creating—to the very best of her abilities.